W9-CNL-451

WOMEN OF THE UNITED FEDERATION MARINES

GLADIATOR

Colonel Jonathan P. Brazee
USMCR (Ret)

Semper Fi Press

A Semper Fi Press Book

Copyright © 2016 Jonathan Brazee

Illustration © 2016 Jessica TC Lee

ISBN-13: 978-0692692783 (Semper Fi Press)

ISBN-10: 0692692789

Printed in the United States of America

Acknowledgements:
I want to thank all those who took the time to pre-read this book, catching my mistakes in both content and typing.   And again, thanks for Sherry Dixon for editing the book. A special shout out goes to my cover artist, the award-winning Jessica Tung Chi Lee. I simply loved the painting she created for the book. You can see more of her work at: http://www.jessicatcl.com/news.html.

Original Art by Jessica TC Lee

Cover layout by Steven Novak

WYXY

Chapter 1

"Don't fuck up, boot!" Wythe told Lance Corporal Tamara Veal, United Federation Marine Corps.

"I'm not a boot, Wythe!" Tamara said. "I'm senior to you by two months!"

"I never saw no CMM on your Charlies. Iffen you got no combat, you're a boot."

"Lay off her, Jessup, or she'll have you for breakfast," Corporal Killington "Killer" Wheng, their team leader said.

"I'm just saying, Corporal. You never know how someone's gonna act when the shit hits the fan," Wythe said as he settled back into his web-seat. "And I need to know she's gonna have our six, you know."

"She will, so leave it," Corporal Wheng said.

Tamara looked across to where her squad leader, Sergeant Vinter, sat, staring at her. Only half Tamara's size, she never-the-less sent shivers down Tamara's spine. Tamara couldn't read into the glare that was in her squad leader's eyes, and she wasn't sure she wanted to.

As much as Jessup Wythe could be a pain in the ass, he was right. Tamara, even with three years in the Corps, had never been with an operational unit. Not only did she not have a CMM, or Combat Mission Medal, which was awarded to any Marine or sailor who saw combat, her uniform chest was bare of any ribbons. Even PFC Korf, sitting on her right, with his nine months since boot, had a CMM.

Tamara's handicap was not only that she was big and strong, but she was a skilled shot putter and discus thrower. Not skilled enough to make the Federation Olympic team, but more than enough to catch the eye of the Marine Corps Athletic Division.

The Marine Corps loved sports, whether that was battleball played between units or organized sports such as rugby or basketball played against civilian, Navy, or other government teams. Competition was in the Corps' DNA, and the MCAD was always on the lookout for prospects.

Tamara had been the Orinoco planetary junior shot put champion while in school, and that was enough to flag her. When it became apparent that she was going to graduate from boot camp, she'd been approached by Lieutenant Colonel Frank Versase, two-time Olympic weight-lifting champion and director of MCAD, and recruited to the Marine Corps track team. After boot and her 12-week School of Infantry course, instead of going straight to the fleet, she joined the team and began training.

Tamara looked the part. Almost two meters tall and 90 kg and blessed with superb balance and reflexes, she had immediately done well in low-level competitions. But Orinoco was not the largest planet in the Federation, and there were many, many great athletes who wanted a spot on the Olympic team. After eight months of intensive training, Tamara managed to take the bronze in the discus, her supposedly weaker event, at the Universal Military Games in New Mumbai in the Confederation, and was ranked number four in the Federation. At the next Military Games, she finished a disappointing tenth in the discus and eighteenth in the shot put.

She blamed a nagging thigh injury on the finish, but deep inside, she knew she had simply lost the drive. Gunny India, her coach, evidently recognized it as well, and after six more months without improvement, she was dropped from the team. The Marine Corps loved champions, but it did not love also-rans, at least in athletics.

That was two months earlier, and since then, she had received new orders and reported to the Second Battalion, Third Marines, the "Fuzos." And now, she was on a Stork, on an actual mission—and she was scared.

It wasn't the fear of death (which was there, but somewhat of an afterthought). Since being dropped from the track team, her feeling of self-worth had been less than ideal. She hadn't been good enough for the track team, so what made her think she'd be good enough for her new team, the infantry?

She was afraid of failure, pure and simple, and Wythe wasn't helping out. She looked again at Sergeant Vinter, hoping against hope for a hint of encouragement. Vinter was a salty dog, with five stars on her CMM and a Battlefield Commendation 2, so she'd been there and done that, and a simple nod from her would have boosted Tamara's self-confidence. But while the sergeant had undoubtedly heard Wythe, she'd said nothing.

Get it together! she told herself. *You're a lean, green, fighting machine, and you're going to kick ass!*

She repeated the mantra, psyching herself up, a technique she'd used in hundreds of competitions. The technique hadn't done her much good in her last year with the track team, but maybe there was a little life left in it. It couldn't hurt.

The Stork suddenly banked hard left. With full battle rattle, the Marines couldn't strap in with the normal seat harness, something that made no sense to Tamara (didn't Marines always go into a fight in full battle rattle?) so the simple lap belt kept them in their seats as the Stork maneuvered. But with 90 kg of Tamara and 60 kgs of warfighting gear, that put a lot of pressure on her gut, and she had to kick out both of her feet to brace herself.

The 70kg Wythe saw that and smirked, making sure Tamara could see his disdain. It was only then that she noticed that every other Marine, even the two new privates—real boots—had already put their legs out to brace themselves.

Great! That makes me look simply cosmic!

The Stork pulled hard right, and the force shifted 180, but now the back of her seat supported her. The force grew as the big bird corkscrewed in, which minimized its vulnerability to enemy ground fire or missiles. This wasn't the first time that Tamara had been in a Stork during this maneuver, but this was the first time there had actually been bad guys on the ground who'd like to blow her ride out of the sky.

She'd heard the term "asshole puckering" before, but now she truly understood just how accurate and descriptive the term really was. At any moment, she expected the alarms to go off, but miraculously, the corkscrewing ceased as the Stork straightened up to flare in for the landing.

"Check your safeties," Staff Sergeant Abdálle, the platoon sergeant passed on the platoon circuit, "and prepare to debark."

Tamara had checked hers about a hundred times during the flight, but she dutifully looked down at her M99A3, the latest and greatest in the venerable M99 assault rifles. Marines had been shot by fellow Marines before during combat debarks, and each Marine lost to friendly fire, particularly stupid and avoidable friendly fire, was one less fighter for the mission and either death or regen for the victim. Tamara's safety was on, but overthinking it, Tamara flipped it off, then flipped it back on. The dim green indicator light confirmed the safety circuit was on and functioning.

The Stork hit the deck with a hard bounce. Tamara joined the rest of the Marines and the platoon's three corpsmen in releasing their seatbelts and standing, turning to face aft. The ramp was already down, and the two guides were stepping off.

The battalion had been practicing MEEP, or Minimal Electronic Emissions Protocol, the newest pet project out of Tarawa. The old salts roundly derided it. The Corps had only recently implemented the new PCS, the Personal Combat System, a few years back, and with the many improvements it offered to command and control and the dissemination of information, all being tremendous assets in the modern battlefield, the Corps was now advocating going back to the middle ages with hand and arm signals.

The two guides turned to face the rest of the platoon, and like traffic cops, each held out an arm pointing to the direction each line of Marines was to take.

Pushing up against Korf, Tamara shuffled forward a meter or so until Korf was able to step out. Tamara followed, ducking under the overhead at the end of the ramp to step onto the grass of the football field that was serving as the Golf Company's LZ.[1]

Enemy soil! I'm on enemy soil! Tamara thought excitedly as she wheeled to follow Korf.

---

[1] LZ: Landing Zone

Except that it wasn't really enemy soil, she knew. Wyxy was a Federation planet. It was the SevRevs who were the enemy, and the Marines had been called in to eliminate the group and return the planet to the control, or lack thereof, of the planet's advisory group. Without a central government, without even a nominal police force, the particularly individualistic population of the planet had been easy pickings for the SevRevs. Since the Wyxies couldn't protect themselves, it was up to the Federation—read the Marines—to step in and restore the planet to its rightful tenants ("tenants," not anything so crass as "owners").

If it had been anyone other than the SevRevs, the planet might have been left to the wolves. The planet was only nominally in the Federation, and their trade with the rest of the Federation hardly made up for the cost of sending a Navy task force and a Marine battalion to restore order. But the Seventh Revelation had been a growing thorn in the side of human space. Apocalyptic groups have risen and fallen throughout history, but the SevRevs employed a particularly violent form of attempting to bring on the End of Days. Coupling their desire to bring about total chaos with their seemingly zero fear of death, they'd conducted some extremely horrific attacks on planets across human space. Wyxy might be low man on the totem pole on the list of Federation worlds, but the SevRevs were a virus that had to be stomped out before it infected anyone else.

Like just about everyone else in human space, Tamara had seen the holos of the SevRev executions, and she had been horrified at the obscenely creative methods they had come up with. She knew the SevRevs intended to shock humanity, and it worked. So on an overarching level, Tamara knew this was a righteous mission, one that had to be accomplished. But on a personal level, it didn't matter of the enemy were the SevRevs or anyone else; Tamara was going into combat for the first time, and she had to perform her duty to the best of her abilities.

Running right on Korf's ass, Tamara reached the football field's retaining walls. She raised her head to scan the empty seats. A recon team had already duck-egged into the stadium several hours before and reported it secure, but there existed some inert explosives that could escape normal detection, and the battalion had been warned to keep alert.

Two more flights of Storks landed on the field, debarking Fox and the battalion headquarters.

"Korf, eyes front," she hissed, feeling proud that she'd been able to take charge over the junior Marine.

With the Storks landing behind them, PFC Korf had glanced back at them instead of scanning the stadium seating area to their front.

"There's nothing there," he muttered, but he swiveled around to observe the seats.

Within 12 minutes of landing, the two line companies were ready to move out. Fox was to lead the assault on the Farmer's Market, where the SevRevs had more than 500 Wyxy hostages. Golf Company was the support element for the assault. Echo and Weapons had established blocking positions beyond the market to cut off any avenue of retreat, not that anyone thought it would get to that. The SevRevs had not shown signs before of retreating in order to play another day. In previous incidents with both the Brotherhood and the Confederation, the SevRevs had fought to the end, trying to inflict maximum casualties. But the battalion CO was not relying on past actions. This was the first major SevRev action within Federation space, and the CO was in the better-safe-than-sorry camp. Her orders had been to eliminate—not defeat—the SevRev forces, and as the sergeant major had briefed them on the ship, that meant every swinging dick of them was to be killed. A message was going to be sent, not to the SevRevs as they were probably lost causes, but to anyone thinking of joining them.

Join the SevRevs and die.

The SevRev philosophy was self-defeating. They expected the End of Days and were willing, even eager, to die. But that meant they had to have new recruits. Given enough time, all the current SevRevs would be gone; without new recruits, they would disappear into the dustbin of history.

In fits and starts, the two companies got up and began to exit the stadium. Tamara could see all the friendlies on her face shield display, but with MEEP in place, no verbal orders were passed. So it was more of a ripple effect as the hand and arm signals to get moving were passed down the lines.

Corporal Hinmein in Second Squad, who always knew everything in the entire universe and liked to let everyone else know it, was sure that using MEEP against what was really an unsophisticated enemy was intended as a dress rehearsal. Tamara thought that the corporal might not be that far off. The SevRevs probably had little in the way of electronic warfare capabilities, nor could they be expected to be much of a threat to a Marine battalion, so this mission could be MEEP baby steps, a field trial and validation of the process.

Tamara wasn't sure she wanted to be part of a field trial, and if the SevRevs proved to have any tricks up their collective sleeves, she hoped the CO would pull the plug on the MEEP and switch to full electronic command and control.

The four columns of Marines snaking out of the stadium moved in fits and starts, accordioning with the point moving quickly, the main body starting and stopping. Tamara's squad was the second to the last squad in her column, and she seemed to spend most of her time either stopped and right on Korf's ass or almost sprinting to catch up with him. She worried every time they were bunched up. It had been driven into her head at both recruit training and School of Infantry that bunching up meant death and dispersion was paramount. Since she had no real operational experience, she had to rely on her training. But she couldn't very well just break out of the column to gain tactical dispersion.

Supposedly, the area was being cleared as they conducted the movement to contact. The two companies were advancing in a misshapen arrow formation, which was a wedge clearing the area and followed by the four columns. This was the second least secure formation after simple columns, but it allowed for a fairly quick movement and covered a narrower front. It provided very little lateral security, though, and as they moved through the city, Tamara was busy watching each building and each road for the enemy. There were people out and about, both on the roads and in the buildings, watching them. Most seemed happy to see the Marines, and more than a few were shouting out greetings. There was even a

Federation banner hanging from one window while a man and young girl leaned out waving small flags as they watched the Marines march by.

Tamara knew the reputation of the Wyxies, that they barely tolerated the Federation and resented paying any taxes. But the SevRevs had some 500 hostages in the neighboring village, and they had already killed another couple of hundred people, so it seemed as if the 30,000 or so remaining people who lived in the main town had suddenly become true patriots.

To last all of a week after we leave, Tamara told herself, ever the cynic.

While everyone she saw seemed welcoming at best, merely curious at worst, it would be easy for a SevRev to hide among the town's populace, ready to fire upon the Marines, or even bring down a building on them. The battalion was going in light with in their skins and bones, their field uniforms with the armor inserts. The armor inserts, the "bones," would instantaneously harden against projectiles, dispersing the force, but there were quite a few energy weapons that were more than a match for them. Heck, a few explosives could tear Marines apart, or if emplaced well, could bring down buildings to bury Marines in the rubble.

It would have been nice to have a couple of PICS platoons, the heavy combat suits providing a far greater punch. Rumor had it, though, that with Wyxy sensibilities, the PICS Marines would have been "too militaristic." Tamara was way, way down in the pecking order, far from the goings on at the battalion head-shed, but from the scuttlebutt, the CO had been royally pissed at the restriction.

Tamara's unease at passing through the town proved to be unwarranted. Either Intel or recon had been correct. The town itself was clear of SevRevs; at least no one had engaged the two companies as they moved forward. Within one-and-a-half klicks, they were leaving the main built-up area and moving into the fields surrounding the town.

"What the hell is that smell?" Wythe asked.

Tamara had to laugh, but it was Korf who answered, "It's chicken shit, Lance Corporal! You never smelt it before?"

"Why would I ever smell chicken shit?" Wythe asked. "What, they can't get rid of it? And I don't see no chickens here nowhere."

"They use it for fertilizer. See those plants? They're strawberries. They use the shit as organic fertilizer."

"Bullshit, Korf! No one uses shit on food. It'd be unsanitary, that's what it'd be!"

"I'm afraid Korf's right," Corporal Wheng said. "That's how they get such high prices for their produce."

Wythe stopped dead for a moment. "You mean, they really use shit on food?"

"Keep it moving, Wythe. We haven't stopped," Sergeant Vinter interjected.

"Fucking A," Wythe muttered as he started up again. "Crazy fucks never heard of fabricators, I guess. I ain't never eating no organic crap, no fucking way!"

Tamara had to start breathing through her open mouth, the stench was so putrid. Even then, she could imagine the little chicken shit molecules coating her throat. Orinoco had a number of the back-to-basics organic farms, and she knew that they used natural fertilizer, but she'd never been close to one of the farms before, and while Wythe was taking it too far, she could sympathize. She'd eaten organics, but only after they were placed in nice stasis packages and sold in specialty stores. After getting socked in the face with the reality on how they were grown, she wasn't sure she'd want to try them again, either.

And their objective, the Farmer's Market was still two klicks ahead in Rose Garden. Tamara couldn't help but hope that the name of the village might be reflected in its smell.

After crossing Renter's Creek, though, either Tamara's nose had gotten used to the stench or they'd gotten out of the nasal kill zone. The fields of knee-high sweet corn, unlike the strawberry fields, were fairly benign. On the other side of the corn fields, Tamara knew, was the assembly area for the assault.

This entire operation was not exactly textbook. There were embedded reporters and drones, and it seemed more like a live-fire dog-and-pony show rather than a combat operation. The assembly area not only did not have cover and concealment, and it was in full view of the Rose Garden Farmers' Market another 600 meters away. It made for great cam shots, though, Sergeant Vinter had noted sarcastically.

Six hundred meters was nothing. Even a half-assed marksman could shoot that far accurately. Most handheld energy weapons would ablate to ineffectiveness over that distance (especially considering the suppressor field generators being emplaced between the assembly area and the Farmers' Market), and their bones would stop just about any projectile at that distance as well. Still, Intel could be wrong, and they could have more powerful crew-served weapons.

The reporters, though, did not have the same protection as the Marines. Most had on helmets of some sort and various types of ballistic vests, but that still left a lot of exposed flesh just begging for the attention of a SevRev sniper. As Tamara followed her column into the assembly area, she could see more than a few reporters and cam operators wandering around, looking for Marines to interview, and entirely exposed.

"What a circus," Korf muttered ahead of her, something to which she wholeheartedly agreed.

Whatever she had imagined a combat op to be, this wasn't it. But she knew she had to focus. The SevRevs were serious enemies, not to be taken lightly. The reporters were superfluous, to be ignored. The mission was to crush the SevRevs and save as many of the hostages as possible.

A Wasp overflew the assembly area and the market, nasty and mean. With the hostages, air couldn't engage the SevRevs, but the psychological effect should be significant. They had to be rattled—at least, that was part of the plan.

As the Marines moved into the assembly area, the psych warfare team was already at work.

Speaking through a small, but incredibly powerful directional speaker, one of the Marines in the team said, "Inside the market, we are the United Federation Marines. You are trapped where you are. If you want to live, release the hostages. If you comply, you will not be harmed.

"If you do not release the hostages and resist us, you are inviting a certain destruction. It is up to you. Surrender and live or resist and die."

No one expected the SevRevs to surrender. Dying was part of their creed. But the formalities had to be observed, especially with the press present. And if the psych warfare team could get a few of them to have second thoughts, to make them less committed to the path they were taking, all the better.

"Check your curtains!" Staff Sergeant Abdálle shouted out.

Tamara dutifully activated the curtain. What looked like fog rolled down from the rim of her helmet, coalescing around her head. Within moments, the fog cleared to invisibility, and a steady lilac light on her heads-up display indicated it was working. The fog had bothered her, but she knew it had only been visible to let each Marine know it was deploying.

On Janson, in the Confederation, the SevRevs, in their burn-the-fields strategy, had deployed a super-aggressive biological that had killed six Confed soldiers, their brains too eaten up for regen. The Marines didn't know what to expect from the SevRevs in the market, so they had included NBC[2] capabilities in their rehearsals for the operation. Tamara shuddered at the thought of a brain-eating biological, and it was hard to believe that a little puff of fog around her head would protect her from that. Still, she was glad she had it.

"Check out the snipers," Korf whispered to Tamara, nodding to one of two scout sniper teams who had been moving with the company. "Uber cool."

The team, a tall, burly man, and a short, very pretty woman, were setting up on top of a small public restroom where the sniper, who was carrying his sniper rifle in a case, could observe the Farmer's Market. Tamara knew their orders were to take out any SevRevs they could once hostilities initiated. If they were successful, they could save untold hostages.

"Uber cool" was probably appropriate. Scout snipers had an air about them, and within the Marine Corps culture, they occupied

---

[2] NBC: Nuclear, Biological, and Chemical

the same niche as recon: the penultimate warriors. Not that Tamara had any desire to join them. She knew that as a Marine, she could be tasked with killing an enemy, but the absolute personal nature of spotting a person through the sniper scope and then reaching out and touching them, lethally, was a little too intense for her.

To her surprise, the large Marine opened the case and handed the sniper rifle to the smaller Marine. She was the sniper, not him. Tamara ruefully acknowledged that she had stereotyped the pair. The larger man was the a-gunner, the smaller woman the actual sniper.

"All right," Sergeant Vinter said. "Let's get into position. We all know our jobs, so think, Marines, think! No bonehead mistakes."

Golf Company was assigned the support element mission. They would provide covering fire, but not enter the market itself. Tamara understood the logic. The market was just too small for anything bigger than a company-sized unit to enter it without max chaos resulting. Still, she'd been disappointed that it wasn't Golf as the assault element. She'd waited three years to be tested in combat, and this wasn't going to be that test. Her enlistment would be over in another year, and 2/3 might not see combat again during that time.

She should be relieved. There was almost no chance of her getting hurt if Golf wasn't assaulting, and logic would hold that was a good thing. But then no one ever said Marines were married to logic.

With no response from the SevRevs—not that any was expected—the assault element started to cross the LOD.[3] Even if Tamara couldn't see much from her position, she felt the excitement rise within her. This was far more intense than anything she'd felt on the track field, and she thought she could get used to the adrenaline rush. She could only imagine what it would be like to be moving forward with Fox, right into the teeth of whatever the SevRevs had waiting for them.

"I wouldn't be doing that," Korf said.

---

[3] LOD: Line of Departure

Tamara looked over at him, and he pointed back to the battalion command group, some 100 meters away. The CO was moving away from a reporter and her camcorderman, trying to ignore the two as she monitored Fox company. A big Marine was trying to pull back the reporter, but the guy was nimble, dodging the Marine and pressing the CO. Tamara tried to smother a laugh. The reporter was putting Marines in danger, but it did look funny.

"Eyes front, you two. To your sector," Sergeant Vinter said, venom in her voice.

Tamara quickly looked forward, afraid to catch her squad leader's eyes.

"Cut the crap, Korf. Don't get me into any trouble."

"You didn't have to look," muttered the PFC.

With Marines to the fore, their sectors of observation were pretty much blocked. Tamara almost wished she was with Third Squad. Their sector was to the rear. Nothing was going to happen there, but at least they had a clear field of vision. In front of her, Tamara thought that the lead Marines of the assault element had to be about half-way to the market. The trail elements were only now crossing the LOD.

A sudden snap broke through her thoughts. Sergeant Vinter's admonition forgotten, she looked over to her right where the scout-sniper team had positioned themselves. The sniper was cycling her rifle while the assistant glassed the market. The sniper fired once more, cycled, and then stopped, still looking through her scope.

Almost immediately, fire sounded from the market. To her front, the Marines from Fox started maneuvering in a bounding overwatch, one unit covering the other while the first moved forward, then that unit stopping and covering while the second one moved forward. Tamara thought she heard a few rounds zipping through the air past her, but she realized that could have been her imagination.

To her right, the sniper engaged unseen targets several more times, rounds that couldn't have been individually targeted. At least, Tamara knew she couldn't acquire a target, aim, and fire that quickly. She guessed snipers had different training.

Just as the lead elements were at the front of the market, the entire building exploded in a huge fireball of flames and smoke. A few moments later, the shock wave swept over them. Tamara could feel it take the air right from her lungs.

"Holy shit!" Korf said from behind her, sitting up to get a better view.

The column of smoke rose 100, 200, then 300 meters into the air, billowing black and angry.

No one could have survived that, Tamara thought in wonder.

But there were survivors.

"We've got people coming out," Sergeant Vinter shouted. "Get ready."

As the support element, one of Golf's missions was to assist with the hostages. First Platoon would be the handling teams, and Tamara's Second Platoon security.

"Remember, these are friendlies, but be on the alert," Sergeant Vinter reminded them.

Ahead them, Third Platoon had moved forward into Fox Company, creating a corridor for the survivors. A few Marines entered the corridor to act as traffic cops, funneling the walking back towards the rest of the company and out of immediate danger. A few corpsmen were active for those who collapsed and couldn't move on their own. There would be more people seriously wounded inside, too wounded to move on their own, and there would be dead that might be resurrectable. Triage teams were ready to move into the ruins of what had been the market, but they couldn't do anything until Fox cleared them. If hostages had survived the blast, then so would some SevRevs. As if on cue, firing broke out from inside the ruined building.

The first of the survivors passed Tamara, dirty and bedraggled, but looking unhurt. After a minute or two, others stumbled past with signs of injury. Tamara knew these were the lucky ones, though. Others would have been hurt much worse or killed. The blast had been huge.

A woman fell right in front of Tamara, and she stepped out to help the panicking woman to her feet. The sheer terror on her face hit Tamara hard, and she felt guilty for being so excited earlier. This wasn't some console game—this was real war with real consequences. These people were scared for their lives, and it looked like many of them had not survived. Tamara pointed the way, and with a choked thanks, the woman stumbled past Tamara and towards safety.

More people ran by, and the Marines helped funnel them towards the initial collection points where they would be searched first, then fed to the processing stations. Each survivor had to be identified and cleared, and each would be interviewed before being released. It wasn't unheard of for hostage-takers to hide among the hostages in order to get away.

At that thought, Tamara looked back at the smoking ruins of what had been the market, dust still rising into the air. Between that blast and Fox's assault, which seemed to be petering out, she didn't think any of the hostage-takers had made it out of that alive.

Their choice, she thought to herself.

She was pretty sure that it had been their choice, to bring down the market around themselves. There had been no plans for the Marines to blow the market, and she didn't think the assault force was carrying anything powerful enough to simply destroy it. No, it had to be the SevRevs.

The stream of fleeing hostages started to thin out. Tamara sobered as she did a quick mental count. There were about fifty of them who had either reached the Marines or who were on their way—fifty out of five hundred. There could be others on the other side of the market, but it looked like the SevRevs had taken out most of the hostages when they decided to end it all.

"Please, sir, help me," one of the hostages said as he staggered up to Wythe, holding a bloody woman around the shoulders.

"Doc!" Wythe called out, helping the man lower the woman to the ground.

Doc Neves hurried up to help and started her triage.

Wythe helped the man to his feet and asked, "Are you hurt, too? Are you OK?"

"I've got information, sir. I need to talk to your commander. Lives are at stake!" the man said, his voice fraught with stress.

"Corporal Wheng!" Wythe called out. "This guy says he needs to talk to the commander."

The corporal was in the process of picking up a small child, assisting who had to be the child's mother to get back to the initial collection point.

He barely gave Wythe a glance over the crying toddler, but he said "Take him, then," as he nodded to where the battalion commanding officer, surrounded by a Marine squad for security, was standing with some of her staff.

Tamara thought Wythe had misunderstood their team leader because he turned to the company commander, who was standing with the first sergeant 20 meters to their right. She started to yell out to him, but something caught her attention, something that didn't completely register with her.

Wythe was struggling to hold up the hostage, but the man had one hand in his pocket instead of using it to lean on Wythe. It didn't look natural. And for someone so seemingly frightened, his eyes were now laser-focused on Captain Mueller.

Tamara broke into a run without realizing just why. With six strides to gather steam, she slammed into Wythe and the hostage, sending both to the ground just as Captain Mueller looked up to see who Wythe was bringing.

"What the fuck?" Wythe started as Tamara lunged for the hostage's hand, the one in the pocket.

The man's hand was wrapped around something, and the closed fist momentarily hung the hand up, trapping it inside. He twisted and got the hand to where he could start to pull it out when Tamara closed her own hands, both of them, around the man's hand.

"Veal! What the hell?" Wythe shouted, rolling away from her. "Are you bat-shit crazy?"

Tamara ignored Wythe as the man, all pretense of fear gone, tried to jerk his arm free. And without ever seeing one before, Tamara knew what was in his hand: a dead man's switch.

This was a SevRev, and he wanted to blow up the captain and anyone else around. She could feel the explosive belt under the man's jacket as he struggled to free the switch. Tamara knew that if she let go, she was a dead woman—along with Wythe, the captain, the first sergeant, and who knew who else.

The man was big, and he outweighed Tamara by 20 kg. He jerked his arm, shaking Tamara like a terrier on a rat, but she was not going to let go. He slammed punch after punch into the side of her head with his free hand, but she focused on clamping her hands into an immovable force.

She was peripherally aware of shouts around her, but her life and narrowed down to the fist in her hands. If she let go, her life was over, so she simply wasn't going to let go.

The man jerked back as blood sprayed over her face. He immediately ceased to fight her. Wary, she held on, but the hole in the side of his head, the blood pouring out of the other side, was evidence enough that he was dead. She started to relax when an explosion by her ear deafened her.

Am I dead? Did he explode? she wondered, dazed from the pounding and the blast. *Did he have a dead man's switch?*

"Don't let go, Marine!" a voice called out.

Moments later, she felt hands close around hers, gentle, but firm hands.

"We've got it now," the voice said, calm and collected. "Keep holding it, and we'll get someone here to disarm this guy."

She looked up to where the first sergeant was standing over her. Sergeant Priest, the company police sergeant, was holding a massive Peidmeister, a huge, short-barreled self-defense handgun, aimed right at the dead hostage—only he wasn't a hostage. He was, with emphasis on the "was," a SevRev. The gaping hole of mangled hamburger that had been his neck and lower face was evidence that Priest had used her Peidmaster to make sure the man was dead. Now, Wythe and Korf were kneeling beside her, their hands around hers.

"Hey, Korf, can you get off me," Tamara said weakly.

"Oh, shit, sorry," the PFC said, moving his knee from out of her side.

"Just don't let go. I'm a little woozy, I think."

The first sergeant, with the captain and other Marines watching, bent over the three Marines and wrapped their hands together with a ziptie. They weren't going anywhere. The three Marines, Tamara in the middle, lay together on top of the dead SevRev for over 20 minutes until an EOD team could get to them. After some initial discussion, the team leader placed anti-ballistic blankets on them, sliding the blankets between them and the dead SevRev, with only their hands sticking out. Tamara had recovered her wits, and underneath the heavy blankets with her two fellow Marines, kept imagining the explosives going off, taking their hands with it. They'd be facing long regens, but at least they'd probably survive.

"Nice work, Tamara," Wythe whispered, his lips just centimeters from her ear. "I guess I owe you one."

"You mean I'm not a boot anymore?" she whispered back with a snort.

"Quiet under there, and don't move!" the EOD tech shouted from outside the blanket. "Unless you want me to make a mistake!"

Tamara froze, not willing to move a muscle.

"No, you're not a boot," Wythe whispered even quieter.

Two minutes later, the blankets were whipped off of them. A happy EOD tech, his faceplate opened revealing an amazing amount of sweat pouring down his face, smiled broadly at them.

"Done and done," he said as he clipped the ziptie that was keeping the three and the dead SevRev connected. "And you guys are pretty damned lucky. He had enough C10 to blow a hole 30, 40 meters across."

Korf looked around, and Tamara could see the mental gears turning.

"Thirty meters? But how could those blanket things protect us from that?" he asked.

"They couldn't," the tech said with a laugh. "But I needed you to keep still, and who knows, maybe they could have scraped up enough bits and pieces of you to regen afterwards. Maybe enough of me, too," he added, slapping his EOD suit.

"And I thought you were bat-shit crazy," Wythe said to Tamara.

"We're clear!" the tech shouted out as he stood up straight, waving his arms.

It was only then that Tamara noticed that there was no one around them for at least fifty meters. No Marines, no hostages, no reporters. A small cam-drone hovered over them about 10 meters up, but that was it.

With the all clear, though, a small tsunami of humanity started forward.

Before they could reach them, Tamara held out her hand to the EOD tech and said, "Lance Corporal Tamara Veal, and thanks for saving our asses."

The Marine took her hand and said, "Staff Sergeant Polinus T'ber, and don't mention it. That's why I get the EOD hazard duty pay. That was pretty ballsy on your part. How did you know he was a suicide?"

"I didn't know. I just reacted, I think."

"Thank God for that," Wythe said.

"Those are the kind of reactions we like in EOD. If you ever want to come over to the dark side, look me up. I'm sure we can make room for you."

Tamara laughed and said, "I may be crazy, but I'm not that crazy! I'd kind of like to live to have kids someday, and this girl isn't one for big risks like that."

"Like jumping on a suicide? Risks like that? Just keep us in mind, Lance Corporal," he said as the wave of Marines and reporters reached them.

TARAWA

Chapter 2

"Hey, it's The Blonde Terror!" Fanny Dolsch shouted out as Tamara walked into the Down 'N Out.

Tamara wasn't blonde, and she had nothing in common with the Blonde Terror's over-the-top braggadocio, but he was a one of the revolving wresting champions, so she didn't protest. She was an MMA fan, not wrestling, but she was enjoying her new-found attention.

If the other Marines had thought her a boot or a dilettante, all of that had vanished on Wyxy. She was part of the team now, and that was something she cherished.

Tamara had not been ostracized at school, but neither had she been one of the Alphas. Big and athletic, other students seemed to take pride in her accomplishments representing the school, and she had friends, but not too many guys gravitated romantically to a girl who could tie them into knots should she get that into her head. With her one boyfriend, if she could call Cyrus that, they had not gotten beyond kissing—something that excited her very being, but didn't seem to do that much for Cyrus. At least they'd stayed together until after prom, which had been better than nothing.

Enlisting in the Marines had been partially instigated because of her size. Yes, she was driven by patriotism and a love of physical activity. Yes, she was following in both her uncle and grandfather's footsteps, but the Marines were the biggest and baddest group of misfits in the Federation, and she thought that among them, boys—no, *men*—might be more attracted to her than a tiny wisp of a woman.

Of course, as she found out, her concept of size had been pretty much mistaken. There were large Marines, small Marines, and Marines right in the middle, and size didn't seem to have anything to do with a Marine's status. It was the size of the fight in the dog, not the size of the dog in the fight that mattered, as the saying went. Heck, the most badass Marine in the platoon was probably the petite—and attractive—Sergeant Vinter. But not even Wythe, who had no social graces, dared to contemplate how the good sergeant might be in a social setting. A tiger was a beautiful animal, but no sane person climbed into a cage with one, after all.

But there were some rather large Marines, Tamara noted, as she saw Lance Corporal Victor Williams, all two-point-three meters of him, already sitting in the large corner booth her friends had staked out.

"Sit down, Veal. I've got a pitcher with your name on it!" Wythe shouted, waving a stein of beer.

Wythe, Fanny, Doc Neves, and several other Marines had gotten a pretty good head start on Tamara at the Down 'N Out, one of the grubby bars located on Hill Street. The Down 'N Out might not be fancy, but the beer was cheap, and like all of the Hill Street bars, it had been pretty much abandoned by the NCOs and higher. Oh, a few corporals might hang out with friends, but not that often. SNCOs rarely made an appearance, and officers pretty much never. And that made the string of bars just about perfect from the point of view of the non-rates.

Tamara, slid in beside Wythe, using her butt to push him aside and stake her own claim. Her fifth-grade decorum teacher, Ms. Garcia, would have been shocked by her manners, but Wythe didn't blink an eye other than hold up the stein higher so as not to spill any of it.

"Took you long enough," Fanny said. "We've almost drunk all the beer Jessie here bought for you, and the next pitcher's on you."

"That true, Wythe? You buy this?"

"True that. I told you on the *Caracas* I was buying, dint I? An' a Marine never goes back on his word, am I right?"

Tamara took the beer from his hand and took a long swallow. It was true that Wythe had said that after embarking back on the ship, and having just gotten back to the base that afternoon, this was the first chance he'd had. Tamara just hadn't been too sure that he was serious or that it had been the raw nerves of almost getting killed that had been speaking. Still, the beer was cold and good, and if she had the next pitcher, she was going to drink as much of this pitcher as she could.

She made a show of smacking her lips, then said, "The skipper wanted to see me. Couldn't get out of that."

There were some good-natured hoots from the others, and Wythe made a fist, put his nose in the hole made by his thumb and forefinger, and rotated it back and forth. Tamara punched Wythe in the arm, and not gently.

I am not a brown-noser! she protested, but silently.

It was OK to hit one of her buddies, but to protest out loud would only invite further trash talk.

"That's 'cause you're a bleeding hero," Fanny said, drawing out the "e" in hero.

"Eat me," Tamara said as the others laughed.

Marines tended to rather earthy language, to put it mildly, but "eat me" was about as vulgar as Tamara could get. She knew that schools on other planets almost never formally taught decorum, but those on Orinoco did, and Ms. Garcia had made an impact on her. Swearing just didn't come naturally to Tamara.

"You getting an award?" Victor asked.

All eyes turned to her, suddenly serious.

"Eh, I don't know. It's no big deal," she answered, attempting to sound nonchalant.

But it was a big deal. Especially to Marines. The old earth general Napoleon had famously said "A soldier will fight long and hard for a bit of colored ribbon," and Tamara was bursting with pride that Captain Mueller had told her she was being recommended for the Silver Star.

A Silver Star! The third highest award for valor. For me!

Of course, it had not been approved yet, and she couldn't let the rest know that she was excited over the possibility. All Marines coveted awards. It was in their DNA, a validation of their service. But no one could seem like he or she was chasing medals, which was a good way to get not only him or her killed but his or her fellow Marines as well.

"Eh, you'll get one, maybe a BC1," Victor said, reaching his stein over the table to clink with hers.

Not a BC1. A Silver Star, she thought as she half stood and reached across Wythe to clink steins with Victor.

"Hey, watch it. I don't need your boobs in my face when I'm drinking!" Wythe shouted out, spilling some of his beer.

Laughter and shouts of "Oh you love it," and "That's as close as you're going to get to any," greeted his statement.

Tamara sat back down, and she could feel her face reddening. Sexual innuendo and jokes were part of the culture in the modern Corps, and a Marine couldn't be too self-conscious about body parts when living in such close quarters. And while Marines did hook up together as relationships developed, sexual harassment was a rare occurrence and was grounds for an immediate General Court Martial.

Wythe's comment about her breasts were as innocuous as if he'd said her shoulder, even if the others chose to ride him about it. However, as an Orinoco girl, Tamara still wasn't used to such casual reference to certain body parts.

Tamara couldn't help but to look down at her breasts, though. Tamara knew she wasn't a beautiful girl by most standards. She wasn't ugly, either, but no head-turner. But she had a deeply held pride in her breasts, which she thought were good-sized and rather well-formed. Without a doubt, she considered them her best feature, and while she didn't flash them in public, when in civvies, she never-the-less wore blouses she thought might enhance their appearance.

She quickly looked up at Victor, and his eyes were on them for a moment before he quickly looked away. Tamara was still embarrassed, but Victor's attention was more than a little exciting. She thought Lance Corporal Victor Williams was one heck of a fine cut of a man, and he seemed nice enough. This wasn't the first occasion that she had reflected that it would be *interesting*—which

Jonathan P. Brazee

was as detailed of a term that she would allow herself—to have a romantic liaison with a nice guy who was so much larger than her. She could feel the flush on her face grow, and she wasn't sure anymore if it was just from the embarrassment or something else.

"This one's on me!" she shouted, too loudly, as she stood up and grabbed the empty pitcher. "What are we drinking? San Miguel?"

"You can't tell? What a lightweight!" Doc Neves said. "That's Wolfshead Red, Tammy."

"That's Tamara, Doc. I'm not a freaking Tammy. But Wolfshead Red it is. What about Corporal Medicine Crow? Did she show up yet? I owe her more than I owe you guys."

Corporal Medicine Crow was the sniper she'd seen back on Wyxy, and she'd been the one to take out the SevRev with whom she'd been wrestling. It had taken Tamara awhile to find that out, but once she had, she'd sent to corporal an invitation to meet them for a beer. Sgt Priest might have blown the guy's head to bits, but it had been the sniper who had done all the real damage.

"The Ice Bitch is coming?" Wythe asked.

"The Ice Bitch?" Tamara repeated, confused.

"Yeah. Crow. Hot as snot on the outside, but cold as Hades on the inside."

He clinked his stein with Vic's in a toast.

Ice Bitch? She hadn't seemed bad when they talked on the PA. Pretty, yes, even beautiful, but it was hard to tell much more than that on the small PA screen.

"Well, she sure 'iced' that SevRev," Tamara said, feeling a need to defend the corporal.

"Touché, Tammy," Doc Neves said. "We girls have to stick up for each other. Wythe's just mad because he's like all the rest of guys in the battalion, lusting after Corporal Crow when she won't give any of them the time of day."

"Tamara, Doc, Tamara. But if its raging hormones talking, then I need to get the beer to cool these guys off."

She walked up to the bar, handing the bartender the empty. He gave it a quick sweep under the irradiator, then started filling it up. She looked back at her group while she waited.

24

Tammy! she thought, looking at Doc.

She'd never been a "Tammy." Her little sister had called her Tamtam, but other than that, she'd always been Tamara. Marines, or corpsmen, in the case of Doc, often gave nicknames to each other, but Tammy? That wasn't very warrior-like. Not like Corporal "Killer" Wheng. That was a Grade A nick.

Fanny, sitting on Korf's left side, was reaching around behind him to tickle his right ear with a rolled up napkin. Korf turned to punch the new boot Lassi Rassiter, who was sitting on his right, in the arm. Lassi, taken by surprised, punched his arm back as Fanny laughed uproariously.

Horseplay, pure and simple: what friends did with each other. This was part of the bonding process, that which made Marines what they were. Combat was a big part, maybe the most important part, but even this was vital in forging the unit. And Tamara was part of that now. She belonged.

"Here you go," the bartender said, handing Tamara the pitcher.

When she tried to pay for it, the bartender waved her off with one hand.

"I saw you on the holo," he said. "Copacetic to the max, Lance Corporal. This one's on me."

Tamara didn't know what to say. She knew the newscams had caught her tackling the SevRev, but this was the first time someone she didn't know recognized her. It felt decidedly weird.

"Are you sure? I can pay," she said.

"I insist," he said, stepping back from the bar and out of reach of the PA she'd held out.

"OK, then. Uh, well, thanks, I guess," she said, pocketing her PA and turning back to the booth.

And she felt whole. This was what Uncle Benjie had told her about belonging, something she'd been missing while on the track team. This was what the Marine Corps was all about.

And free beer! she thought. *It just doesn't get any better than this!*

Chapter 3

Tamara watched the monitors closely. Third Platoon was going through their training run, and Tamara thought they were the platoon to beat. But the lieutenant and SSgt Abdálle had been drilling Second hard, and Tamara thought they had a good chance to not only win the battalion competition, but maybe the division as well. This year, the Corps-wide Premier Platoon competition was on Transcendent Reef, and Tamara would love to make it to the fabled planet.

Second Platoon was up next, and while tomorrow's start of the actual competition wouldn't be broadcast until after every platoon had made all six problems, the run-throughs were free game, and if Tamara could learn something from them, she would.

A crew-served weapon opened up on Third's flank, taking them in enfilade. Two Marines fell, but the flank squad quickly maneuvered through the kill zone while the rest of the platoon providing suppressing fire. Within minutes, the enemy crew-served was destroyed, the KIA tended, and the platoon was back on the move.

Nicely done, Tamara had to admit to herself. *But we can beat that.*

The hype about the new Gen Four RCET,[4] the pride of First Division, seemed to be well-deserved. The enemy in the run-through looked pretty real to her, even over the monitors hanging above the stadium seats in the theater. The Gen Four had only been operational for six months, and this was Tamara's first chance to use it. She'd used the old RCET at Camp Charles, of course, but she could see that this new one put the that old antique to shame. She hoped it would give the platoon, if they could take the division title, the edge on the rest of the Corps. Third Division's Gen Four was

---

[4] RCET: Realistic Combat Environment Trainer. This is a huge simulator used to train Marines and sailors how to fight.

just about to be commissioned, and that would be too late for most of the competition. No other unit had theirs yet.

"Veal! Come down here!" Staff Sergeant Abdálle shouted from the front of the seats, earning a disapproving look from some major sitting right under the platoon sergeant's nose.

What now? she wondered.

She was anxious for their turn in the breach, and she didn't want anything, like some stupid "special" task, to get in the way. She was feeling confident as to her place in the squad, but this would be the first real field training in the three weeks since coming back from Wyxy, and she wanted to work with her fire team, squad, and this time, platoon. She'd read enough to know that the better a unit trained together, the better it would perform in combat, and she was gung-ho ready to make that happen.

"Get down here now!" the staff sergeant said. "I don't have all day, and neither does the CO. She wants to see you ASAP!"

She? That meant LtCol Rhonendren, not Capt Mueller.

Jessie Wythe coughed loudly, then rotated his clenched hand around his nose again, his favorite sign language.

Tamara stood up, making sure to give Jessie a hard kick in the shin as she stepped past him.

"Brown-noser, brown-noser," he choked out, making the words sound like a cough.

Vic was sitting with his squad in the next row down, and he gave Tamara a supporting smile. Tamara was tempted to give his shoulder a brush with her hand as she passed in back of him, but she resisted.

There was no restriction on dating between Marines of the same rank, but a certain decorum was expected, especially while in uniform. With all eyes on her as she made her way to the center aisle, it wouldn't go over well if she openly committed PDA.[5]

It wasn't as if they were a secret, however. Pretty much everyone knew that they two had gone out to town for dinner a couple of times, and they had become somewhat of a thing.

---

[5] PDA: Public Display of Affection

Not that Tamara knew just what that thing was yet. She liked him and like the attention he gave her, and they'd made out at the theater the Saturday before. She wasn't sure if he was really a good match for her or if she was just enjoying the relationship part of it, and with a newly reinforced determination to make good in the Corps, she didn't want anything to get in the way of that. But in the meantime, she planned to enjoy whatever happened between them.

It doesn't hurt that he's easy, oh so easy on the eyes, she thought as the tiniest of smiles creased the corner of her mouth.

"Took you long enough," the platoon sergeant said as she finally reached him. "Look, go report to the sergeant major. He's waiting for you. I've got to get back to the lieutenant and the squad leaders. We're up in about 20."

"Will I make it back in time? I want to do this, too."

"Well, aren't we just too precious," Staff Sergeant Abdálle said, sarcasm dripping from his voice. "The thing is, the CO hasn't confided in me with this, so I think Sergeant Vinter's just going to have to manage without you. So get your ass in gear and report in, Lance Corporal."

"Yes, Staff Sergeant," she said automatically before she wheeled about and hurried out of the RCET.

Dummy! she admonished herself. *Don't be too eager. Be professional!*

The battalion CP was a good two klicks from the RCET. There had been a bit of a flurry of interest by the press in her after the holo of her hit the newslines, and she'd given three interviews (under the watchful eye of a public affairs lieutenant colonel, who made her more nervous than the reporters and camrecorders), so Tamara figured this was probably more of the same. That left a problem. She could run to the CP, cutting down the time anyone, reporter or the CO, was waiting for her. But she'd arrive sweaty and with her hair, short as it was, a mess. If it was a reporter, she should look squared away. If it weren't a reporter, though, appearances would not matter, and she didn't want to keep the CO waiting.

Between military and civilian reporters, the military won out. Tamara broke into a fast jog back to the CP. She arrived less than seven minutes later, only slightly winded. She felt strong as she straightened her utilities in the full-length mirror just inside the front hatch of the CP, then hurried on down the passage to the sergeant major's office.

She knocked three times on the doorjamb of his open hatch, announcing, "Lance Corporal Tamara Veal, reporting as ordered, Sergeant Major."

"Veal! Took you long enough," the sergeant major said, rising from his seat and coming around the desk.

The sergeant major was a good four centimeters taller and thirty kilos heavier than Tamara, and he tried to get around her and out the hatch. The fact that she was blocking the way and he was trying to get out didn't register with Tamara, and she just stood there, expectantly waiting for an order.

"Can I get out, if you please, Lance Corporal?"

"Oh, sure, Sergeant Major. Sorry about that," she replied, jumping out of the way.

She followed him, one step in back and one to his left, down the passage to the CO's office.

"Colonel? Lance Corporal Veal's here," the sergeant major said through the open hatch.

"Send her in," Tamara heard from inside.

"Report to the battalion commander," the sergeant major told her.

Tamara pulled down the bottom of her utility blouse, very conscious of her disheveled appearance, and then stepped through the hatch with as much confidence as she could muster, centering herself in the position of attention on the CO's desk.

"Lance Corporal Veal, reporting as ordered, ma'am!"

"At ease, Lance Corporal Veal," the CO said, looking over her desk.

Tamara had the uneasy feeling that the CO was looking at her as a hawk might watch a mouse, despite the slight smile on the woman's face.

"I'm glad we tracked you down. I believe you know Lieutenant Colonel Versace, and that's Colonel Covington with him," the CO said, nodding over Tamara's left shoulder.

Tamara took that as permission to look around, and it was only then that she noticed the two Marine officers sitting on the couch behind her.

What's Versace here for? she wondered. *Does he want me back on the team?*

Her heart fell at the thought. She was fitting in with the squad, and she rather liked the feeling. She did not want to leave her fellow Marines, her friends—no, more like her brothers and sisters—to go back to the track team.

"Lance Corporal Veal, why don't you take a seat," Lieutenant Colonel Versace said, indicating a second couch kitty-corner to the one on which he and the colonel were sitting.

Almost warily, Tamara took the seat, sitting on the edge of the couch at a modified position of attention.

"Lance Corporal Veal," the colonel said, "I'm Colonel Covington. I'm the Marine Corps liaison to the Combined Human Single Combat Corps. Do you know that that is?"

'Uh, yes, sir. I know what it is, sir."

Tamara was puzzled by the question. Pretty much everyone in human space knew what the CHSCC, or "Chicsis," was. They were the gladiators, the human champions who fought the Klethos queens in hand-to-hand combat to determine the outcome of the challenges. They fought in single combat instead of both species conducting full-fledged wars. They were basically the defenders of human space.

How could anyone not know who they are?

"So, I can imagine you know then why I'm here."

What? she thought, her mind racing. *What does he want me to say?*

"Not really, sir," she said after a few moments hesitation.

"I should think it would be obvious, Lance Corporal, the CO said, interrupting. "The colonel wants you to join the CHSCC. He wants you as a gladiator!"

Chapter 4

Tamara sat there in shock, her ramrod position slumping as she tried to take in what the colonel had just said.

A gladiator? Me?

"I . . . what . . . ?"

When she was wondering why she was being summoned to see the CO, she would never have guessed in a million years that she was going to be asked to volunteer to be a gladiator.

"Why me?" she managed to choke out, momentarily forgetting military courtesy.

Colonel Covington smiled, then said, "Fair question, Lance Corporal. And yes, this has a lot to do with your latest exploits on Wyxy. But that just brought you to our attention, and that was enough for us to initiate an evaluation.

"You have proven yourself to be quick on your feet and a fighter, and of course, those are two of the basic parameters we want in a candidate. But there are many more things involved. One of the first things we look at is body mass."

"Body mass, sir?"

"Yes, mass. And do you know why?"

Like most people, Tamara was vaguely aware of the process of becoming a gladiator, mostly based on the several Hollybolly flicks. She didn't remember anything about body mass being a prerequisite. In fact, Natyly Jutlin, who had the starring role in last year's *Queen Killer*, was not a particularly large actor. Buxom, yes; large, not really.

"No, sir, I don't."

"You do know that our gladiators are genmodded to match the d'relle queens in size and strength, right?"

"Of course, sir."

"Well, as you can surmise, it takes a lot more genmodding to bring someone at 100kg to 400kg than someone who starts at 50kg soaking wet. And it's not just a difference of 50kg. It is a matter of percentage. It takes half as long to build up the 100kg candidate than the 50."

"And do you know why this is important, Tamara?" Lieutenant Colonel Rhonendren interrupted, a note of, was it concern, in her voice?

Tamara didn't know what scared her most: the note of concern or the fact that the CO had just called her by her first name.

The full bird[6] looked slightly annoyed that the CO had interjected herself in the conversation, but he said nothing as LtCol Rhonendren continued with, "Because of the Brick. The longer time it takes in genmodding, the less time a gladiator has to serve humanity. If the Kelthos don't claim you, the Brick will."

Tamara flinched at the CO's comment. The gladiators are the heroes of mankind, feted and admired. They were the very thin line that protected human space from an all-out war, one that no one thought they could win. But they paid a very heavy price for serving. Their genmodding was very extensive, pushing the very limits of what the human body could endure, and Mother Nature did not take that interference lightly. Gladiators were extremely susceptible to the BRC, Boosted Regeneration Cancer. Even if they were not killed in combat, they had a life expectancy of five years or so after starting genmod.

"Thank you, Colonel Rhonendren," Colonel Covington said, although not sounding overly thankful.

Then to Tamara, "What the colonel said is true, to an extent, but there is more to our analysis that just mass and a warrior spirit. We look at things such as biofeedback, fast-twitch slow/twitch ratios, intracardiac electrophysiology rates, and well, a host of other measurements. But perhaps most of all, your G-rating. You can be the world's best athlete, but if you have a low G-rating, the genmodding will just not take root well. And you, Lance Corporal, you are almost off the charts with a 97.4% rating. This is very, very good."

---

[6] Full bird: slang for colonel, due to the rank insignia of an eagle .

He looked at Tamara expectantly, but when she just stared blankly back at him, he shrugged, then continued, "What I mean to say is that you are a prime candidate to fill one of our slots at Malibu, and I think you would make the Corps proud."

"Begging the colonel's pardon, sir, but not everyone thinks Lance Corporal Veal is a prime candidate," Lieutenant Colonel Versace said, speaking for the first time since Tamara had entered the office.

"Well, yes, but that is what the official screening's about," the colonel said.

"Lance Corporal Veal, what Lieutenant Colonel Versace is referring to is what he thinks was a lack of desire when you were on the track team. Or to be more specific, how your competitive edge seemed to fade the longer you were on the team. I'd like to hear your take on that, if you don't mind."

"Well, sir," Tamara started immediately into her set spiel, the one she'd hammered out long ago for just this sort of question. "I joined the Marines to defend the Federation, and while I appreciated being selected to the track team, and I tried to represent the Corps to the best of my abilities, I just thought of the track team as a temporary assignment. I thought it was time to get back to the real Corps."

She saw a slight flinch in LtCol Versace's face when she said "real Corps," and she regretted that. The colonel had been nothing but supportive of her, and she didn't want to insult him or his position. And, she realized, that the spiel she had just recited was just that, a spiel. She knew she hadn't her heart into the track team for her last year or so on it, and she hadn't known why. She worried that maybe she really didn't have that competitive spirit.

"I think that's sound reasoning," Colonel Covington said the other two officers. "Of course, I'm just a liaison, not a psychiatrist, so any evals will be done by them, not by me.

"Lance Corporal Veal, I know this is a lot to take in. But I want you to consider the honor of what is being offered you. This is your chance to serve Corps and Federation in more than just about any other way."

"But I would have to leave my platoon?" she asked with a note of sorrow in her voice. "So I won't be a Marine anymore?"

Colonel Covington looked surprised at her question, then said, "Well, of course, you will have to leave your present unit. You'll be on Malibu. But you will still be a Marine. In fact, you'll get a nice promotion to Warrant Officer, and you'll be assigned to our detachment there. Why would you think you wouldn't be a Marine? Remember, Federation Marines have a strong history with the CHSCC. General Lysander was the first gladiator, after all.

"Look, as I said, I know this is a lot to take in, and the UAM[7] code requires a ten-day cooling off period during recruitment. I've got a team standing by to brief you, and after that, we'd like you to go home and visit your family. Talk it over with them. And in ten days, we'll meet with the commandant himself where you can let us know your decision. Does that sound fair to you?"

"Uh, yes, sir," Tamara responded, really not knowing what was fair or not.

Her world had just been turned upside down. She'd just been offered a death sentence, but one that came wrapped in honor and the chance, a real, honest-to-goodness chance, of serving mankind. She felt a surge of patriotism that was cloaked in a fear of dying, not so much in the gladiatorial ring, but of the Brick.

"I know you have questions, but why don't you hold them until after your brief. I'll meet with you again right after, and then we'll get you on your way to see your family."

"Aye-aye, sir," she said, wondering if that was a dismissal.

The CO came to her rescue by calling out, "Sergeant Major, why don't you escort Lance Corporal Veal to your office for a moment and wait there. Then have the duty driver ready to take her to the head-shed for her brief.

The sergeant major must have been waiting right outside the open hatch because he immediately stuck in his head and said, "Lance Corporal Veal, why don't you come with me."

Tamara dutifully followed the sergeant major back to the office where he indicated a worn couch.

---

[7] UAM: The United Assembly of Mankind, an intergovernmental organization which spans human space

"Do you want something to drink? I've got Coke and Sunset," the sergeant major asked, opening a small stand-alone cupboard.

Tamara's mind was reeling, and her mouth was dust-dry, so she said, "A Coke would be great, Sergeant Major."

He pulled out two Cokes and asked, "Twelve OK for you?"

Tamara liked her Coke really cold, at a 17 at least, but this was the battalion sergeant major, so she said, "Yes, Sergeant Major. A 12 is fine."

The sergeant major dialed 12 on the chiller, popped in the two Cokes, and hit the start. Twelve seconds late, the timer rung, and he pulled out the Cokes, handing one to Tamara and popping the top on his. He sat down on the front edge of his desk, facing Tamara, and took a long swallow of his drink.

Tamara sipped hers a little more hesitantly, but the cold wash down her throat was welcome. It was the first piece of normality to hit her over the last twenty minutes.

"Kind of a hellacious howdy-do, huh?" the sergeant major asked as he took another swallow.

"I'd say that's an understatement, Sergeant Major," Tamara said.

She wondered immediately if she'd been too familiar with the sergeant major, but the man simply laughed and said, "You might be right at that."

He seemed thoughtful for a moment, then asked, "I know you haven't had any time to think this over, but what's going on in that head of yours now?"

"I can't rightly say. I mean, I know it's an honor and all of that, but . . ." she said, trailing off and leaving the rest unsaid.

"But the Brick is an awful way to go. If you even make it that far."

She stared glumly at her Coke as if she could find answers in the labeling.

"Uh, Sergeant Major, what would you do? I mean if it was you."

"I can't answer that, Veal. Aside from the obvious that it could never be me, I just don't know. I can wave the flag and all, I can remind you of the Corp's special position in the Chicsis and give you names like Lysander, Hollis, Singh, and more, but when it boils down to it, this is a personal decision, and one you have to make." He let out a loud an unapologetic burp, then added, "I've faced combat, and I've sent men and women to their deaths, but this is not a decision for me or for anyone else."

Outside in the passage, Tamara could hear the CO and the other two officers talking. A moment later, the CO came into the sergeant major's office, waving Tamara down as she started to jump up to attention.

"You got another Sunset in there?" she asked.

"That's nine of them, ma'am," the sergeant major said, pulling one out and popping it into the chiller at 19.

How cold the CO liked her drink was apropos of nothing with regards to what had just transpired, but Tamara could help but watch the timer tick down. A 19 was almost frozen, and Tamara felt the tiniest bit of kinship with the lofty lieutenant colonel over a shared appreciation for very cold drinks.

"I'll get you a case soon, Sergeant Major. Don't worry about it."

"Just reminding you, ma'am. You've got a habit of getting too much on your mind," he said, a smile and an easy tone letting Tamara know this was some of their common banter.

To Tamara, the sergeant major was next to God, and the CO *was* God, so it was interesting to see them with their guards down.

"So, Tamara, what do you think?" the CO asked as the sergeant major handed her the cold Sunset.

"I don't know, ma'am. This has all be pretty sudden like."

"I can imagine. Look, though. This is your decision. I'm not going to feed you all the bullshit about honor and duty. This is a suicide mission, pure and simple. It might just take a little longer, but that's what it is."

"But doesn't someone have to do it? To keep us out of the war?"

"Yes, someone has to do it. But we have over 400 billion people, and we have maybe six or seven battles a year. So don't feel obligated. If you decide not to volunteer, someone else will. You have to be 100% sure of this decision. If there is any hesitation, then maybe there is a reason for that."

Tamara had taken to staring at her Coke again, but as before, no answer magically arose from it.

"Can I ask the ma'am something?"

"Yes, you can ask 'the ma'am,'" the CO said with a smile. "That would be me, I'm guessing."

Uh, yes, ma'am. I—well, would you do it? I mean if they asked you?"

"No, I would not. As you can see, I'm half your size, and I'd waste more time genmodding. But more to the point, I've got a husband and three kids. I couldn't just abandon them."

"But you go into battle, ma'am. I can see your Purple Hearts there."

"Don't misunderstand me, Tamara. I'll die for my Federation if it comes to that. When I've gone into battle, I'm just taking the risk that soldiers immemorial have taken. I've come out alive, even if I've had to regen twice. And if I were the last human alive to fight a Klethos queen, I'd do it. But there are far better choices out there for this kind of mission. Not just Marines, not just legionnaires or soldiers, but people from all walks of life who would be better gladiators than I could ever hope to be."

"I'm not so sure of that, ma'am," the sergeant major interjected.

"Yeah, I know, I'm a lean, green, fighting machine. But I'm getting older, just like the sergeant major, and my G-rating is only a 52. Good enough for getting cosmetic surgery, maybe, but hardly enough for a real genmod. To be blunt, I'm not the best person for this.

"You, Tamara, you have the intangibles to make it through the course and genmod. But there are millions of others who are suited as well, so don't put the weight of humanity on your shoulders, OK?"

"I won't, ma'am," she answered, but she could feel that weight beginning to grow.

"You're a good Marine, Lance Corporal Tamara Veal, a good Marine. I think you could have a long and impressive career. Yes, your star would be brighter as a gladiator, but it will burn out far quicker, too. So listen to your brief very carefully. Ask questions. And then get home and see your family. Admin is cutting you emergency leave right now, so you'll be on your way before evening."

"Emergency leave?" Tamara asked, wondering for a moment who in her family was sick.

"Yes, emergency leave. So if you decide against the Chicsis, then no one will be the wiser. No one will know that you were offered and turned it down. And there is no shame in that. Turning it down, I mean."

"Oh, OK. Thank you for that, ma'am."

"Well, we've got a ride for you to your meeting. Take your time and make the decision that is right for you."

The CO stood up, immediately followed by Tamara. The CO held out her hand, which Tamara took and shook.

"You'll serve the Corps well, Tamara, no matter what you choose."

Tamara only hoped that was true.

ORINOCO

Chapter 5

"Are you getting kicked out of the Marines?" Diana asked her.

"What?" Tamara asked, shocked at the question. "Why would you ask me that?"

Tamara's younger sister shrugged over her pancakes and mango juice.

"Mom and dad think that's what's going on with you. No one even knew you were coming, and now you've been acting all weird-like."

"No, I'm not getting kicked out of the Corps, so just put that idea to rest," she said sourly.

Tamara knew she'd been somewhat withdrawn since arriving the day before as she wrestled with her decision, but it bothered her that her parents, and now Diana, thought she might be getting discharged.

Do they have that little confidence in me?

Tamara took another bite of her own cloudberry pancakes, but her enjoyment of her favorite breakfast had faded away. She'd come no closer to making a decision, and while she knew she should talk to her family, she frankly didn't know how to start.

Mom, Dad, I'm going to save humanity, and it's a great honor. You'll get a real nice payment, too, but, oh, yeah, that payment will because I'll be dead.

Part of her hoped that her family would help her make a decision, to tell her to turn it down. But another part of her was afraid that they would tell her to accept, to be a gladiator and embrace the sacrifice. Would that be because of patriotism, though, or for the fame and adulation of others, gained at the cost of their oldest daughter? She knew her family loved her, but deep inside, she feared what they would say—and why.

Orinoco was known as a pretty patriotic planet. They'd sided with the old Federation during the Evolution,[8] and ever since, it seemed as if the entire population went out of their way to out-patriot everyone else as if to prove their loyalty. A large percentage of people went into the Navy, Marines, the FCDC,[9] and the newly formed Common Assistance Corps.[10] If word got out that one of her daughters was going to be a gladiator, the planet would probably burst at the seams with pride, and her family would be treated as heroes. Tamara was afraid that the hoopla that would surround such a series of events would color her family's opinion on what she should do, and they all would get caught up in a tsunami of patriotic fervor that just could not be turned back.

Tamara was no different. She bled Federation black and gold, and now the Marine Corps scarlet and gold. She felt a deep need to serve the Federation, and by extension, humanity. The honor was one thing, but the knowledge that she would be making a difference far outweighed anything else.

The thought of death in gladiatorial combat was a concern, but not a major one. She'd accepted the possibility of death in combat when she joined the Marines. And while death fighting a Klethos queen might be a more personal one, it was still combat. You rolled your dice and took your chances, counting on training, skill, and luck to pull you through. But the thought of the Brick scared the living shit out of her.

Tamara might not be the belle of anyone's ball, but she was proud of her physical capabilities. Her achievement in sports had defined her to a large degree. And physical fitness was a religion in the Corps, one to which she worshipped at the altar of the gym. The thought of wasting away as her body fell apart filled her with dread.

---

[8] Evolution: the term used to describe the civil war in which the Marines and part of the Navy conducted a coup d'état against the central government.

[9] FCDC: The Federation Civil Defense Corps, which is a hybrid between a standing army and a federal police force.

[10] Common Assistance Corps: a non-military force of volunteers who spend two years on public assistance projects throughout both the Federation and human space.

During her briefings back on Tarawa, she had paid particular attention to the genmod process. When a starlet underwent genmodding for larger eyes or a wasp waist, the modifications to her DNA were minor, and the body would grow into those modifications within months. The changes programmed into a gladiator were so severe, though, that it might take 15 years or more for the gladiator to grow into the larger, more powerful body. And with the practical aspects of the war with the Klethos, that was just too long. So genmodded gladiators underwent boosted regen, which shortened the time from 15 years to about six months.

Regeneration changes regular body cells into stem cells though the process of epithelial-to-mesenchymal transition, or EMT, thereby allowing them to grow into whatever the programming instructs. However, it also changes cancer cells into stem cells, and that is what results in BRC. BRC can never be cured, only managed. But the combination of extreme genmodding and boosted regen was just too much of an insult to the body, and the rapid degeneration of gladiators kept the cancers too far ahead of medical treatment. Gladiators who survived combat had their bodies simply deteriorate into total system failure. It was a slow and painful process, and Tamara was terrified of it.

The rest of her briefing had been easier to take. She learned that the first six months of training would take place before genmodding. This was both part of the selection process as well as putting as much training as possible while in their normal bodies to not waste time with the basics as a genmodded gladiator. Both made sense to Tamara. If a person could not master hand-to-hand combat, then it would be foolish to genmod her, both to her and to the CHSCC. The Chicsis had to send only its best to meet a d'relle.

At one point in the brief, they'd focused a scanner on her head, then showed her a holo of a fight, one in which a gladiator had been torn apart by her Klethos opponent. It was a graphic death, but to her surprise, Tamara had not felt overly bothered by it. She didn't know if that was good or bad, but the technician took his scanner and left the briefing room.

From Tamara's point of view, the briefing boiled down to a few basics: being nominated did not assure her of being selected, being selected for the SCTC, the Single Combat Training Course, did not mean she would eventually become a gladiator, and if she did become a gladiator, she would either die in the ring or from the Brick.

Oh, yeah. There was also the small matter that she would be keeping all-out war with the Klethos at bay.

Tamara knew that she should accept. No matter what Lieutenant Colonel Rhonendren had said to her, someone had to accept the mantle for the sake of humanity, and if she really was qualified, then why not her? How could she refuse and then make someone else, someone possibly not as well qualified, take her place?

She realized this was a heavy dose of hubris. She'd been selected because of the incident on Wyxy, and then she'd met the prerequisites. Out of 400 billion people, there had to be other women who would make a better gladiator than she would, but the fact was that she had gotten the call, not them. Right in the here and now, it was her decision to make, no one else's.

Diana was studiously staring at her pancakes, but Tamara knew she was waiting for something more from her. And Tamara wanted to talk about it. She just didn't know how to start.

"Eat your breakfast, Di. I'm not in any trouble with the Marines, or anyone for that matter. I've been offered an opportunity, a big one, really, and I'm just a bit preoccupied."

"An opportunity? What kind?"

"It's, uh, well, it's big. What say we go down to Franklin's. I really need a workout, and you could afford to put a little meat on your bones," she said, reaching over to feel her sister's biceps as if evaluating them.

"Not all of us are freaks of nature, Tamtam," Diana said, part of their timeworn banter. "I'll lift with you only if you agree on say, ten klicks? Down along the river?"

Diana was a good 30kgs smaller than Tamara, and while she was nowhere near as strong, she'd always been a better runner. Tamara thought her little sister might be in for a surprise, though. As a Marine, she'd become a better runner, too, possibly not enough to beat her, but enough to give her a run for the money.

"You're on, Di."

As they stood up from the table, Diana placed a hand on Tamara's arm and said, "And when you're ready to let me know what's going on, I'm here, and I'm a good ear."

Tears almost formed in Tamara's eyes, but she fought them back. She knew her family had her back, and they would be there for her no matter what.

"I know you do, Di. And yeah, maybe I'll bounce a few things off you during the run."

TARAWA

Chapter 6

Tamara sat nervously in the Sergeant Major of the Marine Corps' outer office. She was in rarified atmosphere where lance corporals simply did not tread. Soon, too soon, she'd be escorted in to see the commandant himself to tell him her decision.

Since getting back to Tarawa, no one had asked the big question of her. By the stares and sideways glances, she knew that more than a few people knew why she was there, and while they wanted to know her decision, but no one was going to usurp the commandant's prerogative.

Sergeant Major Çağlar stepped through the hatch as Tamara jumped to her feet. The sergeant major *was* Marine Corps history. He'd been at the side of General Ryck Lysander for most of his career and had been an instrumental cog in the Evolution. He'd even been at the general's side when as a colonel, he'd been the first to not only fight a queen, but defeat her, saving an entire world. Tamara would love to sit down and pick his brain about that first fight, but she was frankly in awe of him.

"Thanks for waiting, Lance Corporal Veal," the sergeant major said, holding out his hand.

Tamara took it, her hand disappearing in the man's massive paw.

I never realized he was so big, Tamara thought as she looked up what had to be at least 25 centimeters into the sergeant major's eyes. *He could almost have fought a queen without genmodding.*

That was an exaggeration, she knew. Sergeant Major Çağlar probably topped 2.3 meters and massed 130 hard-as-rocks kilos, but that was a far cry from a four-meter, 400 kg d'relle. Still, the sergeant major was one big man.

"Please, take a seat," he continued, "while we wait for the commandant. Would you like something to drink while we wait?"

"No, sergeant major. I'm fine," she answered.

Two times I've been in a sergeant major's office, and two times offered a drink, she mused. *I wonder if that's part of the training?*

That thought, as light and whimsical as it was, helped to calm her nerves. He may be the Sergeant Major of the Marine Corps and about the size of a T-Rex, but he sure seemed nice enough.

"So, how was your leave? Were you able to spend time with your family?" he asked.

"Yes, Sergeant Major."

She didn't know if he wanted more information, so she said nothing more than that. He seemed to be a bit at loss for words as well.

Finally, he cleared his throat and said, "I'm going back into my office and check on some messages. I'll come out and get you as soon as the commandant is back. Make yourself at home, and if you need anything, just ask Clarissa—that's the blue-haired lady at the big desk who keeps me on the straight and narrow—and she'll get it for you. And don't worry, she's not as tough as she looks."

"I am too, Sergeant Major. Don't you be spreading lies about me," a disembodied voice filled the outer office.

"That's right, Clarissa, tough as nails," said while catching Tamara's eyes and shaking his head in mock denial.

Tamara had not expected the Sergeant Major of the Marine Corps, the famous Sergeant Major Hans Çağlar, to be bantering with his executive assistant, but it sure made him seem human. Tamara thought he'd be a good listener, someone who might even listen to a lowly lance corporal.

"We've got hundreds of years of *Leatherneck* on that library tablet there, all the way back to the old United States Marine Corps. If you're interested, take a gander at them while you wait."

"Thank you, Sergeant Major. I'll take a look."

Tamara only said she'd take a look to be polite, but after pulling up a 200-year-old copy and breezing through it, she got hooked. The cartoons might have been old, but the humor was still valid. Centuries might pass, but Marines evidently were the same over the years. She was deep into an account of the Janson Intervention when the Sergeant Major came back into the outer office.

"The commandant is ready, Lance Corporal Veal."

She followed the sergeant major out though his suite offices. The blue-haired Clarissa, sitting as the gatekeeper, smiled and gave Tamara a thumbs up.

The commandant's office was 20 meters down the passage.

"The commandant is waiting for you, Sergeant Major," a woman who was probably the commandant's version of the sergeant major's Clarissa said as the two Marines entered the outer office.

Tamara followed Sergeant Major Çağlar through two more offices and up to an open hatch.

"Sir, Lance Corporal Veal is here for you," the sergeant major said, standing aside and holding out one arm, indicating that Tamara should enter.

She tried to stand taller as she marched in, centered herself on the desk, and said, "Lance Corporal Tamara Veal, reporting to the Commandant of the Marine Corps as ordered, sir!"

Standing behind his desk, General Joab Ling stood, looking at her. Tamara tried to focus on the bulkhead behind him, about a meter over his head, but the black-with-white-stars Federation Nova on his chest kept drawing her attention.

"Lance Corporal Veal, thank you for coming," the commandant said, his voice surprisingly even and almost quiet.

She hadn't expected that the commandant, one of the most decorated combat Marines in the history of the Federation, to be so low-key, and that almost threw her off stride. But there was a warmth to his voice that was welcoming.

"Please, take a seat," the commandant said as he came out from around his desk.

Tamara dutifully took the proffered seat, sitting at the edge, her hands evenly on her upper thighs, feet planted together and flat on the deck.

"And Sergeant Major, I know you want to hear this, so quit skulking out there and join us."

Tamara felt more than saw the sergeant major enter the office, but when the big man sat down on the couch beside her, is was as if a small earthquake hit her. She thought her seat rose a couple of centimeters as the sergeant major sunk into his side of the couch.

"Well, Lance Corporal Veal, we all know why you're here. You've been offered a unique opportunity, but one with a heavy cost. This is one mission that I would not give to someone, even if UAM regulations didn't prevent me from doing that.

"But I want you to know, that whatever your decision, we will abide by it. If you accept the nomination, we will support you in everything. Colonel Covnington said you seemed worried about your status as a Marine. Rest assured that is not a concern. You are a Marine now, and you will be a Marine while with CHSCC. And to be blunt, you will be buried as a Marine.

"But if you decide to turn down the mission, you will not be blamed, nor will anything be entered into your records. You can go back to the Fuzos and join your squad again, picking up where you left off. No one will think less of you."

No one but me, she thought.

"So, without further adieu, have you made your decision?"

"Yes, sir. I have."

"And that is?" he prompted when she added nothing else.

My decision? Give up my squad, my platoon, my friends? Give up marriage and kids, give up a family of my own? Give up my life? Or give up a chance to do something good, something great for humanity. A chance to make my mark in history? What is worth more, a long, happy and fulfilling life or a short falling star, brightening up the heavens as it burns out?

"Sir, I've thought about this a lot, and I've gone back and forth, but for me, there really isn't any choice. I accept the nomination to be a gladiator!"

MALIBU

Chapter 7

Tamara stood looking up at the statue of General Ryck Lysander, the very first gladiator, in a sense, and the man who first realized the Klethos propensity for single combat instead of all-out war. The fabrisculpter had done an amazing job of programming, she thought. The general, then a colonel, stood in his PICS, battered and close to death, but victorious. Tamara felt a surge of pride fill her very pores. Gladiators came from every planet, nation, and station, but the first one was a Federation Marine. Tamara felt an added burden of not only making it through the training and genmodding, but to uphold the honor of the Corps in the ring. Tamara was in her civvies, but she came to attention and rendered her best drill field salute.

The Chicsiss' "campus," as they called it, did not look like any military base Tamara had seen. It was more like a well-established university campus. The entrance wasn't even secured. She walked around General Lysander's Statue and approached the small white guard shack, reaching into her cargo pocket to pull out her orders.

"Welcome, Lance Corporal Veal," the single guard, a portly man who had to be in his eighties.

"Why thank you," she said, then added, "How did you know it was me?"

She looked around for hidden cameras that might be using facial recognition software, but she couldn't pick anything out.

"Well, Captain Tolbert and Sergeant Hralto have already checked in, and when I saw you salute Big Ryck there, well, it wasn't hard to tell that you were our missing third Federation Marine," he said with a huge smile threatening to crack his face wide open.

"Missing? Am I late?" she asked in a panic.

She'd taken a commercial flight to Malibu via Las Vegas, and while she'd enjoyed the day layover in Vegas, she hoped that had not rendered her UA.[11]

"No, Lance Corporal, no, that's just a figure of speech. Pardon an old man's lack of seriousness. No, you are fine. Only about two-thirds of your class have arrived, so you're fine, fine."

Relieved, she started to fish out her PA, saying, "I was worried for a moment there. Here, let me get out my orders."

"No need for that, Miss. I know who you are, and that's good enough."

"But, what if someone else tries to get in? What about security?"

Her sense of military decorum was frankly shocked. This was the heart of keeping the peace within human space, and it seemed to her that just about anyone could wander in. She doubted the security guard could even get out of his chair and leave his shack until long after someone had broken in.

"And why would anyone try to get in? Oh, yeah, we've got the paramours, but they mean no harm and are easily dissuaded. The objects of their affection are, after all, SCSs, and there's not a man in humanity who is a threat to any of them."

SCSs stood for Single Combat Specialists, the official term for gladiators, but what the heck were "paramours," she wondered. She knew the word, of course, but not how that related to the installation.

"No, you're fine. If you can just go up to Building 19, that red-bricked two-story right over there past the pond, and Bandi will take care of you."

Tamara followed to where he was pointing and saw the building. Its old architectural style, along with the pond in front with honest-to-goodness swans gliding serenely across the surface, was just one more nail in the coffin that this was not a Marine base. She shrugged, thanked Jasper, as she found out was the man's name, and stepped into the installation proper.

---

[11] UA: Unauthorized Absence

"Good luck, young lady!" Jasper called out to her retreating back.

Three swans came up to her, honking a few times as they followed her expectantly around the pond. She didn't know if they were looking for her to feed them, but it was a nice touch.

Bandi was a rather young woman with a very heavy Far Reaches accent. Tamara didn't pry as to exactly where she was from as she welcomed her aboard, handed her a passkey and a follow me, then told her she was on her own for two more days. Until then, most of the installation was open to her to explore as she willed. Meals for nominees were at Terrance House, and the Area 2 gym and pool were at her disposal. Anything she needed could be drawn from the Area 2 commissary. Tamara was pleasantly surprised to learn that she wouldn't have to pay for anything she took from there.

The only areas that were off-limits were Areas 5-7. Tamara knew that these areas were for genmodded candidates and full-fledged gladiators. Bandi hadn't actually used the term off-limits; she only remarked that it would be "appreciated" if she stayed clear of those areas.

Tamara left Building 19, which seemed to be a general admin building despite a lack of personnel manning it at the moment, and with her follow me in hand, walked past a seemingly deserted campus. She caught a glimpse of someone in what looked to be work-out clothes, and she saw a man working on one of the landscaping bots, but that was about it as she made her way to Leung Village, her home for the next nine months.

Leung Village, named for Gasper Leung, the first gladiator to notch up three victories, was as non-military as it could be. It looked like a quiet resort village somewhere. Small houses lined winding streets. Each house had a yard full of flowers and shrubs. Looming over each house was a tree in what had to be back yards.

The follow me guided Tamara to a white house with brown trim. She pushed open the low gate and up the flower-lined walk to the front door. Raising her passkey, she activated the lock. She chose her thumbprint and a combination, and the passkey programmed the lock. When the cycling LEDs hit a steady green, she put her thumb to the pad, and the door silently swung open.

The front entrance was nicely decorated, nothing too busy, but with a homey feel. She could see a cozy front room and a kitchen area, then a large glass expanse that opened up to a beautifully landscaped back yard the simply oozed peace and relaxation. She wanted to check out that lovely back yard, but first, she wanted to shower and change. Her suite was to the right, so she tried the thumbprint access again. The programming worked, and her door opened to a bedroom. Her luggage had already been delivered from the spaceport and was waiting for her.

I could get used to this, she thought as she took in the big, comfortable-looking bed.

One thing was for sure, this wasn't a Marine Corps barracks.

"Hi!" a cheery voice said from behind her.

Tamara, still standing in the open door, turned to see a tall, willowy blonde girl standing in the common area.

"I'm Johanna Sirén, but most of my friends call me Jonna," the girl said with an accent Tamara couldn't place. "I guess we're roomies."

They weren't really roomies, Tamara knew. Each had their own bedroom, but they shared the common area.

"Tamara Veal," she said, holding out her hand.

Johanna happily took it, pumping it up and down vigorously.

"I've been here five days already, and I'm about to crawl out of my skin just waiting. So I'm so glad you're here. I was just about to go for a swim, but if you'd like me to hang out so we can get to know each other, that's cool, too."

Tamara had planned on just chilling until dinner, which Bandi had said started at 1700, but Johanna had such a hopeful look on her face that she didn't have the heart. Besides, if they were going to be housemates, it wouldn't hurt to get things started off on the right foot.

"Well, why don't you come on inside and give me the gouge on what's going on. Let me change, and I'll go for that swim with you."

Chapter 8

Tamara and Jonna stood together in their fluorescent orange running suits, waiting for their PF[12] team. Over the last two days, the two housemates had become quite close, finding each other to be kindred spirits. They'd met others in the incoming class, of course, but the two had already formed a bond, and in the nervous excitement of actually kicking off their journey, they were subconsciously leaning emotionally on each other for support.

The real welcome and start of instruction were to begin later in the morning, but it seemed appropriate that their first formal function as a class was to be a group run. Jonna was not military, so Tamara had filled her in on the chaos and yelling that took place at boot camps throughout the galaxy. It was all part of the tried and true method of breaking down a person's norms and then building that person back up into the mold desired. Jonna was hoping she'd be able to handle it. She'd admitted to Tamara that she'd once choked out an assistant coach, and she wasn't sure how she'd react to authority. Tamara had vowed to stick by her side and not let her do anything stupid.

She took in the gathered candidates: 100 women from 55 different governmental bodies, 100 women from which the next class of gladiators would form. Tamara had met the other two Marines, and there were four other Federation citizens (two from the Navy, one from the FCDC, and an MMA fighter of note). Surprisingly to her, only 53 her fellow candidates came from a military background.

"Here they come," Elei Tuputala, a huge woman from the one of the Oceania Association worlds, said from behind Tamara.

---

[12] PF: Physical FItness

Tamara turned around to see four people, two men and two women, in matching blue running tights and shirts, walking up the group.

"Stand by," Tamara whispered to Jonna as she gathered herself for the expected eruption from their instructors.

But there wasn't any such explosion as one of the men pleasantly said, "Hello, ladies. I'm Derrick, and these are Gaylor, Reba, and Liang. If you would, please join me on a little jog."

As simple as that, the four instructors took off at a quick, but not too fast, pace. A few of Tamara's fellow candidate took off immediately, but the bulk of the women, Tamara included, seem to take a few moments for everything to register. It took Jonna pulling on her arm for Tamara to start moving, and then it took another minute or so of a muddled mess, with elbows knocking into each other, before the class seemed to settle down into something that worked. This was a far cray from the formation runs Tamara was used to in the Marines; it was more of a mob than anything else.

The pace was bearable, but the run went on for over an hour as the group wended its way off the main campus and into the forested hills that surrounded it. By the time they made their way back to the starting point, Tamara was a little winded, but pleasantly so. She looked around at the 80 or so candidates who had finished with the group, glad she hadn't fallen behind to straggle in as they could.

Jonna was not even breathing hard, but her pale skin had turned red around her face and throat. She had a big smile plastered across her face.

"Nice little jog," she said in her accent, what Tamara now knew was Finnish, or more specifically, Mannerhein Finnish.

Jonna was Karjala, or what the rest of humanity knew as Karelian, even if she was born and raised on Pohnjanmaa. Tamara had already learned more about the Karjala, Lappis, Pohjanmaas, and Savos, the four ethnic groups that made up the three planets and one moon that made up the Mannerheim Covenant, over the last few days than she had even known to ask before. She had learned in school that the Mannerheim Covenant was part of the Association of Free States, and that they raised reindeer, but that had been about the extent of her knowledge before Jonna had happily filled her in on more.

"If you say so," Tamara responded.

"You don't think? You didn't have problems on the run, no?"

"No, I'm just kidding. Good run."

"And not the boot camp harassment you told me about."

"No, it wasn't. I can't say I'm disappointed."

But Tamara was a little disappointed—not that she hadn't had someone yelling in her face and getting physically harassed, but that she had expected it and it hadn't occurred. If this was not going to be like boot camp, she was unsure of how things would work. Tamara liked things in a certain order, and not knowing made her uncomfortable.

The last of the candidates stumbled in to the finish. Elei, the Samoan woman who'd alerted them to the instructor's arrival, was second-to-last, breathing heavily as she lumbered up, all what had to be at least 135 kg of her.

"I'm glad I'm not her," Tamara whispered to Jonna. "I can't think she's long for the course."

"Don't tell her that," Jonna whispered back with a suppressed giggle. "As big as you are, I think she could tear you apart, no? She can probably be a gladiator without even genmodding."

Tamara laughed and punched Jonna in the arm, before pulling her in and whispering, "Don't let her hear you! She'll probably want you as her new girlfriend, and then what will you do?"

Tamara knew that was catty, but she wasn't serious, and if she couldn't joke with her new best friend and confidant, then who could she joke with?

"Ladies, if you can gather around me," Derrick shouted out, cutting off Jonna's response.

Tamara and Jonna joined the rest of the candidates as they surrounded the four instructors.

"Welcome to Chicsis and the SCS course. You'll be formally welcomed this afternoon by Warden Mantou, Ambassador San Dolomite and the rest of the staff, but we wanted to personally welcome you this morning. You'll be spending more time with the four of us during Module 1 than you think, and you'll be plenty sick of us before we're done with you.

"Today was an easy introduction to physical training. It will get harder as we go on. But I want to make one thing clear to you. We will not be pushing you. We are not your coaches, we are not your cheerleaders, we are not your motivators. All of you are the cream of humanity, and if you are not already motivated, then you do not belong here. If you are not already 100% dedicated to the cause, then you do not belong here. If you do not have the self-discipline to push yourself to get better, then you do not belong here. So we will guide you, we will set up the training cycle, but if you want a cheerleader, then once again, you do not belong here.

"We are a resource for you. You can come to any of us for assistance, you can ask us anything. We are here for you.

"And with that, we'll take our leave. The formal welcome brief will be in Conference Room 110 at 1300. We will be there, even if we won't speak. There will be a reception immediately following the brief, and please feel free to come up to us then. We know all about each one of you, but it would be nice to get to know the real you, not just what is written in each of your packages."

With that, the four instructors came to an odd position of attention ending with a half nod, half bow, and then turned to walk off.

The candidates broke out into talk, discussing what had just been said.

"I guess that's why no boot camp harassment," Tamara said to Jonna, but also just to voice her thoughts aloud.

"I can't say I'm disappointed, no?" Jonna said. "I think I'll like things this way. This is much better than what you led me to expect. My own roomie, giving me bad scoop!"

"And you can expect more bad scoop from me. I'm a fighter, not a brainiac."

"Well, then my fighter-roomie, what say we get back to the Hilton," as they were calling their quarters, "and shower before lunch. You're kind of reeking right now, and I don't want to lose my appetite."

"Me reeking?   I think you might want to get a whiff of yourself before you start blaming others.   But yeah, let's get back and cleaned up."

As Tamara and Jonna broke free from the rest to head back, Tamara was happy she had lucked out with such a good housemate. She was both excited and apprehensive about the course, and it felt comforting to know she had someone with her who she could count on for support.

Chapter 9

Tamara sat with Jonna, Beth Hralto (it was still difficult for Tamara to refer to the sergeant as Beth—and it was almost impossible for her to call Captain Tolbert Kyra), and Oda Steinbrugger waiting for their first class. The classroom was set up arena-style. There were six tables/desks across, seven rows deep. Each table had four chairs. The four women were in the middle, two rows up.

Tamara still hadn't met many of her fellow candidates. During their welcome brief the day before, Warden Mantou had suggested that they get out to know the rest and throw away national identity. They were representing humanity, not the Brotherhood, the Confederation, the Federation, and the rest. Still, it was easier to stick with Jonna, and while Beth was a sergeant, she was still a Marine. Oda, who was from the Brotherhood, was Beth's housemate, so the four had taken the easy way out and sat together instead of following the Warden's suggestion. There was still plenty of time, Tamara knew, to get to know the others.

The welcome brief had been moderately interesting, but Tamara had thought it more aimed at observers than to the candidates. Warden Mantou was the director of CHCSS, and her selection to the position had more to do with being from the independent world of Pollux and not from one of the major governments. Even Ambassador San Dolomite, the official representative from the UAM, was from the relatively minor world of Vesuvius. The entire feel of the brief was that CHCSS represented mankind, not any particular government, and the candidates would leave behind all their nationalistic feelings when they became gladiators.

Tamara had listened to that with only half an ear. Saving mankind was all well and good, but she was an Orinoco girl, a Federation citizen, and a United Federation Marine. None of that was going away.

Still, she understood that they were all in this together, and despite her problems with meeting new people, she knew she had to make the effort.

Sitting next to her at the adjoining table was Elei, the woman from one of the Oceania worlds. Tamara was familiar with the Kingdom of Hiapo, of course. Their economic might and no fewer than four Federation chairmen were well known. But the Oceania Association went across governmental boundaries, and Jonna had said that she heard Elei was from one of the Samoan worlds within the association, but not in the Federation. How that worked in practice was beyond Tamara, but it really didn't make any difference, especially here at CHCSS.

"Hi. I'm Tamara," she said, turning to Elei, making the effort to be sociable.

"Elei," the big woman said, her voice deep and matching her appearance.

"I saw you on the run this morning," Tamara said, then realizing that could sound like a criticism, given that Elei had come in second-to-last and several minutes behind the front of the pack.

Elei just shrugged, however, seeming not to take the comment poorly.

She patted her belly and said, "There's a lot of me to get around, but I always eventually do."

"I didn't mean it like that. I just, I, well, I just meant I've seen you around, so I wanted to introduce myself. This is my roomie, Jonna," she added, pointing to Jonna.

"Glad to meet you," Jonna said, reaching across Tamara to shake Elei's hand.

Just then, the door by the stage opened, and a 70's-something woman, short and petite, walked in and over to the podium, forestalling any more talk.

"I'm Johanna, not Jonna. Only my friends can call me that," Jonna manage to whisper to Tamara before the lady could begin to speak.

"Ladies, I'm Doctor Ruth Whisperjack," the woman spoke up, her voice reverberating through the classroom. "You are about to embark on a mission that is vital to the very survival of mankind, but before you become SCSs, it is important that you understand the history of mankind's war with the Klethos and the history of the gladiators."

Without any more preamble, she launched right into a short history of mankind's expansion into space, the formation of the various governments of man, and the first contact with the Trinoculars.[13] Unknown to humanity at the time, the Trinoculars, or "capys," were being pushed out of their territory by the Klethos, and the first contact between man and capys was with open warfare. It was only later that the capys, being defeated on one side by the Klethos and unable to push the humans in turn, approached humanity and asked for aid. That led to the discovery of the Klethos and the initiation of fighting between humanity and the Klethos on the Trinocular planet Tri-30, which resulted in a total loss of the planet. It wasn't until the fight on the human world of Yakima 3 that Colonel Ryck Lysander figured out the gladiatorial slant to the Klethos, and half-dead from the Brick, challenged the unnamed d'relle leading the Klethos attack to personal combat, and the rules of warfare, so-to-speak, were re-written.

Tamara felt a surge of pride as Dr. Whisperjack spoke of General Lysander. He was a Marine, after all, and while he later led the coup against the Federation Council, his one flash of inspiration on Yakima had basically saved humanity. Almost all experts have since concluded that mankind didn't then and still doesn't have the ability to stand up to the Klethos in standard warfare.

As Dr. Whisperjack spoke, the screen behind her flashed with images of maps, timelines, and live action recordings. When it came time for General Lysander's fight, she quit speaking and turned around to watch the entire battle.

"And that, ladies, is the start of what you wish to become, Single Combat Specialists," she said, turning back to face them at the conclusion of the fight. "Of course, as capable as a d'relle is, none of them could stand up to a human in a combat suit."

---

[13] Trinoculars: the first non-human intelligent species known to man. The first contacts were in the form of warfare. The trinoculars, or "capys," were being pushed into human space by the Klethos who were taking over world after world from them.

On the screen behind her, images of individual gladiators flashed in sequence, images of each and every one who fought a challenge. Initially, all gladiators were from the few military forces who had Gen-Five combat suits: Federation Marines in PICS, Brotherhood soldiers in Sauls, Greater France legionnaires in Rigaudeaus, and Confederation soldiers in Loricas. Forrest Deltan, from Wayard was the only gladiator from somewhere other than these four governments, fighting in a modified Saul. And in four years of contests, the tally was 17 victories for humans, one for the Klethos.

"The Klethos have their warrior code, but they are also pragmatic enough to realize that the field of battle was essentially being ceded to us. So in 378, they demanded a change to the terms. No artificial battle suits would be allowed. The problem with that is that a d'relle masses about 400 kg, and she is armed with a wickedly effective beak and powerful legs. A large man might mass 140, and human teeth are not designed for combat."

In back of her, two images appeared, side-by-side. One was a Klethos queen, the other a naked man. The man was pretty impressive-looking, and a few appreciative-sounding murmurs from the class reflected that. But as impressive a specimen of man as he was, he was dwarfed by the queen. Even without the d'relle's combat training, it was intuitively obvious that no human could go up against a queen in hand-to-hand and hope to win.

"Without the ability to enter the gladiatorial ring, we could not avoid all-out war. But sending normal humans without combat suits was simply suicide and a guarantee of a loss of both the fight and the planet being challenged.

"Luckily, there was an answer, as you are all aware. Genmodding could render any human the equal in combat to a d'relle. Also luckily, the Klethos code of combat chivalry required them to allow this and to give us two years to create our new breed of gladiators.

"The first to enter the ring was Larry Vistine," she said as the man's image popped up on the screen behind him.

Nicknamed "Shrek" from an ancient flick, he looked like a reject from Dr. Frankenstein's junk bin. The genmod recipe had gotten much more refined since then, but as one of the first to undergo the process, his body was essentially forced through the process for capabilities, not for quality of life.

"Mr. Vistine entered the ring on March 4, 380, New Reckoning, on Fraceline. He was defeated and killed, but he put up enough of a fight to validate the concept. He just hadn't had the time to train properly in his new body. The Vistine Fitness Center, which will be open to all of you who move on to Module 2, was named in his honor.

"Over the next 14 years, we were challenged 53 times. Humans won 29 times, so that means we lost 24 times. Twenty-four planets were lost, ironically, one of them being Talimonde."

Talimonde was the Brotherhood planet given to the surviving capys after they'd been driven completely out of their home-range.

"Then came the watershed moment that affects all of you here today. On April 19, 404, we were contacted by the Klethos liaison, not for another challenge, but by the gender request. We had always known that the d'relle, that all Klethos fighters, for that matter, were female as we understand genders. The Klethos evidently were not as quick on the uptake, and they hadn't realized that they were fighting our males. When they did, the gladiatorial option was almost taken off the table. Fighting a male in Klethos society is a taboo of some serious degree, and by sending males against them, we had besmirched their precious honor.

"Matters almost deteriorated to war before we were finally able to get them to understand that no slight was intended. However, having male gladiators was no longer an option. We had to switch to females.

"Genmodding, thank goodness, is essentially neutral. Yes, there are some minor differences in the process, but the end result is attainable without regards to gender.

"Two years later, almost to the day, Winnie Kim became the first female gladiator, defeating her opponent in her first battle."

An image of Winnie flashed up on the screen, a fierce-looking woman with the same close-cropped hair as had been worn by all male gladiators before her.

"Winnie was killed in her third fight, after which we instituted our current rotation schedule."

Initially, gladiators fought until they were defeated in the ring. But Winnie had become a much bigger personality than most gladiators, a social force that made her the most famous person in all of humanity. Her loss was taken tremendously hard throughout the galaxy.

Dr. Whisperjack went over each of the following gladiators to enter the ring. When she got to Celeste, every set of ears in the classroom perked up.

"As you all know, all previous gladiators went into the ring with their hair either shorn or in a buzzcut. Long hair was considered a liability in hand-to-hand combat. It wasn't until Celeste burst onto the scene that this changed.

"Celeste was, well, Celeste," Dr. Whisperjack said with a smile. "All who knew her fell in love with her irreverent personality. I vividly remember her sitting right there," she continued, pointing to a table over two from Tamara's and up a row. "She asked, well, what she asked isn't important now. What is important was her force of life. And to you, she has left a lasting legacy."

"Our hair," Jonna whispered beside Tamara.

"Celeste was fascinated with the Klethos' crest. We know now that the crest is filled with nerves, and they have some sort of function having to do with balance and spatial awareness. But the colors they display are also a source of pride among them, even to indicate ranking. We don't totally understand this relationship, but take it that the crests are important far more than just as a sensory array.

"Celeste, being Celeste, thought it made sense to mirror the crest, if for no other reason than to instill uncertainty in her opponent. So she approached Colonel-General Molinov, then the director of Chicsis, with a request to grow her hair. Although he denies it to this day, the Colonel-General first turned down her request," she continued with a huge smile. "But Celeste did it anyway, citing that there was no rule against it, and that she was free to do as she pleased. Three days before her scheduled fight, she had her own hair not only accelerated at Illy's out in town, but then she had it died into the pattern you have seen in countless holos."

An image of Celeste flashed on the screen, flaunting her famous hair in the yellow, blue, and pink stripes. Most of the class burst into applause.

Dr. Whisperjack smiled and waited for the clapping to die down before she continued, "Many people were shocked by this, and there was talk about not letting her fight. They thought she had made light of the combat. But her name had already been submitted to the Liaison Committee, and Arapaho was too important a planet to simply let go. Five billion people are quite a few to re-locate, after all. So she was allowed to fight."

An image of Celeste, walking proudly through the crowds to the ring, flashed on the screen. The people of Arapaho who were lucky enough to get in close erupted in cheers as she appeared. One man, looking like a child when compared to her, burst past the holding rope that marked her approach and fell to his knees and kissed her feet. One of her escorts started to haul the man away, but Celeste, ever aware of the stage of life, pulled the man up to her head level, his feet dangling more than a meter in the air, and kissed him. The crowd went wild.

"The first paramour," Jonna whispered.

Tamara had heard the term the day she checked in, but now she was aware of the legions of men who worshiped and loved gladiators. Which was somewhat of a waste as during the genmod process, a gladiator's reproductive system was atrophied to almost nothing, and hormones were adjusted so a gladiator was never distracted with sexual urges.

When Celeste appeared at the edge of the ring, the assembled Klethos simply froze for 10 or 15 seconds, staring at her. Unlike the humans who attended each fight in large numbers, there were rarely any more than 20 Klethos at any contest. On Arapaho, there were 17, and all 17 stepped forward in unison, then by putting out one leg in front, bending at the waist, and spreading all four arms outwards like some sort of 18th Century courtier, they performed their honor bow. Contrary to some initial fears, they seemed to appreciate her actions. The consensus was that the hair was considered by the Klethos as an act that brought the opponents closer together in the sisterhood of combat.

Whether Celeste's hair threw their d'relle off stride or not is still a point of argument. But after a hellaciously wonderful hakka, Celeste defeated her opponent in short order.

Ever since then, a gladiator's hair was her symbol of pride. Each gladiator designed her own color pattern, and this became sort of a coming out ceremony, a visual confirmation of going into combat. In the flick *Queen Killer*, the candidates before and after they had been genmodded spent hours discussing and considering their own hair patterns.

Unfortunately, Celeste did not live very long to enjoy her status. She did not die in the ring, but rather from an extremely early and aggressive onset of the Brick. Less than a year after her one and only fight, she was dead.

It took Dr. Whisperjack only a few more minutes to go through the remaining gladiators, bringing the class up to the last fight only two weeks prior, where Grace Patternik had kept the mining planet Uberto in human hands.

To Tamara's surprise, the lecture didn't end there. Dr. Whisperjack spoke quietly into her PA, and a moment later, Grace Patternik herself entered the classroom, to the thunderous standing ovation from 100 candidates as they recognized her. Even if they hadn't recognized exactly who she was, her swirls of magenta and lilac in her hair and the single braid hanging down the side of her face shouted out that she was the real deal, a gladiator who'd seen combat.

Grace walked over to Dr. Whisperjack, dwarfing the woman, who was small anyway by normal standards. She leaned over as an adult to a toddler and gave her a hug and a kiss on the cheek.

"Candidates, welcome to my world," Grace said in the soft, normal sounding voice of most gladiators that Tamara always felt was a little surreal.

A person that big should have a low, rumbling voice, she thought, but that wasn't the way it was. She'd heard that voices were programmed in the recipe to be kept fairly normal even if louder either to enable a gladiator's hakka to be piercing (where a low voice didn't penetrate as well) or simply to leave the gladiators with an old part of their former lives.

"I'm not much of a speaker, but if Dr. Whisperjack, asks, we all jump to her whim, as you will all learn."

The doctor simply beamed with pride as she stood beside the huge gladiator. Tamara wondered just what the relationship was between someone who she thought was only an instructor and Grace and what sounded like all the other gladiators.

"There are 100 of you, just as there were in my class three years ago. We sent 68 of us through to Module 2. Fifty-nine came out of M-2 to Module 3."

Module 2 was the genmodding process. Nine candidates started genmodding, but didn't make it to the end where they could begin specific and intensive training as a gladiator. Tamara had been briefed back on Tarawa that the genmodding was so severe that not everyone made it through. Some candidates died, their bodies simply not able to take the immense strain. Others were stuck in limbo, neither a normal human nor a functioning gladiator.

Tamara looked around the room. If her class held to the same stats, then nine of them would suffer the same fate. Of course for the remaining 59 who made it to Module 3, all were in the process of dying. But at least some of them would have the chance to defend mankind first.

"Of the rest of us who entered Module 3, two ended up with aggressive BRC and never got out of training. That means just over half of us became potential gladiators. From my class, five have already presented our hair. Two of my glad-sisters died in the ring, and three of us have triumphed, keeping human worlds in human hands."

She had to stop as the class erupted in applause again. Finally, she held up a huge hand to quite them down.

"This is what you have volunteered for. To go into combat for mankind. And it is for this that you will sacrifice your life as you know it. If there is any doubt in your mind about this, if there is any doubt about giving up the chance for children, for volunteering to die in the ring or from the Brick, stand up now and leave. You won't be doing anyone any favors by staying around.

"But if you are dedicated, if this is what you want to embrace, then I welcome you, and I hope I am around long enough to call you sisters, and even be on your side when you present your hair.

"I'd wish you good luck, but that is meaningless here. Instead, I wish upon all of you satisfaction in knowing what gift you are giving the rest of humanity."

As the class rose as one for another round of applause, Tamara saw the glint of a tear running down Dr. Whisperjack's cheek. Tamara wondered exactly for what the tear was, and if one would ever be shed for her as well.

Chapter 10

Elei rushed Tamara, knife held high, an expression of pure hate on her face. Tamara instinctively backed up, holding up one hand to block the blow. That was a mistake, a fatal one. Elei slashed down at Tamara's arm, then at the last moment, diverted it to sweep across Tamara's throat.

"You're dead," Elei said, a smile replacing the grimace as she switched off the training knife's holo-blade.

"You looked like you really hated me," Tamara said sullenly. "I thought you'd gone feral from all the stress."

"Ah, my war-face. You don't have one? How come you don't have one yet?"

"Miss Veal," Combatmaster Hallen said. "What did you do wrong?"

"Aside from getting killed?"

"Aside from that, Miss Veal, yes."

"I, uh, I backed away?"

"Not quite. Backing away can be a logical movement, but only when it is planned. You backed away in panic. You let Miss Tuputala dictate the fight. Try not to let that happen again," he said in his reserved, almost prissy manner.

"Try not to let that happen again," she repeated in an exaggerated bouncy voice—after the combatmaster moved off to the next group."

"Not bad advice, Tamara," Elei said.

"It's not like we are going to be fighting in these bodies," Tamara said, not willing to concede the point. "And they're not even training us to really fight. We get introduced to a few moves, then we fight."

"You know why," Elei continued, her voice calm and reasoning, as if she was talking to a five-year-old.

That voice only grated on Tamara. She knew they were not actually being taught to fight yet. What she had said about not being in their genmodded bodies was correct. Their natural bodies just couldn't do what their genmodded bodies would be capable of. The classes now were only to begin to instill a concept of hand-to-hand fighting, to build upon the warrior spirit—and to see who might never develop one. And so far, Tamara had not shown much in the way of being a true warrior. That filled her with a feeling of not only failure, but a fear that she could be dropped from the program. She didn't want to face that fear, so she projected her distaste to what she considered Elei's condescending attitude.

"You're not doing so well yourself," she countered. "Have you made it back with the pack even once?"

A cloud seemed to form over Elei's eyes for a moment. Tamara knew she should apologize, but she couldn't. And that wasn't fair. Over the last week of the course, they had become friends, and after Jonna, Elei was probably her closest friend.

"No, not once. But we are never going to race a d'relle, only fight her. So, shall we dance again?" Elei asked, turning her blade on once more and bringing it up in a salute.

Tamara turned her blade back on, and the two clashed several more times. Tamara even scored win, the AI giving her credit for a crippling blow. Combatmaster Hallen stood by during one more fight, observing, but he said nothing as Elei notched another kill.

Both women stopped to get a drink when the outer doors opened, and a tall, but wasted figure in a hover chair came into the gym.

"That's Fleetwood Andrews," Elei said unnecessarily.

Fleetwood Andrews was the last remaining male gladiator. He'd been in the last group of men to be genmodded, just before the gender switch. Because of the hiatus in fights, he'd never been assigned a mission. He'd been genmodded for nothing. He'd stayed on at CHSCC as an instructor for as long as his body held out. Now, his wasted body confined to a hover chair, he was just marking time until the Brick claimed him, the last of his kind.

One by one, the groups of women stopped fighting to watch Fleetwood maneuver his chair to the bleacher area. Tamara couldn't take her eyes off of him. He looked horrible, as if the Brick had already killed him a year ago, and now his corpse was somehow reanimated, a zombie.

"Young ladies, please continue," the combatmaster shouted out.

Slowly, the women got back to their training, but everyone seemed to be conscious of Fleetwood as he watched them practice. The gladiators tended to avoid Area 1, where the candidates lived and trained, so any gladiator excited interest. But Fleetwood, was, well Fleetwood, a famous, if tragic figure.

Tamara tried to focus on Elei, but her attention was on Fleetwood. She kept looking over at the man. When the combatmaster went over to talk to the gladiator, she dropped all pretense of training, and simply stood, staring at them.

"I heard that the braided gladiators offered him his hair, but he refused," Elei said as she stood beside her.

Gladiators "received their hair," as they called it, when they were assigned their first fight. Each gladiator chose her colors, and together with her sisters, had it done at a beauty shop out in town. Once a gladiator fought—and survived—she braided one strand of hair that hung down the left side of her face. If she fought twice and survived, she added another braid. As this tradition didn't start until Celeste hit the scene, no men had it done. So to offer it to Fleetwood was simply an honor, like an honorary doctorate.

"I would have refused it, too," Tamara said, not sure she really would have.

Combatmaster Hallen realized he had lost the class, so he called an end to the session.

"Come one, I want to meet him," Elei said, pulling on Tamara's arm as other candidates started flowing to the bleachers.

Tamara pulled back, resisting.

"Come on, what's the matter with you?"

"I don't want to go," she said. "He's going to be mobbed, and in his condition . . ."

Jonathan P. Brazee

"His condition? Don't you think he wants to meet us? Why would he come if he didn't?"

"You two coming?" Jonna asked with Gert D'Amato, her fight partner, as they passed the two of them.

"No, really. If you want to go, fine. But I don't want to bother him," Tamara told Elei.

"OK, suit yourself. But I want to meet him. I doubt we'll have too many more opportunities," Elei said as she left Tamara standing there.

Not too many opportunities because he'll be dead of the Brick, Tamara thought.

She slowly made her way behind her fellow candidates, then slipped out the door into the welcoming embrace of the afternoon sun. She took several deep breaths, calming herself.

Too many candidates mobbing him had only been an excuse. She didn't want to meet Fleetwood because she feared him, or feared what he'd become. What she'd become if she survived the ring.

She had volunteered to become a gladiator, and by doing so, she knew she had a very limited lifespan. The thought of dying in the ring fighting a queen was sobering, but she wasn't too upset or worried about the idea. But surviving the ring and then facing the cold hands of the Brick frightened her to no end. This was the nightmare that woke her up at nights.

Chapter 11

"The lateral tendons are a weak spot in a d'relle's legs," Dr. Cheboi said as Gail's outer skin went transparent, and the candidates could see the inner workings of her legs.

"While these allow the stored energy to unleash tremendous power in front kicks, they offer little in the way of lateral support. No less than 18 victories in the ring have come from disabling the knees in this manner, crippling the d'relle first."

Gail performed several deep-knee bends, the tendons glowing fluorescent pink so there could be no mistaking them. Dr. Cheboi stepped forward, half the height of Gail, and mimicked striking the sides of the knee.

"Do we really know the exact placement of the tendons?" Grammarcy Regent asked as the class collectively groaned.

Grammarcy was a springbutt, the worst in the class, always asking questions, mostly inane or, as in this case, something that had been answered time and time again.

"Ooh, one more and I've got bingo!" Jonna whispered.

With so many springbutts—Grammarcy was just the most prominent—quite a few of the candidates had started playing Springbutt Bingo. A table was drawn with three rows up, three rows across, making nine separate boxes. In each box, a candidate's name was written. If that person asked a question in class, the holder of that bingo sheet marked that box as filled. Jonna and Tamara had only recently found out about the game, but they had eagerly joined, paying 10 credits per game played.

Tamara glanced at Jonna's PA. She had two of the diagonal boxes filled. If she got her bottom right box filled, she'd win the pot of 230 credits. Tamara couldn't quite make out whose name was in that bottom box, but she hoped it was one of the quieter candidates. She didn't wish Jonna bad luck, but she wanted to win once herself.

"As I've mentioned, several times now, the Klethos simulacrum was designed after countless man hours of analysis. Gail's outer form is a pretty accurate depiction of an actual d'relle, but as to the inner workings, well, the Klethos are not about to give up one of their d'relle for us to autopsy. We do have the bodies of the basic warriors recovered on Tri-30, but just as a gladiator's genmodded body is a far cry from that of a normal human's, so a d'relle's physical workings are probably different from that of a normal Klethos.

"However, based on the bodies we do have, and from analyzing recordings of each fight, we think Gail is a pretty accurate construct.

"So now, unless there are any more questions?" Dr. Cheboi asked, pausing to look out over the class.

Jonna quickly looked past Tamara to stare at Elei as if waiting. Then it struck Tamara why.

Ha! Fat chance! Elei's never asked a question in class!

"So, watch while Gail kicks forward," Dr. Cheboi continued, instructing the simulacrum to kick out. "If a d'relle connects solidly with this type of kick, it could disembowel a gladiator and end the fight right there."

"They should just genmod us with stronger guts, like steel," Jonna whispered.

"They can't. Protocol Six," Tamara reminded her.

"Yeah, I know, but still . . ." Jonna said, trailing off to nothing.

Protocol Six was the self-imposed limit as to how capable, and how vulnerable, a gladiator was. A human could be modified to the point where they would practically be invulnerable to a Klethos queen. But as with the gladiators in combat suits, once the Klethos realized the deck was stacked against them, they would demand a change, with the threat of all-out war if their demand was not met. So the gladiators were genmodded to allow them to compete with a d'relle, but still leave them vulnerable enough that they could lose. It made sense from the long view of the situation, but it almost meant that a certain number of gladiators were essentially being sacrificed for the greater good.

Tamara turned back towards the stage where Dr. Cheboi was sending Gail through a series of kicks. It was sometimes hard to believe that Gail was simply a wind-up doll—a very sophisticated and expensive wind-up doll—but still a doll. If you could forget how Dr. Cheboil made parts of her skin transparent when he wanted the candidates to understand the physiology of a real d'relle, Gail looked like a living, breathing creature. She was the pinnacle of Dreamworks-Huawei technology, and she cost the same as a small planet's GDP.

During Module 3, the gladiators would fight other simulacrums, but much cheaper ones which merely moved like a d'relle, not one that had all the inner organs and bones like Gail. Fighting them sounded like fun, and Tamara looked forward to it. As usual, though, she refused to think of what happened before that, in Module 2. She had to agree to enter Module 2 first, and then go through a successful genmod.

She looked over past Jonna to Beth. The seat beside Beth was empty. Oda had quit the day before. Beth had seemed to take it OK, but to have your roomie quit like that had to raise questions. Tamara had made it a practice to ignore Module 2, to act as if it didn't exist. Jonna was the same way, but while they discussed life as a gladiator, they never mentioned that first necessary step. If they didn't think about it, they couldn't brood over it and start having second thoughts.

Thirteen candidates had already fallen to those doubts and quit. The class was getting smaller, and they were still in the first third of Module 1.

Chapter 12

Beth waved from the table she'd staked out, and Tamara and Jonna made their way through their fellow candidates to join her. Tamara had thought the two of them would be among the first to arrive, but there were already at least 25 of their fellow candidates there, most looking like they'd gotten good start on the night. Tamara nodded to several of them as she scooted between the scattered tables; she'd touch base with all of them before the night was over, but for now, she wanted to start with Beth and Elei.

"I've ordered a pitcher of Wolfshead Red, if you don't mind. Might as well go supreme, and it's not like we don't have the money."

And this will be our last night with alcohol, Tamara thought, unwilling to say it out loud.

"Where's Elei?" Jonna asked as she slid onto the bench seat next to Beth.

"In the head. She's hurting a bit after stuffing herself at the banquet."

"Oh, jeez! Me too. That was some feast," Tamara said, patting her still-full stomach.

"The tacos were the best," Jonna said. "I think I'll miss them the most."

The three women were silent for a moment, afraid to say more about what else they would be missing after the first of them started the genmod process tomorrow.

Genmodding and regen were very broad processes. Someone could go in for a skin color change, a straighter nose, or even a double row of teeth (Tamara had never understood that particular craze) and go home the next day. Within a month or so, and with no regen, the change would be completed, and there would be no other effects. A battle-wounded Marine could go into boosted regen to replace limbs, and after nine months, they would be good as new, even if he or she now had a greater chance of contracting the Brick. But a gladiator went through a much more radical genmod that wrought huge changes on her body, and then the regen went into overdrive to make the changes actually grow.

The basic processes were the same, but just as a Cali and a Hyundai were both hovers, the Hyundai was a higher class and needed more care. If the person wanting purple skin was the Cali, the wounded Marine was the Hyundai. And that made the gladiator a Bugatti: an amazing machine, but a very temperamental one that needed lots and lots of care.

Once the candidates started the process, alcohol was out of the question, as were spicy, high fat, and acidic foods. No more beer, no more tacos, no more orange juice. So tonight, the last night of Module 1, the traditional banquet had been served with a huge array of food. And now, all of the candidates were gathering at the Moldy Lion to celebrate or drown their sorrows, depending on their frame of mind. Seventy-nine were still in the class, and Tamara expected all seventy-nine to show up.

Elei made her way out of the head, looking sheepish as she sat down with a groan.

"I lost most of what I'd eaten," she admitted ruefully. "And it didn't taste so good the second time around."

"No problem," Ronna said. "I've ordered a pizza from Gary's, and it'll be here in an hour. So now you have room for it."

Tamara groaned when she heard that, but she was intrigued. Gary's pizza? She might be able to nibble on a piece.

Several more women came in, including Captain Tolbert. Tamara knew she'd have to share a beer with her. They had not become particularly close during Module 1, but along with Beth, they were all three Marines, and that bond still held strong.

Tamara was becoming very close with her fellow candidates, but she would rather have spent her final night with her family back on Orinoco. But while the candidates were told they were free to do what they wished, going home was not an option. The only way to do that was to quit the program. The consensus was that the powers that be knew that if they went home just before Module 2, too many candidates would simply not return. Someone like Angela Timothy, sitting at the next table, for example, would be extremely vulnerable. Angela had two young children, and seeing them might be too much for her. The Federation wouldn't even nominate a candidate if she had children, but Wayward Station, where Angela was from, evidently didn't have the same restrictions.

The next couple of hours were filled with drinking, eating (Tamara managed to put down three pieces of pizza, to her surprise), laughing, and a few tears. At one point, a pitcher of beer showed up unasked. The waiter pointed to a table in the back at which four men sat.

The five women (they'd been joined by Grammarcy as she made the rounds) lifted up their steins in a toast.

"Paramours," Grammarcy said with a hint of disdain.

The Moldy Lion was a large tavern, with seating for at least 400 in all three areas. All 79 candidates were now there, mostly congregated in the upper loft, and they seemed to take up the most area. But scattered along the periphery of the loft, and in the tables below the loft, were quite a few men, most nursing a drink as they watched the candidates.

"Remember us after Module 2," one of them shouted out, only to be hushed by one of his companions.

"Too late for that then," Jonna, who was pretty far gone to the beer, muttered. "After they cut the heat out of us."

"Shit, Jonna," Elei said. "Do you have to remind us about that?"

"Cutting the heat out" was the slang for the genmod neutering. Working ovaries and the uterus would not survive the process. Not only that, but estrogen would be minimalized, and the nerves that transmitted sexual pleasure would be deadened. With no desire and a lack of stimulation, gladiators would be sexless. For some of the gladiators, this was their biggest sacrifice, bigger than their eventual death in the ring or to the Brick.

The given reason for this was that the reproductive system was so full of active stem cells that they would take a huge portion of the genmod process and be far more susceptible to the Brick that it was minimalized for the gladiators' health and welfare. Very few of the candidates believed that, feeling control was more of an issue. But no one still in the course complained about it.

There were rumors that some gladiators did, well, partake with one or more of the paramours who hung around like junkyard dogs looking for scraps, but if they did, they couldn't get physical pleasure from the act. It could only be a psychological benefit.

As usual for her, Tamara tried not to think about things that could upset her, so she tried not to think about having the heat cut out of her. Her experience with men was extremely limited, mostly because of her shyness and a lack of many opportunities. On one hand, she wished she'd had some experiences, but on the other hand, she thought it might be best if she simply didn't know what she was missing.

The night dragged on. Tamara made it to all the tables, and things were pretty fuzzy before she made it back to her original seat. Elei was face down on the table, one hand around an empty stein, and dainty snores emanating from her big body. Tamara ignored her and refilled her own stein.

At midnight, a ragged cheer rose from the women. It was officially the start of Module 2. In 12 short hours, the first 15 of them would start the genmod process. As one of the larger candidates, Tamara still had four more days until it was her turn. Four more days to change her mind.

By 2:00 AM, a few of the candidates, mostly the smaller candidates, started to leave the tavern. Tamara didn't envy them. With only a short time before they had to report in to the hospital, their bodies would never be able to purge themselves of the food and alcohol, so they would be "assisted" in purging, which was by all accounts an extremely unpleasant evolution. At least Tamara wouldn't have to go through that.

Suddenly, it was 3:30. A moment ago it was 2:00, and Tamara looked around confused. She'd fallen asleep. Elie was gone, but Jonna was slumped in her chair.

"Hey, wake up," Tamara said, shaking Jonna's arm.

Jonna blinked her eyes open, stretched her arms, and let out a loud burp.

"Come on, let's go home," Tamara said, pulling her roomie up out of her seat.

Jonna looked to a table where the men who'd bought that first pitcher were still sitting.

"You go. I'll meet you there."

"What? Come on, we can split a cab."

"I think I can get someone to get me a cab," she said as she started to the men's table. "You should join me."

Tamara suddenly realized what Jonna meant, and she was shocked. And envious. A huge part of her wanted to throw caution to the wind, to join Jonna in seeking what would soon be impossible. But fear kept her back. It was only partly fear of the unknown—the biggest part was that she'd heard about drunken one-night stands, and the stories were usually how lousy they were. Tamara was drunk, shy, and inexperienced, and she didn't know any of those men whose eyes were fairly exploding with excitement as Jonna tried to saunter over, only stumbling twice—not that the men seemed to care that Jonna was three sheets to the wind.

It might seem foolish to anyone else, but Tamara had certain ideas on what it would be like, and this wasn't it. She feared her one and only experience would be something far less than enjoyable, much less ideal. If Victor were there, she'd probably give in, but not to the smarmy men who were helping Jonna sit down at their table.

She didn't think less of Jonna at all. Jonna had been a basketball star on Pohnjanmaa, and with her pale good looks, she'd been popular, very popular. It was different for her. This was just one last fling. For Tamara, this would be the benchmark, how she would remember sex. And she didn't want to ruin that.

With a sigh, Tamara made her way out of the bar and into a waiting cab. It was time to go back to her room.

Chapter 13

Tamara drank her fifth glass of passion fruit juice of the morning as she watched the clock tick down the minutes. She thought she could just fit in the 16th and final episode of Season 3 of *Lost Opportunities*. Elei, who'd even heard of the show before, watched intently, now totally hooked.

Jonna had left for her genmod the day before, and Elei's roomie, Keiko, had been in that first batch of candidates. Rather than sit alone with her thoughts, Tamara had invited Elei over to binge-watch the entire season. Together, with junk food and citrus juice, the two had kept silent company while Dieter and Penelope had one failed business venture after the other, the "opportunities" of the title, but not the implied opportunity of love (that everyone could see except for them, it seemed).

The trials and tribulations the two characters faced seemed minor, but they served to keep Tamara's mind away from her appointment. Brooding wouldn't do her any good. Elei, however, didn't seem fazed in the least. As one of the largest, if not the largest, woman in the class, Elei would be one of the last to start the process, and when Tamara left in a few minutes, she'd be alone to watch Season 1 on her own.

"Wow, max intense," Elei said as the credits rolled. "But I don't understand how they can't see they are a match for each other."

"You need to watch Season 1 to see that," Tamara said.

"And you don't mind if I hang out here and watch it?"

"No, of course not. You're always welcome. But speaking of that, I need to hit the head before I go."

Tamara didn't need the toilet, but instead, she stood alone in her bathroom, staring at herself in the mirror. She reached up and touched her face as if seeing it for the first time. She pulled up on her t-shirt and stood half-naked. Her breasts hung large and heavy, and after a few moments, she reached up to cup them with each hand. She pressed softly, feeling their heft, feeling the nipples as if trying to memorize them, how they felt. She closed her eyes for a moment, gathering her thoughts.

With a sense of duty, she let go and slid her shirt back on. She took a deep breath, then left her bathroom and walked back into the common room, trying to muster up a smile.

"You OK, girl?" Elei asked as Tamara walked up. "You want me to go with you?"

"No, I think I'd rather make the walk alone."

Tamara had expected staff members hanging around, making sure each candidate made her appointment, but they'd been completely ignored. The requirement that every candidate volunteer for genmodding was stringent, and the staff couldn't even have a hint of coercion.

Tamara took one last swallow of passion fruit juice, draining the glass and saying, "I'm sure going to miss this."

I'm going to miss a lot of things was left unsaid.

"Come here," Elei said, arms out.

Tamara only hesitated a moment before she rushed forward to be enveloped in the big woman's hug. She held it longer than expected, taking strength from her friend.

She finally broke the hug and pulled back.

"Are you going to be OK tomorrow? I mean, we're almost all gone," Tamara asked.

"I won't be alone. I've got Dieter and Penelope, don't I?" she said with a laugh.

The slightest hitch in her voice, though, let Tamara know that Elei was not quite as complacent as she was letting on.

"Well, I'll see you on the backside," she said, taking one last look around the room.

This had been her home for the past nine months. While she was in regen, staff would take her things and move them to her new quarters at Sichko Village where she and Jonna would still be housemates. They'd had the chance to either switch roomies or even live alone, but the two did not want to be split up.

"Love you, girl," Elei said as Tamara walked out the door.

As when she arrived nine months previously, the campus was almost deserted. The staff for Chicsis numbered over 5,000, and there were some 400 gladiators, both in training, in the force, and in retirement on the campus, but rarely was anyone in sight. It took almost 15 minutes for Tamara to make her way to the campus entrance. She looked into the small security shack to see who was on duty.

"Afternoon, Miss Veal," Jasper called out as if everything was normal.

Tamara knew the staff couldn't say anything that could be taken as encouragement, but she really could have used a bit at the moment.

"Afternoon, Jasper," she said as she continued.

At the pond, the swans paddled up to her, honking hopefully. Tamara pulled out a half-eaten packet of Cheese Strings and tossed the wispy snacks into the water. As usual, the swans went into overdrive to snap them up, pushing each other out of the way. Idly, Tamara wondered if they would recognize her when she was a gladiator.

If she became a gladiator, she corrected.

She could still quit. Looking over at the front gate, she could just turn and walk out, and no one would say a word. And even if she did accept the genmod, there was no guarantee that she'd survive it. Statistics were such that probably five of them would not. They would die before ever getting to serve humanity in combat.

She could see Jasper surreptitiously looking at her through the security hut window. She knew he was watching, wondering what she would do.

How many of us walked out that entrance over the last three days?

They'd been kept incommunicado since the first of them went to their appointments. She'd find out later how many had actually made it to the hospital.

As she started to turn back away from the entrance, she saw just the hint of a smile coming over Jasper's face. He might not be able to say anything, but he was relieved, she knew. And she didn't think that was just because there was going to be one more gladiator to defend human space. She thought he really cared.

Five minutes later, she reached the hospital. It looked like a resort lodge, with its pastel blue walls and towering evergreens around it. There was none of the usual architecture that screamed hospital. But it was one of the most advanced genmod and regen facilities in human space.

Tamara didn't hesitate but rather pushed open the front doors. Dr. Whisperjack was standing by the reception counter, and she looked up with a huge smile as Tamara came in.

"Tamara, it is good to see you," she said, beaming at her.

"Well, it's my time."

"Of course it is, dear, of course, it is. We do have this last finality, first, though."

"Sure, Dr, Whisperjack. I'm ready."

"Georg, if you will?" she asked the receptionist.

"Please look into the scanner and repeat after me," Georg said.

Tamara leaned into the retinal scanner as Georg started, "I, state your name. . ."

"I, Tamara Constance Veal . . ."

"fully understand and accept . . ."

. . . *the consequences of becoming a Single Combat Specialist in the Combined Human Single Combat Corps. I freely and without pressure or coercion accept genetic modification and boosted regeneration and agree to serve humankind to the best of my abilities. I will abide by decisions made by those assigned to administrate contact with the Klethos Empire. So help me God.*

Chapter 14

Oh, dang, that hurts was the first cognizant thought that broke through the dark and troubled dreams that flitted just out of her reach.

Tamara slowly became aware of her surroundings. She was lying down, and above her was a pale blue and lilac ceiling with soft corner lights giving just the minimum of illumination. She was warm, and it took her a moment to remember that she would have been immersed in a high-potency nutrient-and-oxygen-rich bath. She seemed to be breathing OK, so they must have already raised her head and emptied her lungs of the liquid. With lungs like an infant's, she knew the fluid would have flooded her lungs, enabling them to work with less stress as they grew.

She struggled to look down at her body, but with most of it still under the surface of the dark liquid, and with all sorts or hoses and monitors stuck on her, she couldn't see much.

"Tamara, I see you're back with us," a soft voice said.

Tamara looked to her left to see Dr. Whisperjack and a tech she didn't recognize standing at the side of her vat.

"Dr. Whisperjack, I—" she started to croak out.

"Easy, Tamara. Your voice hasn't been used in two months. And please, it's Ruth. Auntie Ruth, most of the girls call me."

Auntie Ruth? Girls?

Her voice had hurt when she'd tried to speak. Her whole body hurt. She'd known it would, but not this bad.

"Dr. Tansiri is with Abby right now, but he'll be in soon to check up on you," Dr. Whisperjack, no, Ruth, said.

"But you've done very well. You're progressing right on schedule. It's up to the medical team, of course, but I think you'll be out of your bath in a few days and into therapy."

"What . . . what do I look like?" Tamara forced out.

"Lire, do you think . . . ?"

"Sure, I don't see why not," the tech said.

She reached over to a control panel of some sort and hit some buttons. Above Tamara, a screen seemed to coalesce out of the air. Slowly, an image began to form, an image of a naked body lying in a tank of blue liquid.

Tamara couldn't get a feel for her new size, but the body that reflected back at her was obviously bigger than before. It was stockier, too, but without much muscular definition yet. The one glaring difference was that her breasts were almost non-existent.

Tamara suddenly didn't want to see anymore. She closed her eyes as a groan escaped through her lips.

"Lire, please," Ruth said.

"I know it is a little much to take in right now, Tamara. But we're here for you. We've got counsellors on hand around the clock, and I'm here, too. If I'm not teaching candidates, I'll be here in Area 2, ready for anything you need.

"Thank you, uh, Ruth. I'm fine. I just hurt now," she said, unwilling to admit that the sight of her, of her missing breasts, upset her.

She had to be strong. What was done was done, and she had to look forward to her training. The stakes were just too high for petty vanity.

She was a gladiator now.

Chapter 15

As far as Tamara was concerned, the less said about Module 2, the better. Seventy candidates had started genmod—nine had refused to report to the hospital and quit that day. Four had never made it out of their medically induced comas. For the rest of them, not including the two months out cold and in the aquarium, as they called it, the module was six months of torture. The human body was not evolved for such drastic genmodding and regen, and it protested its abuse every second of every minute of every hour of every day.

If their bodies were not complaining enough as they molded and grew into new forms, the medical staff, their "agonizers," put them through "therapy" that would put the Spanish inquisitors to shame. Twice a day for the first three months, the agonizers would stretch, pound, and pull on their bodies, then make them do the same on their own.

According to Dr. Tansiri, their nerves had been dampened and their tolerance to pain increased, but if that was the case, Tamara couldn't imagine what it would have been like without the dampening.

What was worse than the manual manipulation was when they were hooked up to the EMNS, or electromyographic neurokinetic stimulation. This fiendish device ran electrical currents through the body to stimulated the nerve endings and muscles to mesh their function together and then closely monitored the progress. While this machine might have sped up the regen, the process was perhaps the most painful experience during the module.

One of the hardest things for Tamara to accept was just how screwed up her body seemed to be. Simple things like getting up and walking across the room took concentration. Her center of gravity was off, and her bones were different from what she was used to. A heavier musculature in the chest and shoulder compensated somewhat for the lack of breasts, even if the balance was different, but the narrower hips and slightly turned out legs were far more problematic. Tamara had been an elite athlete who was well-attuned to her body, and now, that tuning was out of whack.

The staff assured her that the changes were for the better and through neural plasticity, her brain would adjust so her new body would now be the norm. It would feel as if she'd been born to it. She could see the potential in her new form, but she didn't have to like it while she built up to that potential.

During the last three months, the afternoon sessions were replaced with physical activity designed to build up strength and endurance. These sessions were bad, worse than anything Tamara had experienced in the Marines or as a track star, but they were a heck of a lot better than the EMNS.

Jonna, when they were still roomies, had remarked that the trainers were trying to make them so miserable that they would all jump at the chance to meet a queen in the ring just to escape the torture.

And yes, Jonna. The two had wanted to be roomies together, but the stress and pain made all the girls, as they called themselves now (not women, not candidates, and they were not yet gladiators, so somehow, "girls" was the norm), short-tempered. The horrible, bland food was no help. The "gruel" was the same every day. Insipid and tasteless, it would not bother their still-developing digestive systems while providing for all their nutrition, but it did nothing for their souls. All these pressures resulted in more than a few blowups, and Tamara and Jonna were not spared. After a month, the two roomies had a fight. Tamara didn't even remember what started it, only that it escalated until Jonna stormed out of their oversized house. They refused to speak to each other for a month. Tamara missed her friend, her sister, as the girls began to refer to each other, but she didn't know how to fix the problem. It had taken intervention by Auntie Ruth to bring them back together, and they shared a house again for the last month of Module 2.

The gladiators were a help. Whereas they rarely contacted the candidates, they often mixed with the girls, offering advice and a shoulder to cry on. But they had their own issues. Three challenges were issued during their time in the module, and two gladiators had lost. Each time, the rest of the gladiators had withdrawn for a few days.

But luckily, Auntie Ruth was there. She was the den mother, friend, advisor—whatever was needed. She was all of 1.5 meters tall, but no one would dare to argue with her. Tamara owed her a debt of gratitude for helping her patch up things with Jonna, and she thought the entire class would have collapsed without her tireless efforts. Finally, the horrible module was over. Sixty-six girls were moving on to Module 3.

As far as Tamara was concerned, it was high time to learn how to fight.

Chapter 16

Tamara held up the blade, sighting down the edge. It looked beautiful with the faint pattern of the Damascus folding evident. The quillon and langets were gold, the grips white in the pattern of the original US Marine Corps mamelukes. She brought it back down, feeling the heft and balance. It seemed more a part of her than her own arms right after emerging from her coma. She knew the blade had been designed for her and her alone, but still, she reveled in the feel.

And she was more than pleased that she'd been assigned a mameluke. As a Marine, she couldn't have hoped for more. Beth had been insanely jealous, and Tamara understood that.

In an attempt to keep the Klethos off-balance, gladiators were assigned different blade weapons and trained in different styles. Mamelukes and other scimitar-type swords had not been particularly effective, with three wins and four losses, but Tamara didn't care. She was a Marine, and this was the modern poly-amorphous steel version of one: strong as heck and durable to a fault.

It wasn't her position as a Marine that left her with the mameluke; that was just a lucky coincidence. Each gladiator was analyzed ad infinitum by both swordmasters and huge AIs that took into account movement and reflexes before the best type of blade and style was selected for her.

Beth shouldn't be too disappointed, though. She'd been issued an ichi-katana, which was the evolution from the 18th Century, Old Reckoning, Japanese katana. The Japanese family of blades had an eight to three record, and with female gladiators, that was three to zero.

Elei was issued a claymore, which was not surprising given her size—she was still the largest of them even after genmodding. Jonna was issued a sylvian, one of the newer styles. Developed by the University of Garuda, it had less heft than many blades, but with Jonna's long reach and superb reflexes, it could be a deadly weapon.

While she would still be mixing it up with the other girls in the ring, for the next two months, her swordwork would be accomplished with Master Abad along with the other four gladiators who'd been given scimitars. She'd learn how to use her mameluke first before sparring with those with different weapons.

It had seemed odd to her at first that in this day and age, they would be taken to planets in modern warships that could pulverize said planet, fly down in comfort in shuttles, and then meet their opponents with weapons that had been around in some form or another for 10,000 years. On the other hand, anything more powerful would be somewhat of a mockery to the gladiatorial ring. Anyone could stand there and blast away with an energy weapon.

The Klethos technology was pretty far beyond that of humankind's. In conventional, all-out war, they could almost certainly overcome humanity. Luckily, their warrior creed allowed the battle of champions, and if they allowed the champions to be armed with swords, all the better.

Tamara slowly sheathed her mameluke, almost sad to see the gleaming metal disappear, centimeter by centimeter into the silver and gold scabbard. Her first class was not until that afternoon before dinner, and she couldn't wait.

Chapter 17

Tamara stood stock-still, staring straight ahead and with her sword down along her side. Rheina looked confused as she stood in her en garde. She looked to Master Abad for the briefest moment, the tip of her mohannad dipping ever-so-slightly.

That was what Tamara was waiting for. She immediately launched into a fendente, a direct overhead slash with her mameluke. Rhenia was taken by surprise, but she had the quick-twitch reactions of all gladiators, and she was able to raise her sword to block Tamara's at the last second.

It would have been a quick kill had the fendente scored, but Tamara had launched it as a feint. Rheina was out of position for Tamara's second intention. Instead of some fancy fencing move, however, Tamara's second intention was a corps-à-corps, or a body slam. Touching bodies like this was against every rule in modern fencing, but this was not fencing. This was gladiatorial combat, where a handful of sand thrown in an opponent's eyes would be par for the course. And as Tamara's first time facing a live opponent in the ring, she was bound and determined not to lose.

Both gladiators massed close to the same, but while Tamara was braced for the collision, Rheina was not. She was knocked to one knee, her sword-hand on the deck to keep her from falling flat. Tamara didn't let her recover. With a shout, she brought her mameluke down with all her might, connecting with Rheina's neck just as the other girl realized her mistake.

Tamara's sword passed through Rheina, and the fight AI flashed red.

Tamara let out a screech of victory. She could see Rheina starting to protest, so she spun away from her, but making sure her knee hit Rheina in the chest, knocking her on her ass. She flicked the switch in her sword's handle, and the blade, all the way down to the ricasso,[14] disappeared.

"But Master Abad," Rheina cried out from behind her, "she did that corps thing you said. That's not, not—"

"Not *fair*?" the master swordsman asked, his voice dripping with sarcasm.

"Yeah. Not fair," Rheina said, evidently missing the sword master's tone.

"Do you think a d'relle is going to adhere to human fencing rules. Miss Savant?"

"Well, no. But we're in fencing class now, not combat class!"

"And you are trying to tell me that fencing isn't combat?"

"Yes. I mean no, I don't mean that. But Tamara, she, she, and then she kicked me when I was down!" Rheina said, her voice rising as her frustration got the better of her.

"You were killed, Miss Savant. That is all that matters. Now, or when you get into the ring for real. Remember that.

"Miss Singh and Miss Jones, you two are up," he said, forestalling any more whining.

Tamara turned to look at Rheina with only the slightest bit of pity. And that surprised her. While Tamara had always been a fierce competitor, that had been tempered with a large degree of civility. She never wished anyone harm, and she usually felt compassion for those she beat. Now, she'd humiliated Rheina, and she felt proud. It wasn't as if she didn't like her fellow gladiator. Rheina was a sweet girl with a great sense of humor, and Tamara would be happy to share a meal with her.

It had to be the genmodding, Tamara knew. As part of the genmod recipe, her ovaries and been atrophied, so her estrogen levels were extremely low. Testosterone is also produced in the ovaries, so that would lower the hormone's level in the body as well, but the genmod changed the adrenal gland, where testosterone is also produced, making it into a super-factory of the hormone. Tamara's body was literally flowing with testosterone now. They'd been told that the process would not change a gladiator's basic personality, but it could shift things around to let different facets surface.

---

[14] Ricasso: the unsharpened part of the blade that extends out from the handle.

Genmodding didn't make Tamara into an aggressive bitch, but it was allowing that part of her personality surface. Ms. Garcia back in Orinoco might faint with shock at what one of her favorite students had become.

"Aggressive bitch" might be overstating things, but even if Tamara liked Rheina, the other gladiator had better stand the eff by next time, and any time, they fought. There was only room for one winner, and Tamara was going to make sure that winner was always her.

Chapter 18

"A little different from the party at the Moldy Lion, huh?" Elei asked, lifting a glass of lychee juice.

Tamara, Jonna, Beth, and Grammarcy, who'd surprisingly become one of their little group, each lifted a glass of juice or tea in response. The five gladiators were at the Sichko Village canteen, sharing drinks and camaraderie. They rarely went out in town. Even if some establishments had oversized rooms in the hopes of attracting gladiators, the constant attention could be trying. They felt much more comfortable in their own space.

Tamara was drinking mint tea. She longed for the flavor of lychee, but lychee didn't long for her. Her digestive track still could not tolerate it. It was ironic that as one of the 400 or so most powerful people in existence, her stomach was a delicate as a butterfly's. At least she was off the gruel. Her diet, along with the others', was still and always would be limited, but the chefs in each of the four gladiator villages were skilled at extracting as much flavor and variety as possible from the same somewhat dull ingredients.

"Well, we're all a little different than we were then," Jonna said.

"A lot different," Tamara added.

"We thought we were pretty hot stuff then, the crème de la crème of humanity. But that was hubris speaking. Now, we really are the crème de la crème. We're bad ass, fucking gladiators!" Grammarcy said, raising her glass one more time.

"To us," Elei shouted out. "Bad ass fucking gladiators!"

"Bad ass fucking gladiators," the rest shouted out.

Several other small groups in the canteen repeated the toast, raising their own glasses.

That day, each of them had been officially classified as Single Combat Specialists. They had gone into Module 3 with 66 in the class, and all 66 had made the classification. But while no one talked about it, it was common knowledge that not all would ever see combat. They had all developed varying degrees of skills, but worlds were too important to risk, so only the best would be sent out as human champions. Oh, there were rumors that sometimes, for worlds not deemed that important, gladiators lower on the list were sent out as a sacrifice, thereby keeping the Klethos satisfied. But generally, only the higher ranking gladiators were sent into combat.

What that meant was that up to half of this class, depending on how other fights went, would never see the ring. They'd be like Fleetwood Andrews, just hanging on until the Brick claimed them. It seemed like a waste to Tamara, but she understood the need. Humanity had to have a pool of gladiators in order to find the best to fight for it.

Tamara didn't have to worry about that, though. She finished the class ranked number four. There was no doubt that she would see the ring. The Brick probably was not in her future, which was her main goal. She'd die in the ring as a warrior should.

She looked at her friends—no, her sisters. As much as she missed her family, these women were her family now.

Jonna, surprisingly to Tamara, had finished ranked number six. Her willowy frame was only willowy in comparison to the other gladiators. She was tall, had amazing reflexes, and with her sylvian rapier, she had proven to be a match for most of them. She'd beaten Tamara more than once, in fact. Elei was ranked 13th, and Grammarcy was 21st. All four of them could expect to face a Klethos queen at some time.

Beth, though, Beth probably wouldn't. Beth finished ranked 48th. She'd vowed to climb the ladder, and that could happen, but that was a lot of ground to make up.

"Semper fi, Warrant Officer," Tamara said to her, wanting to get that thought out of her mind.

"Semper fi to you, too, Warrant Officer Veal," Beth replied.

With Module 3 finished, both Marines had been promoted to warrant officer that afternoon. Captain Tolbert had been promoted to major. General Williams, the Assistant Commandant of the Marine Corps, had personally made the trip to Malibu to pin on their bars. Her status as a Marine might seem unimportant to outside observers, but to the three Marines, it was part of who they are. Tamara was extremely grateful that the assistant commandant had taken the time to make the trip. It showed that they were not forgotten and still part of the Corps.

Five other Marines, all gladiators and three of them braided, had attended the promotion. Tamara looked forward to getting to know them now that she was a certified SCS.

Each of the newly minted SCSs would go on a week's family leave in the morning. A few of her sister gladiators wanted more time at home, but as Jonna pointed out, their biological clocks were ticking. A year after genmodding, they only had a couple of years of potential combat time before the Brick came a'calling. They couldn't afford more time at home. They needed to continue to hone their skills. Within a year, their class should start providing the bulk of the gladiators needed for combat.

ORINOCO

Chapter 19

"Come on, Tamara, one sip won't hurt," Cyrus said, holding out a glass of champagne.

Cyrus had been a fly constantly buzzing around her since her return, and it was getting pretty annoying. He seemed to think that their brief dating in high school had made a claim on her. What was worse was that her family seemed to think it a good idea, and they continually made time for them to be together.

"I've told you, I can't drink alcohol. You know that," she said, leaning back against the wall of her parents' house and watching the fireflies dance across the back yard.

"Yeah, of course, I know, but one sip? For old time's sake?"

It was just easier to ignore Cyrus, so she closed her eyes and tried to relax. She was still in her blues from that evening's reception, and she knew she shouldn't be sitting on the ground in them, but she didn't have the mental energy at the moment to do anything about it.

It wasn't as if she had much choice on where to sit. Her parents' house was designed for normals, not for gladiators. A crushed chaise lounge was evidence that her parents had attempted to get some gladiator-sized furniture, but that poor chaise lounge hadn't stood a chance at supporting Tamara's weight.

Tamara had been home for three full days, and while she'd been happy to see her family, she was already sick of the trip, to be blunt. She wondered if she could cut it short without offending anybody.

The entire planet, it seemed, had shown up at Davis Spaceport to see her arrive. Newsies and cams had covered every second of the arrival, and she'd had to stand and listen to speeches by the governor and a UAM under-secretary of some sort or another. She finally made it home, but two hours later, it was off of Cascade Valley High School where a ceremony in her honor was planned. Her track number was re-retired (Tamara wasn't sure how that was even possible—the number had already been retired once. Did they "un-retire" it just so they could retire it again?) The school marching band played, even dredging up the saccharine *My Lost Tamara* that she detested. She'd hated it when the Lionel Brothers had sung it, and it was only slightly better as an instrumental. But she'd smiled and nodded as the principal, teachers, her track coach, and several of her classmates stood and told the assembled crowd how they'd always known Tamara would go on to bigger and better things. It seemed as if the assembly had a life of its own, and just as it seemed it was about to end, it would sputter back to life. Finally, Tamara was able to leave and get back home.

The next two days were more of the same, with the planetary government taking charge. She was treated like a visiting dignitary instead of a native daughter. She'd been to Horsten Dam before— she didn't need another tour of it, every moment being recorded for prosperity. Cyrus had been at her side for most of the time making a nuisance of himself. But she was a good girl, smiling and cooperating. She realized the importance of the symbology. The gladiator program was the ultimate and most visual case of all of humankind working together, and the UAM, which for centuries had been a dog without teeth, what milking it for all it was worth.

Today had been a little better, at least. Lunch had been a picnic at the falls with only close friends and family. Someone actually bothered to research what she could and could not eat, and everyone shared the same fare, which was a nice touch. She reconnected with old friends and almost forgot that things had changed—almost.

After the picnic, she'd gotten into her blues and along with a small entourage of Marines led by a lieutenant colonel, made the recruiting rounds. Master Sergeant Haines, the head of Orinoco's small Marine detachment, told her that enlistment requests had skyrocketed since Tamara had been nominated, and now that she'd made it, he had eight times the volunteers that he was authorized to accept. Ten poolees were waiting for their recruit class, and Tamara posed with them while family and newsies recorded the event.

Dinner this evening was more of the same, but this time hosted by the Corps. Nothing much changed, though, from the food (Tamara's was within her dietary restrictions, but she had to sit next to people eating prime rib or shrimp) to the speeches. By the time she got home, she was tired of it all. When the UAM event coordinator showed up with tomorrow's schedule, Tamara had asked Diana to take care of it and snuck out to the back yard. It would have been better had Cyrus not found and imposed himself on her.

"Tamtam, I've sent her on her way. Do you want to go over it?" Diana asked, poking her head out the door.

Tamara shook her head without saying a word.

Diana stood there for a moment before saying, "Cy, why don't you take off now?"

"But we're just enjoying each other's company," he protested. "We're about to have a drink together."

"You know she can't drink," she scolded as if he was a toddler. "Come on, you can see her tomorrow. It's sister time."

He seemed about to argue, but to Tamara's relief, he got up after promising to return in the morning and left.

Diana sat down beside her big sister, dwarfed by her mass. Still, after a few moments, Tamara leaned over, laying her head on top of Diana's.

"You doing OK, Tamtam? I know this has been, well, nothing has been in your control. Everyone wants a piece of you."

"It comes with the territory, Di. I volunteered for it, so I can't complain."

"Yes, you did, but still . . ."

"It's OK."

"Really? Is it really?"

Tamara didn't respond, mesmerized by the fireflies going through their mating patterns. They would find mates, maybe tonight, and create the next generation. Then, they would die soon, their lives complete. Tamara knew she would outlive them, but that didn't give her much solace.

"Yes, it is. Really," she finally said.

"With everything going on, we really haven't had a chance to talk much yet," Diana said.

"I know, and I'm sorry about that."

"I want you to know that I'm getting married."

Tamara sat back up and looked down at her little sister.

"Married?"

"Yeah. I'm sorry to spring it on you like this. But we haven't had time, and I don't know when would be the right time."

"But . . . with who?" Tamara asked, stunned.

"Lars, Lars David."

"Lars David?" she repeated, at a loss for words.

She knew Lars. He lived a couple of blocks over, and he'd played in the neighborhood since childhood. He seemed like an OK guy, but Lars David?

"And I'm pregnant."

If Tamara was surprised before, this statement, out of the blue, floored her.

"Pregnant? How?"

"Oh, the usual way," Diana said, encircling both of her arms around Tamara's left arm.

"I know that, Di. I mean, what happened?"

"I wanted, it, Tamtam. After Lars proposed, we started planning the wedding, but . . ."

"But what?"

"I know you can't have your own children, and I know you wanted them. So I wanted to have a child, one you can meet and love, one who will be old enough to remember you after . . ."

After I'm dead.

"I, I hope you're not angry. I don't want to upset you or anything," Diana said, her voice trembling.

Tears began to flow from Tamara's eyes, streaming down her cheeks. She felt sad; she felt gratitude; she felt love; all mixed together and swirling around her heart. Diana had often talked about delaying a family until after her legal career was in place. She felt family could wait. And now, she'd purposely gotten pregnant so Tamara could vicariously experience at least a tiny piece of motherhood.

She took Diana in her arms and pulled her to her lap, hugging her close to her chest.

"No, Di, I'm not angry. I'm not angry at all."

NEW BUDAPEST

Chapter 20

Jonna and Tamara stood in the back of the open-bed truck as it made its way through the crowded streets to the stadium. People shouted up to them as the truck passed, but the two had gotten tired of waving, so they just nodded down without particular attention to who was shouting.

Bertie Jun, though, was in her element. She had moved to the front of the truck and was standing at the cab, waving and acting like the grand marshall of the parade. You would have thought she was the designated gladiator rather than a witness like the rest of them.

"Look at her. She's loving it," Jonna said, but without rancor.

It would be hard to be upset with Bertie. Everyone loved her, and she loved everyone. She seemed too nice to be a gladiator, but in the ring, she was an absolute terror. Tamara had never beaten her, and she deserved her #1 ranking in the class.

The top ten ranked gladiators of the class, along with ten other gladiators were on New Budapest to serve as witnesses for Marta Haps-Fieldstein's fight. The CHSCC made sure that each gladiator witness a real fight before being assigned her own as part of the preparation process. All of them had seen recordings of each and every battle, all 356 of them, from General Lysander's to the most recent (Latifatu Blue's win on Cyntax 2), but seeing a fight in person took things to a whole new level. Tamara was both excited and nervous. That could be her getting ready to fight in only a few months.

Not for a planet as important as New Budapest, though. With well over a billion people on the planet, this one was too important to lose. That is why Marta, one of the four active two-braid gladiators, had been assigned to the fight. When she won, she'd be only the third ever three-fight winner.

Tamara's first fight would be for a planet not quite as important as New Budapest. But that fight could be soon, which is why the top-ranked gladiators of her class were there, to be ready when called upon.

"Can you imagine having to evacuate this place?" Tamara asked Jonna, looking out at the huge throngs of people. "That would be a nightmare."

"Which is why Marta got this fight, so it won't happen."

When a Klethos queen won a fight, that planet had to be evacuated within 11.32 days. That odd time had astrologists examining the heavens in the direction from which the Klethos came, trying to find a planet where 11.32 days corresponded to an even number of planetary days. Several potential planets had been identified, but the distances were far too great to confirm if any of them could be the Klethos home world.

To date, the largest of the 142 planets to be lost, Harkenson, had something like 120 million inhabitants, and that had come down to the wire to get everyone off the planet. For a planet like New Budapest, the shear logistics would be staggering. The UAM's Office of Relocation had plans, of course, and they had already initiated the movement of ships, but a better plan would be just not to lose the planet in the first place. Hence, Marta Haps-Fieldstein.

The truck pulled around a corner, and the huge Építők Stadion came into view. The stadium could fit over 100,000 people, and Tamara knew it would be full to overflowing.

"We who are about to die, salute you," Jonna muttered.

Only Marta was fighting, but Tamara understood her meaning. The stadium did have a passing similarity to the Roman Coliseum, where the original gladiators entertained the masses of Rome. The numbers of people watching the spectacle bothered her, but the UAM had decided it was the best way to show support and a sense of urgency to the situation. The gladiator fighting was their champion, and they should be able to view how she performed for them. Still, Tamara wondered if there wasn't just a hint of bloodlust for those who fought for seats.

The truck pulled up behind a line of busses that were already disgorging various noteworthies there to witness the fight. The 20 gladiators vaulted over the sides of the truck. An open-bed truck might not be glamorous, but even with a population as large as New Budapest's, they didn't have a normal vehicle large enough to transport them comfortably.

"This way!" a young man called out, making his way past the other dignitaries.

He reached up to take Bertie's arm—a huge breach of protocol—and pull her as if he could physically move her. Bertie didn't seem to take offense, which was lucky for the man as someone like Chaina might have broken his arm in two, and she motioned for the rest of them to follow. They went through a large door and straight out onto the playing field. As gladiators, they were witnesses, there to lift their sister to their shoulders in victory or take away her body in defeat.

Tamara nudged Jonna as they marched, slightly nodding her head at the enthusiastic group or 200-300 people, mostly men, of the self-styled *Spectacula* who were packed into one of the stadium's lower sections. These people traveled to as many of the fights as they could, embracing the concept of gladiatorial combat, making the fights a way of life. Some wore Roman togas, which Tamara thought was strange. Others wore shirts or lofted banners emblazoned with their motto, *sine missione*, which essentially meant a fight to the death without reprieve. While Tamara thought the paramours were a little sad in a way, lusting as they did after gladiators who could never return their passion, the Spectacula frankly gave her the creeps.

The pomp and circumstance of the fight were surprising to Tamara. New Budapest was rightfully proud of their contribution to the war with the Klethos first on Tri-30 and then on Roggeri's World, and there was an almost festive atmosphere to the proceedings. If Marta lost the fight, all of these people would be uprooted and evacuated from their planet, however, so Tamara had expected somewhat of a more solemn atmosphere.

The ring was set up in the middle of the stadium, a 15-meter-in-diameter-wide circle. The grass within the ring had been cut out and replaced with clean white sand. The Klethos had never indicated a specific size, nor even a designated area for a fight, but humans, being humans, liked to standardized everything, and the Klethos didn't seem to mind. For a species that had evidently cleared a huge swath of the galaxy, eliminating, at least, two other species and driving the capys to a tiny fraction of their former population, they seemed to be pretty complacent about many aspects of their stylized combat.

Tamara took her place with the other gladiators and settled in for the wait. Her nose began to itch, an itch that grew in intensity and screamed for attention. Conscious of the fact that billions of eyes might be on her now, she resisted, standing still. For awhile, at least. Finally, she reached up quickly to swipe at her nose. No one said she had to stand completely still, after all.

A sudden roar of the crowd filled the stadium. Tamara swiveled her head to see Marta, the "Quicksilver Fox," accompanied by her closest surviving friend, Kelly June Han, marching out of the tunnel and into the stadium. The crowd was going wild.

Part of her understood the frenzy. She'd never actually met Marta before, only seeing her a few times around the campus, and Marta was a galaxy-wide hero. Her silver, magenta, and turquoise striped hair were her trademark, something emulated by little girls throughout human space. Another part of her, however, felt uncomfortable about the festive atmosphere. Marta was going to fight to the death, and the entire planet's future hinged on her ability to win. Tamara thought this was a more serious occasion than the Galaxy Cup finals which it was resembling from the spectator aspect. She realized that gladiatorial games had always been something for the masses, but this wasn't a game. This was war.

Marta moved gracefully from the tunnel to the middle of the playing field, Kelly June at her side. She didn't acknowledge the other gladiators, but rather stepped up to the edge of the ring before sinking into a *seiza*, or kneeling posture, hand on her thighs, eyes focused straight ahead. With her fighting skins, branded to match her hair, the definition of her muscles were evident. She looked the warrior, and Tamara was not surprised that she had two braids.

They stayed in this position, Marta kneeling, Kelly June at her shoulder, and the rest of the gladiators standing, for over 20 minutes, the crowd growing restless. People started shouting out, some over-enthusiastic spectators issuing challenges of their own. Those challenges stopped short when at last, the d'relle entered the stadium. Except for the Spectacula and some of the UAM staff, very few of the spectators in the stadium had probably seen a d'relle in real life, Tamara included. Tamara, at least, had fought simulacrum after simulacrum, but still, the Klethos queen was impressive, to say the least. She moved with a grace that did nothing to hide the power that her limbs possessed. The muscles on her thighs bunched and relaxed with each step, muscles that Tamara knew could unleash in a deadly kick that could end the fight immediately. Tamara watched her, trying to remember all the xenophysiology classes she'd had back on Malibu.

And this queen strolled into the stadium alone, with no entourage. One Klethos queen facing over 100,000 humans. At a signal, the people could rush the field and tear the queen apart. It had almost happened before, on Milan-Santiago after the human gladiator had been defeated, but luckily, the UAM Guard had managed to keep the d'relle safe. No one knew what would happen should a victorious d'relle be killed, and no one wanted to find out.

There had only been a thousand or so spectators on Milan-Santiago. There were over 100,000 people here on New Budapest. If they charged, then the 100 or so UAM Guard detachment and the 500 or more soldiers at the stadium probably couldn't stop them, which is why some governments advocated that spectators not be allowed on the scene at all. But the UAM did not have the authority to ban the people, so it was up to the host planet, the one whose ass was on the line.

Despite the obvious threat, the d'relle showed no signs of nervousness. Slightly taller, but with slightly less mass than Marta, she seemed at ease as if just out for a walk in the park. Twenty-three

Klethos had landed on New Budapest in their personal craft (craft which human scientist still hadn't been able to reverse-engineer), yet this warrior had entered the stadium alone. Sometimes they faced the humans without an entourage, sometimes they did. On Diamode 3, over 500 of them had shown up. Xenobiologists could not agree upon the reason for the differences. Tamara felt it might just be up to the personal preference of the d'relle.

The gladiator eye in Tamara checked out her armor and sword as she entered. Unlike the humans who entered the ring in their fighting skins, the d'relle fought naked, or nearly so. They had their own style of armor, plates on pieces of a hard substance that covered vulnerable spots such as shoulders, thighs, and chest. The armor didn't look like much, and it functioned differently from the gladiator's armor, but it could turn a human blade. Nothing in this d'relle's armory looked out of the ordinary. Her weapon was the typical scimitar-looking blade that most d'relles carried. It looked like simple steel, but it was actually a ceramic-type material. It was an excellent slashing weapon with enough heft to it to cause some serious damage. But a gladiator could not ignore the point, which could be used for stabbing. Tamara had fought with mock-ups of the sword, as well as with the mace-like weapon some d'relle used, and while it was close in function to her own mameluke, Tamara much preferred her own weapon to it. That was probably not surprising as the mameluke was a human weapon—and hers had been fitted to her—while the d'relle scimitar was designed for the Klethos physiology.

Jonna's sylvian, which was a type of rapier, never-the-less had a sharply forward curved quillon that was designed to catch the d'relle weapon as it slid down the length of the sylvian's blade. It was a pretty good defensive measure, as Tamara had discovered when she'd tried using a sylvian, but that kept the weapon locked and unable to be thrust home.

The d'relle strode to the middle of the ring, eyes locked on Marta for a few long moments. When she lifted her head back and screeched, her neck feathers suddenly flaring out, Tamara flinched despite expecting it. Then came the stomp, where she lifted one leg high in the air, then brought it forward, slamming it into the ground, clawed toes pointing forward as she leaned over the leg, looking back at Marta.

Marta didn't move, and the d'relle she jumped up in the air, at least two meters high, and kicked out with one leg before spinning around in a circle. While the initial challenge was basically unchanged from any previous d'relle's, the bodies of the hakas themselves were more personalized. This d'relle seemed to favor the spins more than anything else. Tamara, standing a good 20 meters back, could hear the whistle of the blade as it sliced through the air. Whatever the style a particular d'relle danced, and some looked like nothing more than an epileptic fit, the intent was obviously to show off skill and power.

The haka went on for almost five minutes before with a final fury of spins, the d'relle slammed to a stop, leaning forward. Marta was still kneeling, but the d'relle had bent over, so her face was less than a meter from Marta's.

Marta waited less than ten seconds before responding. From analysis of combat footage, the d'relle had about a 30-second window in which a challenge could be accepted or refused. No one knew if this was a hard and fast rule among them or not, but the gladiators were taught never to go beyond 15 seconds. It could be catastrophic if a dramatic pause led a d'relle to believe that the challenge was being turned down.

Marta smoothly rose to her feet. She held one hand behind her, eyes locked on her opponent. Kelly June opened the case she was holding, removing Mercury, Marta's shortsword. The crowd gasped in unison, many then breaking out into applause. Not many gladiators named their swords, but with two wins, no one thought her naming hers was bravado. Marta had walked the walk, so if she wanted to name it, so be it.

Kelly June slapped the hilt of the sword in Marta's hand, and Marta immediately jumped into her haka. "Jumped" was right. Marta's haka was mostly a cross between kendo moves, full of grace, interspaced with thrusting actions more in line with the design of her weapon. While some gladiators spent days and days mastering her haka, Marta's was quick, powerful, and to the point. Along with many other gladiators, she thought wasting energy in an elaborate haka was stupid when her life was on the line. With two kills within the ring, Tamara thought her opinions on hakas had to carry some weight. Tamara had only played a bit with hers, but she still had time to decide on which way she would go on that.

Marta circled the motionless d'relle several times, coming close to slicing or stabbing her more than once. It didn't seem to faze the d'relle, though, who never even flinched. At about a minute, which the xenobiologists had somehow determined was the minimum duration of one to be accepted (how they determined that was unknown, and the gladiators thought was utter BS, just something they said to justify their jobs and lack of concrete insights), Marta moved well back from the d'relle and came to a stop facing her. Marta let out a scream, accepting the challenge.

During past combats, d'relle attacked immediately upon the conclusion of the human gladiator's haka 14 times, coming out victorious eight of those times. Gladiators now ended their haka as far as possible from the d'relle in order to have at least a moment of transition between haka and combat.

In this fight, the d'relle seemed amenable to the slight delay. She turned, then slowly brought up her sword, pointing it at Marta with her heavily muscled lower arm. As with most d'relle, this one was left-handed. Marta was right-handed, so the two would be mirroring each other.

Tamara was behind the d'relle, so her view consisted of her back and the red, gold, and tan crest. The crest looked like feathers, but they were chock full of nerves. Once again, the xenobiologists differed on their purpose, but when cut, they threw off a d'relle's balance. After Celeste had started the trend of long, dyed hair, the d'relle spent several fights attempting to cut the gladiators' hair, but when that proved to have no effect on them, the d'relle ceased to target it.

Tamara felt the excitement build up inside of her. As a new gladiator, she felt honored to be there for Marta's third win, even if she knew it was merely a coincidence of scheduling. As one of the first ten in her class, her first fight as a witness had been up to the mercy of which fight was next. Still, she appreciated being able to watch a master at work. She leaned forward to watch. Unlike in the

Hollybolly flicks, swordfights tended to last less than an average of 30 seconds, and much of that tended to be feints and posturing. Fights going past a minute were rare. Tamara didn't want to miss a single move.

It was Marta who moved first, lunging forward to the d'relle's left side, outside her guard. Almost quicker than the eye could catch, she flicked her wrist to bring her shortsword's tip inside the d'relle's weapon, ready to drive it home to her opponent's exposed neck. A thrill swept through Tamara as she realized Marta's strategy. A longer sword could never make that change in direction in order to get under her opponent's guard, but a shortsword could.

And just like that, it was over.

Tamara started to jump forward, a cheer in her throat, but something was off. The d'relle was not falling. It was turning around and lifting a defiant head to the sky. A thunderous screech filled the stadium as just beyond her. Marta, the Quicksilver Fox, fell to her knees, and with a look of incomprehension, fell face first to the sand, blood pouring from her right side.

The crowd, which had been so vocal only a few moments before, fell silent.

"Marta!" Kelly June shouted, dropping the sword case and rushing to her friend.

The d'relle ignored her, stepping past as she walked the perimeter of the ring, sword held high as she screeched half-a-dozen more times. A small line of blue blood trickled from her collar where Marta had scored her.

Tamara felt as if she'd been kicked by a mule. Her breath was heavy and didn't seem to have enough oxygen in it. Marta had been one of their best, if not the best gladiators still active, and she'd been assigned for this mission because New Budapest was just too important to lose. And now, she was gasping out her last breaths on the sand of the ring in the arms of her crying friend. It wasn't supposed to act this way.

Shouts started reverberating from the crowd as they realized what had happened. Marta had lost, and now so had they. They all had to leave, and more than a few seemed to want to fight that edict.

The d'relle gave one last screech of victory, then stalked out of the ring and to her tunnel, never looking back at her defeated opponent. Tamara watched as she disappeared from view. Someone belatedly threw a cup at her, but she was already gone.

"Get it together, girls. We need to bring Marta home," Kristani Hobario, the senior gladiator in the witness team said.

Tamara gathered herself. She was in shock, but she had a job to do. They had to honor their fallen sister. Marta was strong, though. Despite the d'relles sword cutting clear through to the spine, she was not giving up. Tamara didn't think she could last more than a handful of seconds, but she gurgled and fought, gasping to breath, for over two minutes—two horribly long and painful minutes. Finally, she slumped and was silent. Kelly June nodded at Kristani, and the twenty witnesses moved forward, unfolding the stretcher that they hadn't expected to have to use. As a team, they picked Marta up and placed her on the black stretcher. Eight of the senior gladiators picked her up, and with six in front leading the way and six, along with Kelly June, behind, they started to leave the stadium.

The stadium was emptying quickly as people realized they had little time to leave the planet, their home. Many remained, though, to give respects to the fallen. The Spectacula stood silently, arms held out, palms down, in the ancient Roman salute.

Not everyone wanted to honor Marta, though.

One middle-aged man burst his way through the Spectacula to the rail, and leaning out, he shouted, spit flying, "You stupid bitch! This is my home, and you couldn't do your job!"

Tamara was in the lead six witnesses, and anger flowed through her as she heard him.

How dare that worm get angry at Marta! she thought, wanting to break ranks and jump up there.

She didn't have to. The members of the Spectacula near him took care of it, pulling the man down. Tamara could see fists rising and falling as they took their own form of punishment on the hapless man.

Tamara had thought the Spectacula creepy, but now she was glad of their presence. At least, they cared for what the gladiators were doing for mankind.

As the witnesses carried Marta through the tunnel to where the UAM staff waited, the Spectacula dropped rose petals on them.

MALIBU

Chapter 21

Tamara trudged back to her home. Swordmaster Abad had put her through the ringer, and she ached. She didn't understand how he'd been able to keep up with her in the torture—wrist strengthening, he called it. He was unmodified, and she had been designed for this. Yet he'd been able to outdo her easily, even with her mameluke, which was designed for a gladiator-sized fighter.

She'd been back on Malibu for a week after Marta's loss. The newlines were full of the story of New Budapest's evacuation. Most experts doubted that it would be done in time, and no one knew what would happen then. The more dire predictions were that the Klethos would kill anyone left. More than a few politicians said that if that happened, humankind should go to war with the Klethos, full-out war instead of combat by champions.

That was inherently stupid, Tamara thought. The Klethos had wiped out planet after planet, exterminating at least two entire species. Anyone getting killed on New Budapest would be a tragedy, but moving to all-out war would be even worse. The UAM and almost all governments agreed that war was not an option, but a surprisingly high percentage of citizens thought war should be the only response.

Not that you will fight yourselves, Tamara thought. *It will be the Marines, the Host, the Legion, and all the navies and armies that would be expected to fight for you.*

There had already been one more challenge. Luckily, Wanda Quezon had won, so transport resources needed to get people off New Budapest had not had to be diverted to that planet.

Tamara reached her home and opened the front gate. The tulips lining the walkway to her front door were a nice touch. The groundskeepers tried to keep the villages pleasant as possible, and while Jonna had liked the peonies that had lined the walk for the last couple of weeks, Tamara thought the tulips, with their taller forms, were a better fit.

Too bad they don't have an aroma. If they can genmod us, why not put jasmine in them?

She pushed open the door and entered the common area.

"Jonna, you here?" she called out.

The house was silent, which was surprising. Tamara's training had gone on longer than normal, and Jonna should have been home an hour ago. Tamara dropped her kit in the laundry basket and pushed open the door to her room. . .

. . .and was drenched with water as a bucket bounced off of her head. No, not water. It smelled far worse. Tamara was afraid to imagine what was in it.

The sound of laughter reached her as feet scurried, if feet 40 cm long could scurry, towards the back of the house. Tamara bolted back out into the hall just in time to see Jonna and Elei's backsides as they ran out the back door and into the garden.

"You bitches!" she shouted after them. "Just wait!"

She tried to wipe some of the water—or whatever it was—off her, but it was also sticking to her. It was going to take some time to get clean.

She had to give them credit. A buck over the door was about as old-school as it got, but they had nabbed her. She'd have to come up with something good to get them back.

The gladiators had taken the art of pranks to a new level. With a short future and with the weight of humanity on their shoulders, it would be easy to crack. That was why there were more mental health professionals in the campus than gladiators. Some gladiators found religion to help them, some found hobbies and activities. Pets were popular. But one thing seemed to bind them all together, and that was practical jokes. The pranks tended to come and go in waves, but at the height of one of those waves, the campus was more of a battleground than anything else.

Tamara was chuckling as she stripped and stepped into the shower. She didn't find it nearly as funny as it took over 30 minutes and losing more than a fair amount of skin to get whatever it was off of her. She stepped out and looked into the mirror. The skin on her shoulders and chest was red and angry where she'd had to rub hard to get the stuff off of her.

Her PA grabbed her attention.

"Ah, I see they got you, too," Beth said, eyeing Tamara's red skin. "Look," she added, taking off her T-shirt to reveal a red swatch of skin, if not quite as extensive, covering her right side.

She panned the PA's pick-up down, to where the red went all the way to her thigh.

"I can't believe I fell for that. I think Neanderthal pulled that one on each other," Tamara said. "So what are we going to do about it?"

"Payback's a bitch, Tamara. I think me and you need to come up with the most best-est, perfect-est, revenge-est prank yet."

"And what might that be, pray tell?"

"I don't know yet. But we're Marines, damn it! We were trained in combat long before these pussies ever thought of it. So if we can't come up with something, then we need to turn in our warrant officer bars!"

"Sounds good to me. Look, those two took off like frightened rabbits. Why don't you head over here, and we'll think of something, OK?"

"Semper fi, do or die. I'll be there in five."

Tamara took one last look at her red skin. It was a good prank, she had to admit, but with two Marines coming up with a response, those two little girls had better stand-the-eff by.

Chapter 22

Tamara stood in front of the mirror, brushing her hair. She hadn't had long hair since she was a child, before she started track. Growing up, then as a Marine, short hair had been more practical. It seemed odd that after the genmodd not only cut the heat from her, but took away many of her feminine traits, both outwardly physical and in her inner make-up, she now had long, and frankly beautiful blonde hair. Elei had mentioned that putting makeup on a cow didn't make her beautiful, but Tamara disagreed. She regretted the atrophying of her breasts, but with her long hair, Tamara thought she looked quite attractive; not runway model attractive, but a fit and healthy attractive.

Her hair had been boosted, of course. The process was related to normally boosted regen, but it worked differently enough so that it posed no threat to the gladiators. If it had, the practice would never have been approved. But the psychs thought it was good for them, and the gladiators now took long hair as a badge of honor, and like Sampson in the Bible, felt it gave them power. Tamara's new hair really made no difference, but she enjoyed the routine maintenance. Every day, she brushed it 100 times, and she felt it helped her connect with herself. In the practice ring, she was becoming more and more aggressive—and more than a little mean, she had to admit—but here in her bathroom, brushing her hair, she felt calm and at ease with herself.

She was only up to 55 brushes when her PA called for her attention. She was tempted to ignore off. Jonna, Beth, or whoever could wait. This was her time. But when it kept ringing, she stopped brushing and picked it up.

It was scheduling.

Tamara's heart skipped a beat.

Scheduling? I shouldn't be up yet. I'm still number 4!

Bertie Jun had just come back from her fight, the first in their class. But there were still two in front of Tamara. Their ranking did not necessarily reflect when a gladiator would fight, but still, Tamara hadn't hoped to get called so soon.

Tamara slammed down the brush and bolted from the bathroom.

"Scheduling wants to see me!" she shouted at Jonna, who was on the couch watching a holo.

"Really?" Jonna asked, jumping up. "Wait, let me go with you!"

But Tamara was already out the door and on her way. Scheduling was in Raster Hall, a good five-minute walk from her home. Tamara made it in just under three minutes, skidding to a walk as she reached the front gate. Like the gladiator homes, Raster Hall had a laid-back feel, more like a community center than an administration building. Tamara paused in front of the main doors, stopped to take a couple of calming breaths, then pushed her way in. Scheduling was on the second floor, and Tamara took the gladiator stairway, three steps at a time, to go up. The door to scheduling was open, so Tamara rushed inside.

"Warrant Officer Veal," Hiram said, "please, Mr. Light Heart is waiting for you.

Hiram was a Federation citizen, and he always used ranks when addressing military gladiators instead of the more common "Miss."

"Is it . . .?"

Hiram smiled and nodded, but he didn't say a word.

Tamara felt a rush of excitement as she went around Hiram and knocked on the doorjamb of the open inner office.

"Miss Veal, please come in," Mr. Light Heart said in his favorite uncle manner. "Please, sit," he continued, pointing to one of the gladiator-sized chairs.

The scuttlebutt was that the psychs had determined that this style was the best one when assigning a gladiator to a fight, but Tamara wouldn't have cared how she'd get the word. She was ready, and she wanted the ring now.

She knew this wasn't a normal survival trait, to be excited and want to enter a to-the-death fight. She also knew that her hormones and who knows what else had been manipulated during the genmod, and that probably was affecting her. But deep inside, she thought she'd always had the fire to compete with others. She'd lost some of that on the track team because she'd lost the adrenaline rush. It hadn't been a thrill anymore. But this, how could this not be a thrill? This was the ultimate challenge for a competitive adrenaline junkie.

"So, are you doing well, Miss Veal? I must say, your hair has come in beautifully."

Cut the compliments. Just get to the point!

"Thank you, Mr. Light Heart," she said instead, trying to keep her voice calm. "Can I ask if you've got a match for me?"

"Ah, no time for chit-chat, right? But that's OK. I'm sure you are anxious. Yes, you have a fight."

Baby! Tamara thought, closing her hand into a fist and giving it a half pump.

"The planet is in the Halcon system—no name yet, except for Number 4. It is unpopulated except for the terraforming staff, about 2,000 people. It's about 75% completed, and it has oxygen, about 65% Earth normal, so you'll be able to function without external devices. . ."

Mr. Light Heart went on, giving her more details, but most of that went beyond her. She'd be thoroughly briefed later, and she could get what she needed to know then. At the moment, her mind was swirling. In three short days, she'd be leaving Malibu for that unnamed planet where she would defend mankind. That was almost too much to take in.

No more waiting! It's time!

Chapter 23

Ronna, Beth, Elei, and Grammarcy escorted Tamara to the front gates. Several candidates saw the group as they walked by. One stopped dead to watch, but the others hurried on, not wanting to interfere with five gladiators.

At the front gate, where Jasper was on duty—he was always on duty, Tamara thought—the five stopped. By tradition, only Tamara would continue outside the campus.

"I can't wait to see you," Jonna said as she hugged her. "I'm sure it will be killer."

"Thanks," Tamara responded. "Sorry about, well, you know, keeping it quiet."

"Eh, I didn't think you'd let it slip, but you can't blame a girl for trying. I could have cleaned up in the kitty."

The other three gave Tamara hugs and words of encouragement, and with one last blown kiss to the group, Tamara broke off to walk past the gate.

"Have a good evening, Miss Veal," Jasper said, as if he didn't know what she'd be doing.

"You too, Jasper."

"See you soon, Miss."

Outside the gate, Bertie, Giselle Fujioko, and Kaster McAult, the senior braided gladiator still well enough to be mobile, waited.

"You ready?" Bertie asked.

"Sure am," Tamara replied.

The four gladiators piled into one of Chicsis' black panel vans. Inside, two over-sized benches provided plenty of room for the four women. They could have walked, but this was something that was for them alone. Official holos would go out tomorrow, issued by Chicsis, but this was for gladiators alone.

Even in a van, however, it would be hard to keep the trip secret, and the hangers-on and paramours knew what was happening, but for the most part, they tried not to interfere.

Ten minutes later, the van pulled up behind the small strip mall. The back door to one of the shops opened, welcoming them in. The shop had been there for a long time, and while a special chair had been installed for gladiators, the building itself had not been re-engineered, so the four of them had to duck and hunch over to move into the main shop. The shop's curtains were closed; the shop itself had closed early as well. Tamara gratefully sidled over to the large chair and sat down.

Frank and Illysha Delbert, the husband and wife owners of Illy's Salon, waited quietly side-by-side, hands folded in front of them.

"Tamara, you have to tell them what you want," Kaster prompted.

"Oh, of course. Well, I was thinking of something simple. I want to keep my blonde, but only one other color, red. I want them to flow top to bottom," she said.

Tamara didn't mention that red and gold were traditional Marine Corps colors, which had been a major reason she had chosen them.

"I think that would look great," Frank said. "So if you let me, I'll just lean you back and get started."

Tamara glanced up at the other gladiators. Kaster and Giselle nodded their approval, but Bertie seemed a little disappointed. Bertie had decided on a swirl of bright, almost luminescent colors, six of them. She probably thought Tamara's choice was too boring.

Illysha brought the other gladiators cups of lavender tea while Frank lowered Tamara into position. Illysha ran the salon, but Frank was the beautician. They'd been pretty much unknown outside of Orroville until Celeste had asked Frank to boost her hair and then color it. Now, the two had become minor celebrities. Other celebs had even come to Malibu to get their hair done at Illy's. They never charged gladiators, but their business had done quite well since that first dye job. None of the gladiators resented that.

The couple was well-liked, and if they profited from doing gladiator's hair, then so what?

After Module 3, all of them were officially gladiators. But it wasn't until they were assigned their first fight that they "got their hair." What design and colors a gladiator picked were fodder for the masses. By tradition, what she chose was to be kept a secret until the reveal, and that would be the official image released by Chicsis.

Tamara was in the chair for 45 minutes while Frank worked his magic. Meanwhile, he and Illysha kept up a running gossip commentary with the other three gladiators. It was all surprisingly mundane, and that suited Tamara just fine. She knew the next couple of days would have their distractions, but for now, with her sisters with her, within the confines of Illy's, all of that could be pushed aside.

"I think I'm done," Frank finally said. "Do you want to see it?"

"Yes, I'm ready," Tamara said, suddenly unsure of herself.

Frank stepped down on the chair's control, raising the seat to a sitting position. He'd murked the mirror, and Tamara stood looking at the blank surface, waiting for her reflection to appear.

"Bam!" he said, flipping the switch to turn on the reflection.

"Oh, wow!" Tamara said as a lion-maned woman faced her, her hair subtle but stunning. "I'm beautiful!"

HALCON 4

Chapter 24

The shuttle's pilot had a soft hand; the craft landed with barely a perceptible bump.

Finally! Tamara thought.

The last couple of days had been hectic. She'd have rather prepared in her own way with light workouts and practice bouts, but things got out-of-hand quickly. The CHCSS campus was serene and low-key. The world outside the gates, though, were a different story, and Tamara could not shut it out. With Lester, her UAM handler almost constantly at her side, she had interviews, meetings, and briefs seemingly around the clock. With 12 challenges so far this year alone, she'd have thought the public interest would be dying out, especially as Halcon 4 was uninhabited, but interest seemed as high as ever. At least on the ship she'd had some time to herself and to get in some light sparring.

"You ready, Iron Shot?" Jonna asked, unhooking her belt and standing up.

Tamara rolled her eyes. The newsies had previously researched her past, and they'd been lying in wait with her gladiator nickname. It didn't matter that Tamara had only put machined steel or brass shots; "Iron" evidently had a stronger image.

"Right. Just wait until they name you, Reindeer Girl."

"Ah, I'm thinking Louhi, the goddess of the underworld," Jonna said, striking a theatrical pose.

"Ladies, if you're ready," Lester said, poking his head into the passenger compartment.

"Coming, Lester," Jonna said in a little girl voice, which caused Tamara to break out into laughter.

Tamara checked her PA. She had about 20 hours before the fight, which was enough time to gather herself, mentally and physically. The interviews were over. Her calls home were over. Now, it was her, Jonna, and of course Lester until the bout. She could have invited more people. Some gladiators liked to have posses with them. But Tamara wanted to keep it simple and quiet.

Her witnesses, which by coincidence included Beth and by invite Elei and Grammarcy, would arrive six hours before the fight, but Tamara wouldn't see them until she walked into the ring.

Halcon 4 had very little in the way of facilities. There were about 2,000 terraforming team staffers scattered around the planet, with about 800 in the main camp. The staffers had to double up in their quarters to make room for the 200 or so people who were there for the challenge. No one had to move for Tamara and Jonna, though. The camp's quarters were just too small for them. A temporary shelter had been erected with a small set of quarters and a workout area. Tamara was eager to get into the quarters. She wanted to get in a mid-level workout, then get in some sparring with Jonna before going to sleep. In the morning, she'd scheduled a light massage, and if she felt it necessary, she'd have another few bouts with Jonna. It depended on her mood.

And Tamara just wasn't sure what her mood was. She thought it should be serious, concentrating on the fight. There would be serious repercussions from it, after all. But in reality, she felt more excited than anything else. She couldn't even detect a wisp of fear within her, which really wasn't that healthy. Fear can be paralyzing, true, but it also served to heighten awareness and mental acuity. Maybe as she got closer, things would change, but for now, she was eager to get past the next 20 hours.

The camp was small, so the shuttleport was only minutes from the dome erected for her. Tamara was ready for that workout, but first, a team of two doctors not only ran a scanner over her, they extracted a vial of blood. She'd already gone through a battery of tests not once, but twice after being assigned the fight, and this made it a third time. She wasn't sure what they expected had cropped up over the last three days.

To her surprise, Colonel Covington showed up as well. She'd met with him a few times since arriving at Malibu when he did his command visits, but no one had told her he would be there. He was the Marine Corps liaison to the CHCSS, but he spent most of his time recruiting volunteers or at the UAM headquarters at Station 1.

"The commandant wants me to pass his best wishes to you, and he's confident that you will prevail," the colonel told her as the medical staff left, evidently unable to find anything that would keep her from fighting.

"Thank you, sir, but he told me that on the phone just as I was leaving Malibu."

"He did? OK, then, I guess you get his wishes twice," the colonel said with a laugh.

"Sir, this is Johanna Sirén. Johanna, this is Colonel Covington."

"Ah, yes, Miss Sirén. I've heard great things about you. I look forward to your first bout."

"So do I," Jonna said, leaving it off at that.

"Um, well, I guess I'll leave you to your preparation. I'm here, though, if you need me. Just give me a shout."

With the doctors and Colonel Covington gone, Tamara had a chance to look around her home for the next 20 hours. It was Spartan, without a doubt. The two racks had obviously just been fabricated. A chiller and a heater were on a large table, as were packages of food provided by the UAM. Ever since one of the early gladiators had chosen to glut on forbidden food prior to his fight—and get himself killed as cramps wracked his body, making him easy pickings for his opponent—that UAM provided all food. Tamara knew the food would provide sustenance, but not much more than that.

"Even a condemned prisoner gets a last meal," was a common phrase used back on Malibu.

At least the equipment looked reasonable, so Tamara turned to Jonna and said, "Let's hit the weights and get the kinks out. Then I'm going to kick your ass a bit to warm up."

"You can try, Iron Shot. You can try."

Chapter 25

"How do I look?" Tamara asked Jonna for the third time in 15 minutes.

"You look great, Tamara, great. Nothing has changed since you asked me last."

Tamara thought she did look great. She loved her hair, of course, and the gold and black shark suit looked striking. The shark suit, or fighting suit (no one knew why they were called shark suits) was a tight, form-fitting, full-body suit. With pressurized lattice-wear, it helped to contain bleeding and tissue damage from sword strikes. It traded armor for mobility. Early gladiators had more overt armor, more in line with what the d'relle wore, but that had gradually shifted to the tight shark suit Tamara now wore.

The suit had not given up on all armor, though. Using the same technology as in a Marine's "bones," the fabric itself immediately formed crystal-like structures that served to deflect oblique blade strikes, to immediately "de-crystalize" a fraction of a second later. This gave some protection without affecting mobility to any noticeable degree.

Another feature of the shark suit was that it left nothing—nothing—to the imagination. Every curve, every nuance of a gladiator's body was revealed. The first time she'd put on her fitted suit, the Orinoco girl in her had almost been mortified. She hadn't considered herself a prude, but with three technicians swarming over her, taking readings, *touching* her, she'd been highly embarrassed. It had taken her a bit of time to get over that. She'd sacrificed so much for this body, she realized, and she shouldn't be ashamed of it.

Some kind soul from the terraforming staff had put a full-length (normal human full-length) mirror screen in the room, but by stepping back, Tamara could get a good look at herself. She made a few combat movements, studying her image.

Yeah, I guess I do look pretty good.

Looks shouldn't matter; she was here to fight and win. But she was still human, and her appearance did matter to her. Idly she wondered if her image would make the cybernet rounds. She'd have to win this fight, of course, first, but the paramours and gladgeeks who collected images could be pretty tough judges.

"Tamara, the d'relle and her entourage are on their way, about five minutes out," Lester said as he stepped into the dome.

Tamara had finally gotten him to call her by her first name instead of "Miss Veal." He was actually a pretty good handler, all things considering. He looked young, and if her sex drive was still in working order, he had the looks that probably would have elicited a response from her. Tamara knew he probably had about five Ph.D.'s in psychiatry and psychology and whatever—almost everyone who had any contacts with gladiators were highly educated and trained—but his manner made it was easy to forget that and think of him as a younger brother.

"I guess we're a go, then," she said to Jonna. "You've got my—"

"Yes, I've got your weapon," Jonna answered, picking up the sword case. "It's my only job here, so I'm pretty much on top of it."

"You've got another job, girl. So come do it and give me a hug."

Jonna stepped up and into Tamara's arms. Tamara squeezed her friend tight, thankful for the comforting contact.

"You're going to do fine," Jonna whispered in her ear.

Tamara held the hug for about 10 seconds longer than was comfortable, then broke it off.

"Lead on, Sir Lester," she told her handler.

The moment she left the dome, her attitude changed. From the calm woman inside the dome, which had kept her from burning nervous energy, she started to focus. She could feel her body come alive, a wonderful machine that would eviscerate any d'relle who dared to stand before her.

You're a lean, green, fighting machine. You're a lean green, fighting machine . . .

Her mantra took over, the rhythm honing her nerves. With every step, she felt more powerful and deadly.

You're a lean, green, fighting machine. You're a lean green, fighting machine . . .

Ahead of her, all 800 or so of the humans in this sector of the planet were waiting for her. A cheer broke out as she came into view, but that barely registered.

This was a far cry from New Budapest and the hundreds of thousands that had been there to watch Marta's fight. Tamara's fight would be broadcast throughout human space, of course, but here, at the scene, she had no Spectacula, no fans. Civilians were not allowed on the planet. The 800 terraforming staff and 100 or so UAM staff would make up the observers. And of course, the 20 gladiator witnesses. As Tamara walked up the slope to the camp's small LZ, where the ring had been constructed, the gladiators came into view. Tamara saw them with her peripheral vision, but she refused to catch any of their eyes.

You're a lean, green, fighting machine. You're a lean green, fighting machine . . .

She stepped into the ring and stood there, feeling the consistency and footing. As usual, the ring was filled with 12 centimeters of packed sand, but as all planets are different, the sand could vary. Tamara slid her feet forward and back. This was pretty good, she realized, close to the main practice rings on Malibu. Tamara liked her footing firm, unlike Jonna who liked a "slipperier" ring.

You're a lean, green, fighting machine. You're a lean green, fighting machine . . .

Tamara's nerves almost started singing in a counterpoint to her mantra. She felt more alive at that moment than she'd ever felt in her life, which had its own irony because she could be dead in ten minutes. Still, that didn't seem possible. She was invincible!

The devil's advocate in her tried to surface. Over-confidence was a recipe for disaster. A lack of confidence was even worse, but a true warrior tried to balance the two. Tamara knew that over-confidence was winning out at the moment, and she just accepted it, going with the flow.

You're a lean, green, fighting machine. You're a lean green, fighting machine . . .

Motion to her right signaled the arrival of the d'relle and her team. Tamara stared straight ahead refusing to look at her, but she could still see this d'relle had, at least, a dozen other Klethos with her. Differences between a d'relle and a normal Klethos soldier were minor, but it looked to Tamara that at least three of the other Klethos might be d'relle as well. She'd find out after the fight, though. It was hard for her to tell without really looking at them, and she was keeping her eyes locked to the front.

Her opponent stepped into the ring and immediately launch into her challenge screech and lunge. She barely waited any time at all before launching into her haka.

You're a lean, green, fighting machine. You're a lean green, fighting machine . . .

Now, Tamara paid attention. She watched the movements of her opponent, looking for anything that might help her. This d'relle was more graceful than most, and her movements lacked many of the strength-type moves. She twirled and spun, all four arms intertwining in continual motion. Her sword looked the same as any other d'relle weapon, but it didn't sing through the air as had Marta's opponent's. It was more as if it was slipping through the air instead of cleaving through it.

With ten or twelve blindingly quick pirouettes, the d'relle kicked up a small cloud of dust before landing back in the challenge pose, one foot stretched out and pointing at Tamara.

You're a lean, green, fighting machine. You're a lean green, fighting machine, she thought one last time.

The time for mantras was over.

Tamara had thought long and hard about her haka. Some gladiators tried to mislead the d'relles by performing a haka in a style opposite of her fighting style. Other's tried to create the most exciting haka, hoping to strike uncertainty in her opponent. Tamara rather thought that was over-thinking it. She doubted that it really mattered other than as a formal acceptance of the challenge. So she decided to honor the people from whose culture the word haka had come. She would do her version of a Maori haka.

With a shout, she jumped into the center of the ring, centimeters from her opponent. She stuck out her tongue as she squatted, legs bent and spread. Slapping her hands on her thighs, she then raised her hands high before slapping them down again.

"Prepare your feet! Stamp with fury and gusto!" she shouted, slapping her thighs in time with her words.

It is death, it is death.
It is life, it is life!
Behold the hairy woman
Who reigns in the sun
And so it shines

Tamara started twisting her body, right arm flexed, the left reaching around to slap at the first arm's elbow.

Arise, arise
Rise up to the heights of the rising sun

She flung her arms up, still keeping the beat with her stomping feet.

It is death, it is death.
It is life, it is life!
I'm going to die. I'm going to die.
I'm going to live! I'm going to live!

She held her left arm high, bent at the elbow as she held her right arm straight and down at a 45 degree angle, turning her head to look down that arm.

Because I am so strong,
I will bring back the sunny days of peace.
Up the step! Up the step!
I'm making progress to prolong the sunny days of peace!

Tamara slapped her chest, stomped harder and faster, and stopped, still only centimeters from her opponent, who hadn't moved a muscle.

For the first time, Tamara seemed to take notice of her opponent. She leaned in closer to the d'relle, canted her head, and the best warrior face she could muster, yelled out at the top of her lungs.

After a moment, she casually stood up, turned as if not aware of the d'relle anymore, and walked back to the edge of the ring. The crowd behind her erupted, which Tamara barely noted. She turned back to face her opponent and held her right hand behind her. A second later, she felt the hilt of her mameluke slap firmly in her hand. She paused only a moment, then with one more shout, fell into the challenge lunge.

Nothing she had done had been normal procedure, and it had been a far cry from the haka she'd shown the staff at Chicsis. She'd danced the haka without her weapon. She'd stopped within range of her opponent, and then casually sauntered back, exposing her back, before she finished her final lunge. Tamara knew she'd hear about it if she survived the bout, but she'd figured she was safe until she'd finished the haka with the challenge acceptance lunge and shout. And since she was still alive, she'd obviously been right.

The d'relle slowly stood up, then started twirling her sword in an intricate pattern. Tamara almost smiled. While patterns like these looked good in the Hollybolly flics, patterns were a warrior's enemy. An opponent can read the patterns and plan an attack. However, a pattern can lull an opponent into a sense of complacency so that a quick change in the pattern can catch the opponent off-guard. Tamara vowed that would not happen to her.

The d'relle almost casually advanced to Tamara, all the time her sword moving, twirling. Tamara watch her, though, not the sword. A sword never telegraphed what it was going to do next, but a swordsman did. Tamara had studied enough recordings of d'relles in action to be fairly confident in her abilities to watch and understand the tells. The problem with a d'relle was that even with an obvious tell, the d'relle could be just too quick and too powerful to do anything about the action, even knowing it was coming.

Tamara was not going to wait for her opponent to take any more of the initiative. With a short lunge, she executed a vertical parry, not expecting to gain any advantage, but more to interrupt her opponent. To her surprise, the d'relle immediately backed up, then began another different pattern of almost lazy sword movement.

If she was really that hidebound, she would be easy pickings for Tamara, but Tamara refused to fall into what had to be a trap. No warrior could be that vulnerable, and d'relles didn't have a reputation of being easy pickings.

The d'relle began to move in again, but there seemed to be a slight a degree of uncertainty to her pattern. Tamara was just beginning to accept that this d'relle might not be experienced when the slightest tell alerted her instincts before her mind realized what was happening. At the height of the swirling pattern, the d'relle reversed the swing to slash down at Tamara. If she'd done it an instant before, she might have scored, but the extra height of the d'relle's arm gave Tamara just enough time to parry the slash down and riposte. She'd hoped to hit the d'relle at the juncture of her sword arm, but her opponent ducked lower, and Tamara's blade slashed through the flesh and tendons of the smaller upper left arm. It would be painful, and given time, the loss of blue blood would weaken her, but it was hardly a killing blow.

Take the initiative! she admonished herself.

Except for Bertie, who calmly parried whatever Tamara threw at her, Tamara scored more wins by her relentless attacks than through fancy skills.

Tamara pressed forward, driving the d'relle back. Her opponent had given up the swirling patterns and had reverted to the defense, parrying each blow Tamara sent her way.

Tamara had not fully committed yet as she felt out the d'relle's defense while still maintaining her own. A too aggressive attack could leave her open to a deadly riposte. She had to be aware of not only what was her best offense, but what the d'relle was doing.

Even after admonishing herself about being too aggressive, that was almost her undoing. The d'relle stumbled, and in her eagerness to take advantage of that, Tamara leaped into an attack.

Leaped, not lunged, a cardinal sin in sword fighting. It might look dramatic in the flicks, but a swordsman did not leave her feet—ever. There was no way to change direction in the air, no way to control movment until back down on the ground. Luckily, the d'relle's riposte missed her leading thigh, and Tamara was able to counter her opponent's second intention. No serious harm done due to her breach of training, she quickly gathered herself to fight as she was taught, not like some Hollybolly superhero.

She almost forgot, though, that the sword was not a d'relle's only weapon, and that could have been fatal. The d'relle's sword tip drifted too high, and Tamara moved in for the kill when unbelievably quick, the d'relle's right leg snapped out at her belly. At the last instant, Tamara twisted so that the large claws grazed her hip, but not with enough of a connection to spin her around. Tamara immediately wrapped her left arm around the leg and pulled forward. The already extended d'relle gave a screech, too close to use the point of her sword. Incredibly, she hopped on her right leg, which was almost bent under her, preparing to launch a kick up into Tamara's unprotected crotch.

The d'relle was too close to use the point of her weapon, and that meant Tamara was, too. But a mameluke had a long, sharp edge. She yanked the d'relle closer, so the kick she unleased didn't have time to generate too much power, and the shin connected instead of the deadly claw. It still slammed Tamara, but not with enough force to do any damage. And now, the d'relle was completely exposed. Tamara was not in position to generate an executioner's stroke, but she managed to bring the forward curve of her mameluke to the base of the d'relle's neck, and as if cutting carrots in her kitchen, simply pushed forward, letting the sharp edge bite into the d'relles neck, slicing a good five or six centimeters into muscle and nerves. And an artery.

Blue blood spurted out, covering Tamara as the d'relle screamed and struggled, kicking her right leg free and falling to the ground. She put both right arms on the ground to right herself, a true sign that she was hurt.

Tamara didn't know how long it would take a d'relle to bleed out, and she wasn't about to find out. Her opponent was hurt, possibly fatally, but even so, she could still win the bout. She didn't have to live, only live longer than Tamara.

Tamara kicked out the lower right arm, and to keep from falling flat, the d'relle swung around her sword arm to catch herself. Even so, she managed to swing it in an arc which almost caught Tamara.

Tamara ducked back, then with the Klethos queen on her hands and knees, lunged forward like a matador on a bull, driving her mameluke into the back of her opponent's neck, right at the base of her feather crest. A Klethos had a spine similar to a vacuum cleaner hose. It was a very tough cartilage-type tissue, supported by bony strips that ran its length. Tamara could feel the tip of her sword slide alongside one of the bony strips until it found an opening and pierced through the cartilage as she rammed it home. The d'relle didn't even shudder but simply collapsed to lie motionless in the blue-stained sand.

It only took a few moments for Tamara to realize that the d'relle was dead. She'd been acting almost on instinct, and now her conscious mind was regaining control. She jerked free her mameluke, raised it to the skies, and shouted out her pure joy.

She had won!

MALIBU

Chapter 26

Tamara and Jonna rode through the gate of the campus, and of course, it was Jasper manning security. He stepped out of his shack and rendered a passable salute. Tamara knew he couldn't see her through the heavily tinted windows of the van, but she saluted anyway.

I'm glad to be home, she thought, a feeling of calm sweeping over her.

And that made her pause. This was her home now, not Orinoco. She'd been born again here, her sisters were here, and she would die here—well, unless she lost a fight somewhere else. But she would be buried here, at least.

Things had been pretty hectic since the fight. After some immediate interviews, she'd been whisked back to the ship for the trip back. Normally, she might have had some time to decompress on the ship, but it had been set up with full meson comms, so there had been more interviews as well as calls from her parents and Di, from the Chief Executive of Orinoco, from the President of the Confederation of Free States (to whom Halcon 4 belonged), some under-secretary of the UAM who called with congratulations from the Secretary General. Most surprising were the calls from no less than three heads of state of the Oceania Association. Her haka had gone over well with the general population, if holo feedback tallies were indicative, but it had been a huge hit in the association as well as other planets with large Pacific Islander populations.

The van zipped past the admin building. Tomorrow, she'd start her official debriefs, and she knew Swordmaster Abad would be waiting to dissect her fight (and probably tear her a new one for leaving her feet, even if she had beaten her opponent). But for now, she was untouchable. Her PA, which had something over 80,000 messages with more coming in (she reminded herself to get AI help to get through them all) was turned off. The staff was out of her hair. Now was time for the ceremony.

The van took them to Gustavson Village, letting them off at the community center. "Sunset Acres" was essentially the gladiator retirement home. Gladiators who were no longer well enough to be on the active list, while they could stay in their original homes, usually chose to come to the village to live out their last days among others in the same situation. Tamara didn't like to come to the ceremonies, but this time, she didn't mind.

The van stopped, and Tamara and Jonna got out. The van immediately took off for their home where a staffer would unload it of their gear for them. The two women strode up the immaculately trimmed walkway. Elei, a huge grin on her face, stood by the front hatch like some sort of oversized doorman, opening it with a flourish as the two reached her.

Inside, every gladiator was packed into the center.

"That's a lot of beef," Jonna whispered. "And all here for you."

In the middle of the group, Fleetwood hovered in his chair, the senior gladiator. He still made her uncomfortable, but she'd managed to learn to control her feelings while around him. At least he was still mobile, still somehow hanging on to life. Several of the senior sisters could not even sit in a hover, they were so far gone. They were here for the ceremony, though, even if one or two might not completely realize what was happening.

"Senior Gladiator," she announced to Fleetwood in a loud voice. "I have returned victorious!"

Loud cheers and foot-stomping greeted her proclamation.

"So I see. Then I must turn you over to the ministrations of our sister, Naomi."

Naomi Van Sustern wasn't the senior braided gladiator, but she the senior who was still cognizant of her surroundings. She was in a hover next to Fleetwood, and she beckoned for Tamara to come and sit before her. Tamara complied, turning around to face away from her as she sunk to the ground.

Naomi's body might be wasted, but her hands were firm as she separated a handful of the hair on Tamara's left side and quickly braided it the telltale sign of a victor. Within moments, she was done, and she asked Tamara to rise. More cheers and foot stomps greeted her as she raised an arm in acknowledgment.

And that was the ceremony—short, sweet, and to the point. Classmates and friends crowded in to congratulate her, but more people seemed interested in the fine layout the chefs had put together. The ceremony was for her, but they'd had nine already this year, so it wasn't that unique. After she'd been braided, it turned more into a social gathering, a time to eat, gossip, and simply be family (albeit a very large family).

Tamara had barely gotten used to having long hair again after so many years, and now she was acutely aware of the heavier braid laying against her cheek. It felt good, she decided. Everything felt good. She wasn't even bothered by the Brick sufferers.

Tomorrow might be different, but for now, all was well with the world.

TARAWA

Chapter 27

General Joab Ling, Commandant of the Marine Corps, had to stand on a small stool in order to be able to reach up to pin the Single Combat Service Medal on Tamara's chest. Tamara kept her eyes locked straight ahead during the process, wondering what would happen if the commandant fell off the flimsy stool. She had to fight back the smile that threatened to creep onto her face as she pictured that.

He got the medal fastened, though, without incident.

"We're proud of you, Chief Warrant Officer Veal, really proud."

Her victory in the ring had also resulted in her promotion that morning to chief warrant officer. Colonel Covington had arranged the ceremony, and Tamara's mother had proudly pinned on her new bars.

Her family had been a little miffed to find out that she was not coming home after the bout. Tamara had begged off, telling them she had no choice, that she had to go to Tarawa for Marine Corps duties. In the end, she had invited them to Tarawa for the promotion and medal presentation.

The truth was that she could have gone home; she simply didn't want to. The Marine Corps had requested her presence, so that hadn't been a lie, but as she was attached to the UAM mission, not even the commandant himself could order her presence. But she decided would rather go reconnect with the Marines than spend another couple of days back on Orinoco attending every possible ceremony that they could devise.

She still had to explain to them why she'd stopped off at the Kingdom of Hiapo to become an honorary *kao'o'e*, or bodyguard of the king. She'd even received her own *lei-o-nano*, only the third non-citizen to ever received one of the war clubs. Evidently, the king had been more than impressed with her haka, and as the prime figure in the Oceania Association, he'd evidently appropriated the Maori haka as part of overall Pacific Islander culture. Frankly, Tamara didn't care. The ceremony had been interesting, the lei-o-nano strikingly beautiful, and the party was out-of-this-world. Sitting around the luau with the rest of the kao'o'e, who had to all have been genmodded as well to get so large, she had felt a degree of kinship that she hadn't felt outside of the Corps or with her sister gladiators.

With medal pinned on her, she moved to the commandant's left and faced the parade deck while a lieutenant snuck in to grab the stool and take it away.

A lieutenant colonel from the division staff march forward, took his position, and shouted, "Pass. . .in. . .REVIEW!"

Two-thirds of First Marine Division was stationed on Tarawa in the vicinity of Marine Headquarters, and to Tamara, it looked as if almost all of them had taken part in the parade. She'd done enough parades in her career and knew what went into preparing for one that she both felt sorry for putting them through it and honored that they had. As the band started playing, she felt a surge of pride sweep through her body.

One-by-one, the battalions taking part in the parade marched past the commandant and her. Tamara remained ramrod straight, but if she stood a little taller when 2/3 marched by, that could be excused. Her old battalion was hosting a picnic for her after the parade, and this was one event to which she was looking forward.

Just as 2/3 reached her, the breeze picked up, lifting both the battalion colors and her own hair and streaming them in full view. She could almost feel the excitement of the camcorder operators as both they and cam-drones rushed to the right vantage from which to frame the shot

Her hair, or course, was decidedly non-reg, but she was not about to cut it, and no one expected her to. And in her Marine alphas, tailored to her huge frame, she thought the red and gold looked great against the green of the uniform.

As soon as 2/3 passed, the breeze died back down. It was almost as if it had been planned, but while most junior Marines thought the commandant was God himself, or might as well be, he couldn't command the weather.

With so much of the division in the parade, the entire pass in review, to include the company in PICS, the armor company, and the flyover, took almost 20 minutes. Tamara enjoyed every second of it. She was a gladiator, true, but she was a Marine first, and this touched her heart.

Finally, though, the parade was over. Various high-ranking dignitaries came forward to shake her hand while holocams recorded everything. Tamara introduced her family to the commandant, and she thought her mother might faint from the excitement. The commandant's eyes almost glazed over as her mother went into a story about Tamara in the second grade, but he was a seasoned warrior, and he kept a smile on his face as he nodded while her mother blathered on. The commandant—and Tamara—were rescued by Colonel Covington.

"Chief Warrant Officer Veal, I hate to interrupt, but you have an appointment now at the Wounded Warrior Battalion."

"But—" her mother started.

"I'm sorry, Mom, but I promised to do this. Then I've got 2/3's picnic coming up. I'll meet you tonight at the Lodge."

"And we've got that tour ready for you, Ms. Veal. The bus will pick you up at 1130 sharp," Colonel Covington added.

Tamara's mother had been tickled pink to get a room at the VIP Lodge. Well, her father and Diana had been pleasantly surprised as well, to be fair, but her mother had taken her approval to a higher plane. And now, she was getting a lunch and a tour of the city by the mayor, and that quickly mollified her about not finishing her story."

"OK, dear," she told Tamara. "You have fun, and we'll see you tonight."

She let a captain escort them off as the commandant turned back to Tamara.

"I'll see you again tomorrow," he told her. "But if you need anything else, you call me directly."

"Or me," Sergeant Major Çağlar said.

Tamara let Colonel Covington steer her through the press and well-wishers to the waiting van, the same Ford model that was used at Chicsis, but this one Marine Green and with a huge gold Marine Corps emblem on the side. The Marine Corps had only one of the gladiator-sized vehicles, but this one would be at her beck and call for the duration.

While her trip to Orinoco had been chock full of events, the Marine Corps was letting Tamara pick and choose what she wanted to do. They had *requested* her presence at the welcome press conference and for the parade, but the rest was up to her. Tamara wasn't the Marines first gladiator, of course, while she had been Orinoco's first, but she thought there was more to it than that. In a way, it was as if they were honoring her, but that as a Marine, it was simply expected of her to serve the best she could. What she was doing was not out of the ordinary: laudatory yes, surprising, no. She was a Marine performing her mission.

Tamara could take offense at that, given the accolades she'd been receiving from just about everyone else. She'd volunteered to give up her life, after all. But as she walked into the Wounded Warrior Battalion, she knew that was nothing new for Marines. They'd been putting their lives on the line in the most desperate situations for hundreds of years.

It was obvious that the battalion had been eagerly expecting her. Marines were groomed, sheets crisp and clean, and staff standing by each rack. The smiles on the Marines touched her heart.

"What's your name?" she asked the first Marine in the ward.

"Lance Corporal Tenzing Friar, Ma'am," the Marine answered trying to sit up straighter in his rack.

Which was pretty difficult for him to do, given the fact that a regen chamber was where his lower body would have been. His

Jonathan P. Brazee

right arm was in a smaller chamber as well, and half of his face was covered.

"Where were you, Tenzing, if I might ask?"

"Jericho, Ma'am. I got hit by an IED. Took my legs off at the hips."

Tamara had only been vaguely aware that there had been a minor Marine mission on Jericho, but she wasn't sure of the details. Minor mission or not, for Lance Corporal Friar, the mission had been life-altering.

"And how much longer for you? Until you're back with your unit, I mean."

"I just got out of my coma, ma'am, so for me, I've got another year-and-a-half, the docs tell me."

Tamara tried not to flinch. That was a long time in regen, and with so much of his body undergoing treatment, his chances of contracting the Brick were far more than someone who'd just lost an arm or who'd had minor internal injuries.

"You just stick with it, Tenzing. You'll do fine," she said, putting a hand on his good shoulder.

"Uh, begging the ma'am's pardon, but do you think I could get a holo? I want to send it to my girlfriend. She's a huge fan of yours, and she's so jealous that I'm meeting you."

That took Tamara by surprise. Not that the Marine wanted a holo. That was why Colonel Convington had brought along a holoman, after all. But the pride in Lance Corporal Friar's voice that he was the lucky one to meet her, and that someone was jealous of him. He had only half of his body, but he felt lucky, just for meeting her.

"Oh, of course! Here, let me come around for you," she said, motioning for the holoman. "And if you want, you give me her address, and I will personally zap her the holo."

"Oh, really? Fucking yeah I will—oh, excuse my language, ma'am. Of course, I'll give you it. She'll about die!" the happy Marine said, the good half of his mouth curving up in a grin.

Tamara posed for the holo, got Friar's girlfriend's address, and gave him a hug before moving on to the next, eagerly waiting Marine. Colonel Covington had blocked out an hour for the visit, to

140

be followed by 2/3's picnic. Tamara took almost two-and-a-half hours. Other than the lone holoman, there was no press, no fanfare. This was just Tamara and the Marines and sailors undergoing treatment, not a puplic holo-op, even if every one of them, got a holo with her. Not all of the patients were combat casualties. One of the Navy corpsmen had been in a horrendous hover accident and had burns over 2/3s of her body. Tamara tried to spend time with each of them, giving them encouragement.

When she finally left, she felt uplifted. What she was doing as a gladiator was important, but it was the Marines and sailors who were keeping the Federation strong and serving the citizens. No one was giving them a luau on Hiapo. They didn't have newsies following them around. They didn't get the accolades, but what they were doing was every bit as important as what she was doing.

"Do you think I can visit the other Wounded Warrior battalions?" she asked the colonel after the visit as she rode to the 2/3 battalion area.

There were six of the battalions, and she felt a need to see the other five.

"Of course, as far as the Corps is concerned, we would love that and would bend over backwards to make it happen. But the UAM might not be as sanguine for you to spend much more time away from them."

He was beating around the bush that with each gladiator's clock ticking down to the inevitable, their time had to be maximized. This trip could be her last ever off Malibu or whatever world she'd be sent to next.

That put a little bit of a dent in Tamara's high, and she just sat back in her seat until the van pulled into the 2/3 area. As the door pulled back, a cheer erupted from the gathered Marines as they greeted her.

The entire battalion was in PT gear, and in her alphas, Tamara felt overdressed. She was about to turn to the colonel when Fanny Dolsch stepped forward, a huge set of PT gear in her hands.

"We're guessing you might want to get more comfortable, ma'am?" she said.

"I'll 'ma'am' you, Fanny, but yeah, let me get changed," she said, happy to see a face she recognized.

She scanned the crowd, easily picking out Jessup Wythe. She pointed a long arm at him."

"About time you showed up, ma'am! We're starving here!" he said to the laugh of the crowd.

Lieutenant Colonel Rhonendren was standing near her, in her PT gear like everyone else. But she didn't rush up to greet her. It was as if she realized that Tamara wanted to see her friends first. This was about Tamara, not her, and Tamara appreciated that.

She followed Fanny and Doc Neves through the crowd, high-fiving—well low-fiving for her, high-fiving for the other Marines—making her way to the battalion CP. Fanny led her to the sergeant major's office. She had to hunch over, but she managed to get her alphas off, which she gave to Doc to hang up, and slipped into the PT gear, the 2/3 emblem emblazoned on the front of the shirt. They didn't have shoes for her, and she thought she looked silly with her florsheims on, so she simply kicked her shoes off and went barefoot.

"I heard Jericho was pretty rough," she said to Fanny.

"Yeah, it kind of sucked," Fanny admitted. "The ROE[15] was messed up, you know."

"You heard about Wheng, right?" Doc asked.

"No, what about him?"

"They brought a wall down on him, him and Korf. Korf was messed up, but he pulled through and was casevac'd, but Wheng didn't make it."

Tamara felt gut-shot. Corporal Wheng? She'd always liked him.

"Don't let Doc downplay it. When the wall went down, we got hit bad, and she went all badger there, digging like crazy while rounds were bouncing everywhere. She pulled Korf out and saved his ass. She's getting a Navy Cross for it."

"Really?" Tamara asked, pretty impressed.

"It was no thing," Doc said, but Tamara could tell she was proud of what she'd done.

---

[15] ROE: Rules of Engagment

142

As she should be.

In a way, Tamara thought what these Marines, or in Doc's case, sailors, were doing took more courage that what she was doing. She'd had this conversation with Jonna, Elei, and Beth. Elei didn't agree, and the other two were non-committal, but when they all had undergone genmodding, the die was cast. They had limited time left, so going into the ring wasn't that big of a deal. No one wants to die before their time, but a gladiator's time was limited, and their life outside of Chicsis was non-existent. These Marines, however, or soldiers or militia from other forces, had the potential for a full life. Corporal Wheng had only been 22 years old. He had a good seventy or eighty years ahead of him, years that had been cut short on Jericho.

The three left the CP and emerged again to the cheers of the battalion. The Sergeant Major took a throat mic and welcomed Tamara "back home." He made a few comments about her service, focusing on her actions on Wyxy, and barely mentioning her fight on Halcon 4. To the battalion, her service as a gladiator was almost secondary. What mattered was that she was a Marine.

When he gave Tamara the mic, she was stumped. She'd figured she'd have to talk, but looking over the eager faces of her fellow Marines, she suddenly felt shy.

"Thank you for your welcome," she managed to get out. "I.. .I'm glad to see some friendly faces. And some not so friendly, Staff Sergeant Abdálle. Yeah, I see you there," she said, pointing down at him.

The battalion broke out in laughter and "ooh-rahs" while her former platoon sergeant had the grace to smile and nod, raising his hand in acknowledgment.

"I've followed your deployment on Jericho, and I have to say, I'm proud of you, all of you. I just found out that my friend, Doc Neves, is up for a Navy Cross, and I'm, well, I'm bursting with pride at that. I just wish I'd been with you in person instead of just in spirit."

More "ooh-rahs" reached up from the crowd.

"I'm detached from the Corps right now. But there are eight of us serving as gladiators, and we remember our roots. And my roots, where I feel at home, is with Second Battalion, Third Marines! Fuzos!"

Tamara hadn't thought she was finished, but the battalion did. They simply erupted into chants of "Fuzos, Fuzos!" The battalion, whose patron unit was the Portuguese Corps de Fuzileiros, had a long and storied history. Ryck Lysander, the most storied Marine in Federation history, had even commanded it. And now, Tamara was just one more link in the chain, one more Marine to bring the battalion glory.

The chants continued with no sign of letting up, so Tamara gave the mic back to the sergeant major. She waved to the crowd before allowing herself to be led to the food tables. As the guest of honor, she was being offered first dibs at the food, which looked to be gladiator-safe. That was a far cry from the meals on Orinoco, where regular food was served at which Tamara had to pick and choose food which was allowed her.

Guest of honor or not, Tamara was not going to be fed first. Marine tradition was that the junior Marines go first, senior after that. As a chief warrant officer, Tamara now out-ranked a good portion of the battalion. So instead of taking a plate, she grabbed a serving spoon instead, shouting "Where are those privates?"

The CO, the sergeant major, and another Marine who Tamara didn't recognize (but later found out was the battalion XO) joined her, and the line started. Tamara positioned herself by the macaroni salad, dishing out a spoonful to each Marine as he or she passed by. She had a greeting for each, asking the names of those she didn't recognize, happily greeting those she did.

She gave Jessup Wythe two scoops of salad, telling him that was for making him wait. When Victor Williams came through the line, she hesitated for just a moment while he stood in front of her. She'd felt a strong attraction to the handsome Marine before, but that feeling was gone, and that made her sad. He looked nervous as he held out his plate.

"Here you go, Victor. You're looking good," she said as she gave him a scoop.

"Thank you, ma'am," he said, still looking nervous, but a smile creasing the corners of his mouth.

Several of her recruit training classmates had come to the party, and Tamara was pleased and happy to see them. Baker Suarez had even made sergeant already, which was well ahead of the rest of the class.

When a stunningly beautiful Marine stepped up in front of her, Tamara hesitated for a moment before recognition kicked in.

"Corporal Medicine Crow, it's good to see you!"

"It's Sergeant Medicine Crow now, ma'am. I was promoted last year."

"Oh. Well, congratulations! I never bought you that drink, you know, the one for saving my ass on Wyxy. We waited half the night for you, and then after that, you know, I had to leave."

"Yes, Ma'am, I didn't make it. But don't worry, you don't owe me anything. You took on that SevRev suicider. I wasn't in any danger myself."

"Well, you still saved my ass, and I'm grateful for that."

"Sergeant Medicine Crow was one of our best snipers on Jericho," the CO said, the first time she'd interjected anything into Tamara's interactions with the Marines.

"It doesn't surprise me," Tamara said.

"Thank you, Ma'am," the sergeant said once more before starting to step to her right to get the dinner roll served by the CO, then hesitating.

Tamara looked up at her expectantly.

She seemed to war within herself on whether to speak, but then asked, "Uh, Ma'am, have you met Chief Warrant Officer Falcon Coups?"

"Of course, I have. There are only eight Marines serving as gladiators, you know. Why, do you know her?"

"Yes, ma'am. She's my cousin," the sergeant said before turning and holding her tray out to the CO for the dinner roll.

The sergeant was certainly withdrawn, Tamara thought, surprised that nothing else was forthcoming.

And that is probably why she earned the nickname "Ice Queen." But she did her job in saving Tamara on Wyxy, and from what the CO had just said, she'd done it on Jericho as well.

The rest of the enlisted came through the line. She gave Staff Sergeant Abdálle another hard time, feinting giving him his salad, then pulling it back. He laughed, thank goodness, and she ended up giving him two scoops. The man was a certified hard-ass, but he was a good leader, and that was what mattered.

When Chief Warrant Officer 4 Morrey came up and told her to join the line, she refused. Yes, he was senior to her, but she was enjoying herself, and this was a good way to meet everyone. He relented and let her serve him. The rest of the officers filed through. As with the enlisted, it was not just 2/3 officers, though. She was surprised, and pleased, to see Lieutenant Colonel Versace there. She respected the man, even if he thought she might not make it as a gladiator.

After Colonel Covington was fed, the four servers made a show of filling each other's plates. Tamara glanced down at the meal, which looked surprisingly good, just as her stomach rumbled. She realized she was starving.

She gave her respects to the other three, then made her way to where her old squad was waiting for her. To her surprise, no one had eaten yet. They had been waiting for her. Tamara squatted on the ground so she would be at eye level with them and dug in the food. She asked to be brought up to speed on everything that had happened since she'd accepted the nomination.

It was almost 0200 when she finally left, missing her meal with her family and anything else they'd had planned. She'd make it up later in the day to them. But the Marines of 2/3 were also her family, and spending time with them, probably for the last time, had been something she'd had to do.

TARAWA

Chapter 28

"Nemesis-One, this is Nemesis-Two," Beth passed over the child's Walky-Talky-Panda. "What's your pos, over?"

"Quiet!" Tamara sent back in a forceful whisper. "There's no mute on this thing!"

"Nemesis-One, that is not correct communications procedure. Please say again, over."

Tamara ran back out of the room and collapsed in the common room, her back against the wall. She tried to suppress her laughter.

"Uh, Nemesis-Two, this is Nemesis-One. I am at the target's location. Be advised, this thing does not have a mute, and you almost alerted the target."

When there was no response, she remembered to say, "Over."

"Roger that. Be advised that the secondary target is not at the objective. I say again, the target is not at the objective, over."

Heck! What do we do now? Tamara wondered.

She came to a decision and passed, "Understood, Nemesis-Two. Come to my location and assist me, over."

"Roger that. I'm on my way, out."

Tamara looked leaned back and put the pink plastic child's radio on the deck. She'd been amazed to see them in the commissary, and she just had to pick them up. Beth had been delighted with them, especially the panda imbedded in the plastic, its open mouth the microphone pick-up.

Tamara sat alone in the darkened room, waiting. She heard the front door slowly creep open and waited.

"Nemesis-One, this is Nemesis-Two. I am at your position, over," Beth said, both into her Walky-Talky-Panda and while standing over Tamara.

"Jeez, Beth. Why don't you wake up the whole village," she responded, lurching for her radio to turn it off.

"Roger dodger, 10 by 10, wilco, over and out," Beth said into her radio.

The original idea was Tamara's, but Beth had pretty much taken over the operation, fleshing out the op order. All the details were Beth's, even the call signs. Nemesis was the ancient Greek goddess of revenge, and that fit the bill. At least she'd let Tamara be Nemesis-One.

"So, Objective One is still a go?" Beth asked.

"Right there," Tamara said, nodding at the closed door.

"OK, then let's do it."

The two gladiators silently got up and carefully crept to the closed door. Tamara put her ear to it, but there was no sound from inside. She looked to Beth, needlessly put her forefinger to her lips, and slowly pushed the door open.

Inside the dark room, a large lump was motionless on the bed under some heavy blankets. Tamara crept up, fearful that the lump would spring up, ready for action. She needn't have bothered.

Gladiators slept soundly. There was no reason for them to be on the alert around the clock, and deep sleep was thought to delay the onset of the Brick, so deep sleeping was programmed into them during genmod. A gladiator could be woken, of course, but it normally took some effort, and Tamara and Beth were determined not to wake their target.

Carefully, oh so carefully, they took their rolls of Orangutape, and passing it over and under the bed to each other, they slowly created a cocoon around their sleeping beauty. Tamara was afraid of making it too tight, waking her up, but she slept on, the slightest of snores filling the room.

They used all 50 meters of Tamar's roll, then another half of Beth's before they quit. That would be enough to hold even a gladiator secure.

Next came the tricky part. Sleeping deeply was one thing when applying the tape, but now they had to move her for phase two of the plan. Together, the gladiator and bed weighed close to 500 kilos, and the bed would barely fit through the door leading out. The burden was not too much for the two of them, though. With Tamara at the head of the bed and Beth at the foot, they carefully lifted the bed and gladiator up. Slowly shuffling out, they managed to maneuver their burden out of the bedroom, down the entryway, and out the big double doors.

"Is that her?" Elei whispered, coming out of the dark.

"Sshh!" Tamara hissed.

They carried the bed out the gate and carefully deposited it in the middle of the street. Jonna never stirred under her blanket and Orangutape cocoon.

"I thought you said Elei wasn't there!" she whispered to Beth as the backed away.

"Well, she wasn't. She was here," Beth said.

"What happened?"

"Your partner in crime was testing her comms while I was there, and she couldn't keep a secret when I asked her what was up," Elei said. "Don't blame her."

"Of course, I'm blaming her. What about OpSec?"

"Don't get your panties in a twist. You got back at your roomie, and that's what's important, even if it took you two girls long enough. Great plan, though. I wish I'd come up with it," Elei said.

It had been a good plan. Jonna slept on, trapped in her bed in the middle of Deerwood Street. And no one seeing her would wake her. It was an accepted rule that no one interfered with a good prank.

Tamara put the small holocorder she'd gotten at the commissary on the front gate post. She wanted to have everything recorded when Jonna woke up.

Yes, it had been a good plan, and revenge was always sweet.

Chapter 29

"Are you sure?" Tamara asked, astounded at the news.

"Yeppir. Maxi sure," Grammarcy said, shrugging her shoulders.

"But it hasn't even been two years!"

"I'm so sorry," Jonna told their friend. "Are they, I mean, can you still fight?"

"Nope. That's out of the question now. I guess I go into retirement," she said in the same dull voice in which she'd told the two roomies that she had the Brick.

There wasn't an official gladiator retirement. They just fell out of the pool for fights. Most gladiators in that position eventually moved to Gustavson Village to join the rest of the inactive gladiators. Many initially tried to stay in their homes, but surrounded by other gladiators who still had a mission, few ended up staying for long.

Tamara was shocked, to say the least. Grammarcy hadn't even fought yet, and it didn't seem possible for her to already have the Brick. Tamara had been keeping thoughts of the Brick at bay, refusing to talk about it. If she didn't let it into her thoughts, it didn't exist. If—when—it appeared in two or three years, she'd deal with it then. But now, to have her classmate already contracting it, she couldn't ignore it. She could be next, she realized.

That's so messed up, she thought as she reached out to take Grammarcy's hand in hers. *All of the sacrifices, all the work, for nothing.*

"So what are you going to do?" Jonna asked.

"What can I do?" Grammarcy said with the first hints of bitterness in her voice since she'd knocked on their door. "I can't turn back the clock."

"Do you want to, do you want to stay here for awhile? You know, to talk?" Jonna asked.

"Talking won't do anything," Grammarcy snapped. She took a deep breath and brought the calm Grammarcy back. "Sorry, I didn't mean that. Thanks for the offer, but no. I've got to get going. I just wanted to tell you to in person before the word gets out. I've still want to tell a few others before that happens."

She stood up, and both Tamara and Jonna rose as one to envelope their friend in hugs. After a long 20 seconds, Grammarcy broke the hug, thanks them, and left.

Tamara and Jonna stared after her long after the front door had closed. If they survived the ring, that was their future, and that was a future that scared the crap out of Tamara.

Chapter 30

Jonna wheeled around, briefly exposing her back as she ducked, then sprang up, sword tip aimed at the d'relle's underbelly, right at the juncture of her breastplate. She had telegraphed the move, however, and the d'relle's sword swung down in a move to pass Jonna's guard and hit home.

The Klethos blade hit Jonna's sylvian high, knocking aside the tip as it plunged down in a coulé—only to get trapped in the sylvian's quillon. Jonna, using the momentum of the d'relle's strike, carried both weapons to the sand surface of the ring where she stepped on the tip of the d'relle's sword. Driving up with her long thighs, she unleashed a tremendous uppercut with her left hand, smashing through an attempt by the d'relle to arm-block it and connecting solidly with her opponent's beak. The d'relle staggered, and with a smooth motion, Jonna freed her sylvian blade and brought it up, the tip hitting the d'relle low before delving deep into her inner workings. The d'relle stopped all motion, still hung up on Jonna's sword.

Jonna looked up with a huge smile on her face and turned expectantly to her swordmaster. Master Kath Win Li nodded her approval as the techs rushed forward to repair the damaged to the simulacrum.

While most gladiators fought the d'relle simulacrums with virtual blades, the sylvian blades were so new that the trainers wanted this test to be with Jonna's actual weapon. The techs were probably beside themselves that their baby, one of only four at Chicsis, had been abused so cruelly.

Tamara didn't care much about that. She rather destroy a hundred simulacrums than give up even the slightest advantage. She smiled and gave Jonna a thumbs up. She had to have just passed the evaluation, and she'd be cleared to go on the active list.

Ten of the class had already entered the ring, but with their new swords, neither she nor Jackie Prescott-Alercia had been cleared yet.

Another d'relle was ordered forward, techs fretting over it as Jackie stepped forward to take her turn. Jonna whispered something to her, then slapped her on the shoulder before sauntering over to Tamara, hips swinging too much and shoulders rocking, her version of a victory walk.

"Not bad there, Reindeer Girl, not bad. You might even have a chance against a real d'relle," Tamara told her.

"Not bad my lily white ass," Jonna said, punching Tamara in the upper arm. "That was hot shit great!"

Tamara merely snorted her response as both friends turned to see if Jackie would be cleared to the active list as well. She had to admit, though, that Jonna actually had been "hot shit great."

Chapter 31

"I don't see why you have to leave," Jonna said, sitting on Tamara's bed.

"I told you, Jonna, it's nothing against you. It's just that some of the braided girls are taking over part of San Simione, and I need to make sure I get a home."

"But can't you wait? I mean, I'm on the active list now, and I'll get my own braid, too. We can go together!" she whined.

"If I wait, it might be too late. But don't worry. As soon as you get your braid, you can join me. And if I already have a roomie, you can get someplace close to me. Look, I need to get going. The house drawing is in 20. If the staff leaves anything, just give me a call!"

With that, Tamara left the room, leaving Jonna to fall back on Tamara's bed in despair.

She was still lying there 20 minutes later when the door chimed. Jonna slowly sat up, scratched her forehead, and went to the door. She opened it to another gladiator who marched right into the home.

"Excuse me?" Jonna said. "And just who are you?"

"You know me. I'm Queen Forsythe, from the new class. I'm your new roomie," the gladiator said cheerfully before opening the door to Jonna's room. "This mine?"

"No, that's my room. And who the hell said you were my roomie. I didn't ask for anyone!"

"Eh, they assigned me to you. I, well, none of my own classmates wanted me. Hell, I tried three roomies in Module 1 alone. But since your other roomie left you—"

"She didn't leave me. We're going to room together again later," Jonna protested.

"Sure, I bet that's what she told you. But hey, if that happens, then I've got the place to myself," Queen continued, opening up Tamara's room. "Hey, I like yours better. Do you wanna switch?"

"I most certainly do not! And you're not coming in here. I'll talk to Auntie Ruth about this!"

"Auntie Ruth was the one who suggested it. She seems to think you'll be a good influence on me."

With that, Queen lifted a leg and let out a tremendous fart.

"Sorry about that. That's one of the reasons no one wants to live with me. I was bad before, but now, after genmodding, I can really blast them out."

Jonna wrinkled her nose and jumped back.

"Oh my God, that's vile!"

"Sure is. Watch, here goes another," she said as another blast filled the house.

"No, no, no! This isn't happening!" Jonna shouted.

"Oh, wow, this is classic," Beth said from where she, Tamara, Elei, and a few others were watching everything on a monitor from next door. "But maybe it's time to rescue her?"

"No, let her suffer!" Elei said gleefully.

"Hey, you don't get a say in this. You were in with her with the buckets over the doors, so we should be pranking you, too!" Beth said.

Tamara was tempted to let it play out longer, but Jonna was her friend, after all.

"OK, let's go get her."

Six gladiators, all laughing, ran out of the house, jumped the fence, and burst into Tamara and Jonna's house. Jonna looked up in confusion.

"Jonna, meet Queen," Tamara said.

"I just met her," Jonna said sourly, obviously wondering what was going on.

"Queen is a Federation Marine, and being a Marine, she agreed to help me out here."

"What do you mean?"

"You've been pranked, sister dear."

"But the, I mean, what about her not having any roomies?"

Queen sheepishly pulled a small rectangle from her pants and waved it in the air.

"I can't believe the commissary actually had a Fartmaster Deluxe on the shelves, but it sure helped out here."

"I thought I was going to die when I triggered it. That was some foul shit!" Queen said as the others laughed.

"But that means. . .you. . ."

"I'm not going to San Simione. Do you really think I can leave my bestie?" Tamara said, putting her arm around Jonna's shoulders. "I was just getting you back, my dear."

"But you already did with taping me in bed. It took me an hour to get out of that."

"Jonna, honey, you should know me better than that by now. A Marine does not just get even, no. A Marine always goes one better!"

Chapter 32

The mood was somber as Naomi Van Sustern braided Elei. Tamara was still in a state of shock. She'd been at Elei's fight, and she'd have to review the holos to understand exactly what happened. She'd been overjoyed, of course, when Elei's d'relle slowly sunk to the ground, Elei's claymore run through her body. But when Elei sunk to her feet a moment later, she had to contain herself from rushing forward. Beth, as her second, rushed in instead and led an obviously wounded Elei from the ring.

Tamara only had a few moments with Elei before the medical staff tore her away. The witnesses were escorted to their ride, and on the long flight back to Tarawa, Tamara had chewed her nails to the quick.

Now, she watched Elei sitting in the chair while Naomi slowly braided a lock of Elei's striking turquoise, green, and blue hair. It should have been a joyous occasion. Another one of them had gone out to combat and returned the victor. But the empty left sleeve of Elei's tunic was a stark reminder that something had gone wrong.

Elei had killed her opponent, and so she was the victor. The d'relle, however, had scored on Elei, and scored big. Without an arm, Elei was finished as an active gladiator. She couldn't go through another boosted regen. By the time the arm would have grown, the Brick would be ravaging her body.

Naomi finished the braiding, and the rest of the gladiators stomped their feet and cheered, but without the enthusiasm they normally exhibited. Tamara rushed forward to greet her friend.

"So what the hell happened?" Jonna asked. "I couldn't see anything."

"I won, that's what happened," Elei said, shutting everyone up.

She looked around, then said, "Sorry. I haven't had a moment to gather my thoughts since then. I grabbed the d'relle with my left hand," she said, raising her stump, "And pulled her in to run her through with Gege."

Gege was a Samoan god who had rid the islands of demons, according to mythology, and Elei had named her sword after him.

"Gege did his job, but when the d'relle tried to stop him, she sort of sliced my arm right through the bone."

"Holy shit," Jonna said quietly.

Those surrounding Elei went silent in counterpoint to the low buzz of the bulk of the gladiators who were already helping themselves to the food or breaking up into groups to socialize.

"Are you OK?" Tamara asked lamely.

Elei snorted, then said, "About OK as a one-armed gladiator can be."

"But they can reattach the arm, right?" Queen asked. "It was cut cleanly, right?"

"They could, but I said no. I'm getting a prosthetic. Without regen, it would take two, maybe three years to get back any useful function. I'd rather they just keep the hunk od useless meat and give me some hi-tech wonder like Mesonman's."

That brought out a laugh from the crowd. Mesonman's "meson arms" could morph into the most interesting forms as he fought evil in the galaxy. The fact that most of the forms had no basis in logic didn't take away from the franchise's popularity.

"How about Meson-X-man's?" someone asked, bringing even louder laughter.

Meson-X-Man was an adult-rated parody of the Mesonman flicks, and his arms took on more salacious tasks.

"I would, but that won't do any of us any good," Elei said.

"So you are off the active list," Holly Walton, one of the new class of gladiators, said needlessly.

"Yes, young lady, that I am. But don't feel bad. I'll enjoy my time as an inactive, making life miserable for all of you. I've got my braid, after all," she said, dramatically swinging it with a head flick. "I'll outlive all of you, so you can all start calling me granny!"

Elei was taking everything well, Tamara thought. Maybe too well. She hoped there wouldn't be a huge breakdown somewhere.

Tamara looked up to see Grammarcy at the back of their little group, staring hard at Elei's braid. Elei had just joined her on the inactive list, the first two from their class, but there was a huge difference between them. Elei had her braid, and Grammarcy did not.

Grammarcy spun around and quickly strode off for the door. Tamara almost went after her, but as there was nothing she could say, she just let her friend disappear into the night.

FRIESON

Chapter 33

Tamara had been quite surprised to get the call again. Not everyone in her class, even in the top half of her class, had gone into combat yet. Jonna, in particular, had taken it hard. It had been bad enough when two gladiators in the following class had been given fights, but now Tamara was getting her second.

Tamara knew Jonna was upset, and she understood why. But the choice wasn't hers to make. The staff, aided by some pretty heavy-duty AIs, made the decisions, based on parameters that were kept from the gladiators themselves. But Jonna was a good friend as well as a good soldier. She swallowed her disappointment to be Tamara's second. Know how Jonna felt, Tamara had considered asking Beth or Elei to take the position, but she thought that would just make matters worse for her friend.

"Not quite like Halcon," Jonna noted as they stepped into the Escalante.

The upscale hotel chain, only 50 years old or so, competed with Earth hotel chains hundreds of years old, and they continually tried to outdo the more established chains. Tamara had never been in one. There wasn't one on Orinoco, but there was one on Tarawa. However, as a lance corporal, the rooms had been more than a little out of her reach. Now, she was in the penthouse, a most VIP guest of the planet.

"Not bad. I could get used to it," Tamara said, running a hand along the silky-smooth top of a couch.

A couch in a hotel room. Posh to the max.

"Well, the gym has been closed to the public if you want to use it. If you're not up to it right now, I'm going to jump in the bath. Have you seen that tub? It's big enough for two of us."

Two gladiators might be a little tight, but Tamara agreed that the huge tub should fit a single gladiator comfortably.

"No, you go ahead. I'm just going to chill out here for a bit. We'll hit the gym later."

Frieson was a well-developed independent world that excelled at trade. It had very few resources of its own, but it had managed to almost will itself to become the quadrant's premier trade hub. As in independent planet, it was not bound by the same rules and regulations as most planets and nations, but still, their rise to success was noteworthy and something other planets often tried to emulate.

Frieson also had a strong military, and their army was well-regarded. They had even fought side-by-side with the Marines in the war with the Trinoculars. According to her briefing team, the planet was overjoyed that it was a Federation Marine who'd been assigned to defend them.

Tamara had suggested to Jonna that her status as a Marine might have had something to do with her selection, but in reality, no one knew if politics ever entered into the assignments.

Tamara walked around the suite. The furniture was huge, gladiator-sized. There couldn't have been enough time to make the furniture after the challenge had been issued, so they must have had all of it in storage just waiting until it might be needed.

No, not like Halcon 4 at all!

The next 26 hours, though, went by much as the 20 on Halcon had gone. Tamara used the gym, sparred lightly with Jonna, ate (the food, cooked by the hotel chef, was quite a bit better than they'd had on Halcon), and got in two good, deep, eight-hour sleeps. Gladiators slept deeply, but they almost always awoke after exactly eight hours, refreshed and ready to go.

The combat ring was not in a stadium, to Tamara's surprise. The Friesonians loved their sports, and they had hosted the Olympics seven years prior, so that would have made sense to her. But the Friesonians had constructed the ring at the landing site of their founder, Major Fedde Bovenlander. Carruthers, her handler this time, told her that only the planet VIPs would be at the fight itself.

None of that mattered to Tamara. Whether crowds as in New Budapest or small numbers as on Halcon, she didn't care. She'd tune them all out when in the ring. The only one she cared about was her d'relle opponent.

Tamara and Jonna spent the last hour before leaving the hotel playing Shields, a new card game that had caught on with the gladiators. Tamara imagined that the citizens of Freison might be surprised at her choice of activity, but it kept her mind clear and on the game, not on the fight. Jonna was up by over 100 spears by the time Carruthers poked his head in the room.

"We'll continue after the fight," Tamara told Jonna. "I'm not going to leave you spanking me so bad."

"You got it, Iron Shot."

Tamara rolled her eyes. Ever since leaving Malibu, Jonna had reverted to using Tamara's press nickname, and Tamara knew she wouldn't let up until they got back. Tamara prayed that when Jonna did get the call, her nickname would be equally as lame, and then she'd use it as often as possible as Jonna's second.

The fight site itself might be limited to the bigwigs, but a huge crowd surrounded the hotel, and when the two gladiators emerged to get into the van, they erupted in cheers. The landing site was a good 20 kilometers from the hotel, but it took the van driver (not the autopilot that drove most vans) almost 40 minutes to slowly drive through the pressing crowds that lined the way. It wasn't until they reached a police cordon at the base of Landing Hill that he could speed up to a more normal rate of travel.

At the top of the hill, the driver stopped the van, and the two gladiators got out. "VIP" was obviously a loosely-held term. There had to be over 2,000 spectators crowded at around the crest of the hill. Tamara spotted Colonel Covington and the UAM liaison, but that was about it. There were too many people in too little space.

A huge statue of Major Bovenlander dominated the area. He was gazing out over the city of Leeuwarden below. The ring was at his feet. To the major's left, Tamara's 20 witnessed stood. To the major's right, and empty path split the VIPs, a route for the d'relle to arrive.

Tamara nodded once to the witnesses. All seven other Marine gladiators were there, as was Elei. She'd left the rest of the witness list up to the Chicsis staff.

As on Halcon, Tamara stepped out onto the ring to feel the consistency of the sand. She was impressed: it was as good if not better than their rings back on Malibu. The better the ring, the more the results depended on skill. A poor ring could throw a wrench in things, and more than a few gladiators had lost their lives to poor footing.

Tamara then settled in to wait.

Carruthers had told her that only two Klethos had arrived on the surface. As normal, they came in their little one-person (one-Klethos?) ships and landed a good deal away from the combat ring. How they selected a spot at which to land was a mystery. On Saint Baltimore, over 100 of them had landed over 400 klicks away from the site, yet they'd walked up on time for the fight. How they even got to the site itself was only theorized. Surveillance on them was famously erratic and even contrary from one site to another.

A murmur from the crowd let Tamar know that the Klethos was in view. She didn't move, but kept her eyes locked straight ahead.

I'm a lean, green, fighting machine. I'm a lean, green, fighting machine. . .

From the corner of her eyes, she saw her opponent walk up to the ring almost nonchalantly. She stood for a moment and looked at the gathered observers, then with the familiar screech, stomped her foot forward in the initial challenge. Without hesitation, she launched into her haka.

I'm a lean, green, fighting machine. I'm a lean, green, fighting machine. . .

This d'relle, like her last opponent, seemed to be more about grace than pure strength, albeit to maybe a lesser degree. She twirled and spun, but that was punctuated by more than a few foot stomps. She even slammed her sword into the sand, burying the tip at least 20 centimeters deep, which meant she thrust it into the rocky soil under the sand.

Swordmaster Abad would have her ass for that, Tamara thought, interrupting her mantra.

Nothing else the d'relle did was noteworthy to Tamara. She didn't display hints as to her fighting style, nor did she show any weaknesses.

I'm a lean, green, fighting machine. I'm a lean, green, fighting machine. . .

It seemed like a longer-than-normal haka, but with a last spin, she finished with the final challenge pose.

Without taking her eyes off the d'relle, Tamara held her hand in back of her, a surgeon waiting for her scalpel. Ronna slapped the hilt of her mameluke into her hand. There was a murmur from the gathered observers, and for once, Tamara cracked a smile. She knew everyone had expected another Maori haka, but she didn't always do what was expected. After Marta had been killed, she'd wondered if the Klethos kept track of individual gladiators. The accepted truth was that they didn't, but she thought it odd that only three gladiators had ever won three times in the ring. In ancient Rome, there were great gladiators with 50 wins. She thought the Klethos might observe fights and the train up d'relles to face specific gladiators when they fought again. If the Klethos did follow them or not, it didn't hurt to shake things up. If the observers didn't like that, so what. She was there to defend them, not entertain them.

She wasn't very well prepared, though, unlike when she danced her last haka. She hadn't expected to be called again so soon, so she hadn't quite worked out all the steps. Luckily, the Turkish Sword Dance was somewhat repetitious. The mameluke was derived from sabers used by the Maluks in Egypt, and those, in turn, were derived from the Turkish kilij, so the Turkish Sword Dance seemed appropriate.

Keeping her eyes locked on the d'relle, Tamara brought her sword to the vertical, with her right arm cocked 90 degrees at the elbow. She reached over with her left arm and took ahold of the blade half-way up it and then began to march backwards, circling the d'relle.

The Klethos queen never moved, even when Tamara was behind it, but Tamara thought there was the tiniest relaxing of the d'relle's shoulders as Tamara completed the circuit. Stopping, she lunged forward with her right side leading, right arm extended, the point of her mameluke touching the sand centimeters from the d'relle's feet.

Hah! She flinched! Tamara noted, strangely exulting over the fact.

A flinch didn't signify much in the way of combat, but she felt it was almost a moral victory. Tamara sprang back erect, then lunged forward again, a meter or so to her right. She repeated this: lunge, spring back, lunge, spring back until she completed another circuit.

She looks nervous, Tamara thought as the d'relle eyed her.

Tamara didn't actually know how a Klethos exhibited nervousness, but something in the d'relle's carriage gave her that impression. It was like she was wondering just what Tamara would do next.

The final circuit was not really taken from the ancient holos of Turkish sword dances Tamara had been able to find. In those, the sword dancers slapped their swords on small, round shields. Tamara didn't have a shield, of course, so she substituted her left forearm for one. She performed a sort of hop-skip, her right knee coming high, slapping the sword on her forearm at the height of each hop. She covered more ground with each hop, so it only took a few moments to make the circuit around the ring. She came back to her position in front of the d'relle, then lunged forward in the classic challenge acceptance.

She was still too close to the d'relle when she finished, and her opponent didn't hesitate but immediately launched into a furious attack. As Tamara had watched what she considered to be a growing nervousness in the d'relle, she had anticipated that the d'relle might do that. It didn't look like Tamara was in any position to defend herself, extended and low to the ground, and the d'relle brought down a crushing blow to cleave Tamara's head—which Tamara deflected with her quillon just enough to send the Klethos blade a few centimeters to the side. The d'relle was left handed, as normal, and Tamara was right handed. This meant Tamara's mameluke was now inside the d'relle's guard. She pronated her wrist to cant her blade tip a few degrees to the left and the d'relle impaled herself with the force of her lunge, driving her body all the way to the quillons. Blue blood drenched Tamara's hand as the d'relle slumped over.

Tamara stood up as the d'relle's sword dropped from her hand. There was life in her opponent's eyes, life that was fading but still there. With a wrench, Tamara pulled her sword from the d'relle, who fell to her knees. Tamara stood still for a moment, staring at her opponent as she shuddered and gasped for air. D'relles were tough, very tough, and they'd been known to injure and even defeat gladiators while grievously wounded, as Elei could attest. This one didn't even have her sword in her hand, however.

Tamara didn't care.

With an executioners' blow, she took the d'relle's head off at the shoulders. The body fell to the side while the head flew up a meter, feathered crest splayed as the head spun, spraying blood in graceful curve, before falling down to the clean sand, sand that was immediately stained blue.

Tamara spun about and marched out of the ring without a victory shout. The entire fight, from the moment she finished her challenge to when the d'relle's severed head hit the deck, had been less than ten seconds. She'd done her job, nothing more, nothing less. She didn't need to scream to the heavens to advertise that.

MALIBU

Chapter 33

"Nice passata-sotto," Beth said as the van dropped Tamara and Jonna at the Gustavson Village rec center. "You're in the running for the top move of the year."

A passata-sotto was when a swordsman went low, putting his or her non-sword hand on the ground and raising the sword hand to come up under the opponent's guard. Tamara knew that her move on Frieson could have looked like that—and maybe her countless hours of training had kicked in. But she'd been in that position because of the traditional final lunge of the challenge, not because she'd wanted it that way. She just had thought that the d'relle might launch and immediate attack, and she'd reacted to that.

The reaction to the move had been immediate and frenetic. The cybernet had lit up with messages, some 8 billion within the first fifteen minutes, the UAM debriefer had told her. Challenges were becoming more numerous, and as could be expected, the public interest had flagged, something that the UAM Single Combat Directorate seemingly couldn't accept. Tamara was not sure why. What mattered was the win, not whether the ratings were high, at least in her mind. But the immediate and profound reaction from the public to her fight was candy to babies to the UAM, and they were beside themselves with joy, giddy, even. Tamara's flight back had to be delayed as more interviews were scheduled. Beth and the rest of the gladiators had been back for a full day before Tamara and Jonna had been able to return.

There would be more obligations for her tomorrow, but once again, the braiding ceremony had become sacrosanct to the gladiators, and the rest of human space could just tune out for an evening as far as they were concerned.

Beth opened the front door, and the gathered gladiators broke out into applause. Tamara was about the join the fifteen total and eight active two-braid gladiators. While Jonna and her friends were beaming, it wasn't that huge of a deal to Tamara, and she wasn't quite sure why. Sure, she was glad she had won, and she knew she was joining some elite company, but the pride she'd felt after her first win was surprisingly dampened. To her mind, she'd done her job, nothing more.

Still, she let herself get caught up in the general mood as she was led up to Fleetwood. He'd shrunken further into himself over the last eight months, if that was even possible, but his gaze was still clear and strong as she marched up to him.

"Senior Gladiator," she announced, "I have returned victorious!"

"Again!" several voices called out as cheers and foot-stomping reverberated through the center.

"So I see. Again," he said, his mouth turning up into a smile. "Then I must turn you over to the ministrations of our sister, Shareetha."

That saddened Tamara just a bit. Naomi, who had braided her first braid, was no longer cognizant. She had passed the torch to Shareetha Wilson, a frail gladiator who probably wouldn't be around long enough for many more braiding ceremonies."

Her hands were firm, though, as she took another lock of Tamara's hair from just behind her first braid and wove the strands of the lock into another heavy braid. Within moments, two of them hung down her cheeks.

As soon as Shareetha was finished, as many of the gladiators who could fit gathered around her to offer her congratulations.

"Hey, what happened to the haka?" Elei asked. "Did you forget my people?"

"You're Samoan, not Maori," Tamara said with a laugh. "Besides, I've got to keep things mixed up."

"Was that haka Turkish?" Flower Mataraci asked."

"Sort of," Tamar admitted.

"I knew it!" Flower said. "I told you so," she said to someone just out of Tamara's view.

As the gladiators, her sisters, crowded around, Tamara realized that this was what was important. The saving of planets was the key thing, of course. But more than the interviews, more than the attention of the various bigwigs who wanted her attention, it was her sisters here who mattered. Tamara was a Marine and intensely proud of that. And she missed the Corps. But her sister-gladiators were also her family. With them crowding around her, the blasé feeling that had enveloped her since the win on Frieson disappeared.

This is who she was, and she was damned proud of it.

Chapter 34

"OK, let's make the grand entrance," Tamara told Jonna as the two walked up to the Sichko Village rec center.

"You look good, there, Iron Shot," Jonna said.

Tamara did look good, and she knew it. The fact that anyone looked good in Marine dress blues was beside the point. *She* looked good, and that was what mattered.

"Am I OK?" Jonna asked for the tenth time.

Jonna's tall, comparatively lanky frame, pale skin, and almost white hair made her one of the most attractive gladiators from what most people considered beautiful. She'd had numerous requests for meetings from the paramours, something that didn't usually happen until after a gladiator was braided. And now, in a long, tightly fitted deep blue dress, she looked great, "gladiator standards" or not.

"Yes, yes, let's go in. You got your certificate?"

"Right here," she said, pointing at the small clasp she carried in her left hand. Marines in uniform were not allowed to carry purses of any kind, but then again, Jonna was not in uniform.

The door opened as they approached it. Tiktik, one of the maintenance staff, stood tall and proud in a tuxedo, one hand on the door and the other pointing the way.

"Wow! You look great, Tiktik!" Tamara said.

"Thank you, ma'am. And may I say the same for you? And for Miss Sirén, too, of course."

"You may say anything you like, dear sir, if you keep up the sweet talk like that," Jonna said with a curtsy.

Other than with the direct staff of trainers, there wasn't too much in the way of interaction between the gladiators and the norms who ran and took care of the campus. However, there were a few who'd become almost pets of the gladiators. Tiktik was one of them. A short man, even by normal standards, with a huge blotch of white skin along his face and neck, his personality lent itself for him to be a sounding board for them. A deeply religious man, he could have had the blotch that marred his ebony skin fixed easily enough, but he said that if God made him that way, then who was he to argue? Dealing with about 500 genmodded women, that could have been taken poorly, but his attitude and demeanor precluded that. He was one of perhaps a dozen support staff who not only had access to the gladiators, but was their friend. Along with Auntie Ruth and maybe Deseree Lee Caspin, the three were probably the favorite staff members for most of the gladiators.

As if on command, Auntie Ruth walked over to greet them.

"Tamara, welcome. And Johanna? You're attending, too?" she asked, sounding surprised.

"Yes, I am," Jonna said brightly.

"Oh, OK," she said with a shrug. "If you just go inside, Colonel Covington is waiting."

The two gladiators turned the corner into the main hall where the colonel and three Marines jumped up from the small table.

"Happy birthday, Chief Warrant Officer Veal," the colonel said, a huge smile on his face.

"Happy birthday to you, too, sir. And to you, Sergeant. . ."

"Sergeant Nelson, ma'am. And these are Corporal Singh, Lance Corporal Teller, and Lance Corporal Look-Wanson. We're your color guard," he added needlessly.

"Happy birthday to all of you. And thank you for coming. I'm afraid this isn't quite what they had planned on Tarawa, but we really appreciate it."

"We're from Gobi, Ma'am, not Tarawa. First Recon," the sergeant said with more than a little pride.

"Well, thank you, sergeant. We really appreciate it."

"Not as much as we appreciate you, begging the ma'am's pardon," Lance Corporal Teller interrupted.

Tamara felt a warm wash of gratitude sweep over her. Sometimes, she thought being cooped up on the campus isolated them from humanity. Out in Orroville, the townspeople were used to them, grateful for their boost to the economy, and of course the paramours trolled the streets for their own reasons. When fighting, they were isolated as well, preparing for the fight and being hustled back after the required holo-ops and interviews. But right here, these Marines, who gave up the birthday balls and celebrations back with their friends and family just to be a color guard for six Marine gladiators, that meant something.

For a moment, she actually thought she was going to cry, so she got out another thanks and pushed open the door into the main hall. The other seven Marines were already there, and the smiles they had changed to puzzled glances when they saw Jonna behind her.

"Uh, Johanna, it's nice to see you and all, but the first part of this is really only for Marines," Major Tolbert said. The major (Tamara still could not call her Bev), who had recently been braided, was not the senior gladiator of the eight, but she was the senior Marine.

"Show them, Jonna," Tamara prompted.

Jonna pulled out the certificate and held it at arm's length so they could see. "I'm an honorary Marine. It says so right here, signed by General Joab Ling, Commandant!"

"What? Really?" the major said, snatching the certificate. "Yeah, that's what it says, all right," she added, passing to Queen who took a quick look.

"Uh, I've got to ask, how did you get that?" the major continued, her brow wrinkled in confusion.

"I asked him," Tamara answered for Jonna.

"As simple as that?"

"As simple as that."

"Well, slap my britches," the major said. "I'd never thought of that. Did you have to justify it?"

"No. I just asked his secretary, and an hour later, it arrived."

"If you want me to wait, I can," Jonna said. "I was going to, but Tamara asked me to come."

"No, if it's good enough for the commandant, it's good enough for us," Falcon Coups, the senior Marine gladiator said. "Everywhere else, the ball is open to everyone anyway. I don't know why we closed this off to others, but it's been that way since I got her, at least. No, Johanna, stay."

Jonna looked relieved.

"Well, I guess that's all of us. So Beth, if you will?" Falcon said.

Beth stepped to the door and opened it a crack. She didn't have to wait. With Tamara's arrival, the color guard had prepared for their summons. Beth opened both doors as an electronic drum played out the cadence. The guard marched through, the Federation and the Marine Corps colors in the middle with the other two Marines, under arms, flanking them. The six Marines—and one honorary Marine—came to attention as the color guard passed them, reached the far bulkhead, and performed their counter-march. They came to a stop while the drum beat continued until the colonel managed to stop it and play first the Federation anthem, then the Marine Corps Hymn. Tamara stood tall as the familiar notes filled the room.

"Bev, if you will," Falcon asked as the last noted died away.

At units across the Federation, the ball was quite a bit more stylized and rehearsed. Not so much at Chicsis.

The major picked up an old-fashioned manila envelope from one of the tables and pulled out the first piece of plastisheet. She held it up to start reading, then stopped.

"It's for you, Tamara. From Sergeant Major Çağlar," she said, handing her the sheet.

"Me? Why me?"

She took the sheet and looked at it. Yes, it was addressed to her and written on the Sergeant Major of the Marine Corps' letterhead.

Dear Chief Warrant Officer Veal,

> *I just wanted to send you a small personal note. I watched the transmission of your fight on Frieson, and I was surprised to see your haka. You may not recognize the background of my name, but I am from Cennet, which was settled by Turkish pioneers. We kept*

many of the customs from old Turkey, so I readily recognized your sword dance.

You've done the Marines and the Federation proud in earning your second braid, but you made me feel proud of my roots. I sometimes forget about my warrior heritage. I have not been back to Cennet in years, but I'm taking my next annual leave there, thanks to you.

I wish you more success in your mission. I don't need to tell you how vital it is to humanity.

Semper fi
Hans Çağlar
Sergeant Major, United Federation Marine Corps
Sergeant Major of the Marine Corps.

"What is it?" Queen asked.

Tamara looked up to see seven eager faces. Instead of answering, she smiled and simply folded the sheet and slid it into the breast pocket of her blues.

"OK," the major said, extending the "oh-kay" almost into an interrogative. "I guess it's personal."

She seemed a little frustrated, but the note was personal. It was nothing earth-shattering, but it was written to her.

The major pulled out the next sheet, and this time, after reading the heading, she seemed relieved.

"OK, this is General Ling's birthday message," she said, holding it out and clearing her throat.

Message from the Commandant of the Marine Corps

On this, our 399th anniversary of our founding, I want to wish all Marines, sailors, and families a most happy birthday. As I write this, Marines are in harm's way from Dupree to Possington 4, serving the needs of the Federation. Eight Marines are serving all of humanity as Single Combat Specialist, as Gladiators, and another two are in training.

The major had to pause as the other Marines let out a few ooh-rahs.

We are the Federation's reaction force. We keep her safe and secure from all enemies. If you choose to fight the Federation, you choose to fight the Corps, and let me be one hundred percent clear on this, if you chose this route, you will die. It is that simple.

We are a proud force, proud of our heritage and history. But all of you, from recruit to general, are the new history makers. What you are doing today will be written down and read by people 10,000 years from now. Think of that as you perform your missions. You are history in the making.

I want all of you to enjoy your birthday. Relax and enjoy the camaraderie of your brothers and sisters in arms. Eat your birthday cake, and lift up a few in memory of our fallen. Then tomorrow, I want all of you to kick ass and take names. The Marine Corps never rests on past laurels, but on what we will do today.

Joab Ling
General, United Federation Marine Corps.
Commandant of the Marine Corps

The major put down the envelope, then nodded at Colonel Covington. The colonel marched up in his best drill field manner, holding a smallish, one layer caked. It was vanilla, of course, one of the few flavors that seemed to be programmed into their genmod recipe. In the middle of the cake was a gold Marine Corps emblem.

The major had brought her mameluke to Chicsis—not a gladiator-sized mameluke, but her original she'd gotten upon being commissioned. It looked ridiculously small in her hands as she sliced the cake.

As per Marine Corps tradition, the first piece went to the oldest Marine present. Actually, it went to the oldest gladiator Marine present, Beniful Terez. Benni had been a staff sergeant when she'd been nominated, and she was two years older than the major. Colonel Covington was technically the oldest Marine in the room, but none of the gladiators would ever reach much older than they were at the moment, so he was politely ignored for this purpose. Benni took a bite of the cake, then the major cut another piece and gave that to Queen, who was 24 days younger than Tamara.

After that, the other six received their pieces of cake. The color guard stacked arms and put the colors in their stands and along with Colonel Covington, got their cake as well. They stood around, eight gladiators dwarfing five norms, but all chatting as if family. The bonds of the Corps were strong.

The ceremonial part of the birthday ball was over. It might not have been fancy, it might not have been organized, but that didn't matter. What mattered was the simple fact that they'd remembered it.

A knock on the door was followed by it cracking open.

One of the major's friends poked her head in and asked, "Are you guys done yet?"

Within twenty minutes there were at least 300 gladiators and more than a few norms in the hall. Any excuse for a party was always welcomed, especially one that was officially a ball. Music turned on, and the "ball" part began. Mostly, it was gladiator dancing with gladiator, but Elei, complaining about too much estrogen in the room, grabbed Sergeant Nelson and took him out to the dance floor, much to the delight of everyone else. The sergeant acquitted himself well, and before long, each of the color guard, Tiktik and other male staff members, Master Abad, and even Colonel Covington were dragged out to the dance floor. "Dragged" was the operative term for what happened to the reluctant but laughing colonel. It wasn't as if he could put up much of a fight against a gladiator, after all.

When Fleetwood showed up in his hoverchair, he was pretty much mobbed as other gladiators lined up to dance with him.

"So, what do you think?" Tamara asked Jonna as the two sat and watched the dancing.

"Thanks, Tamara. I'm glad I could have been part of the ceremony. I've always been a little jealous of you and your bond with the Marines. And now, I've gotten a tiny taste of that before it'll be too late."

"Hey, don't be a downer. You've got plenty of time, Reindeer Girl. There'll be more birthday balls, and you're an honorary Marine now, invited to every one."

Jonna nodded but looked out at the others without saying anything else.

And Tamara knew she was right. Not about her. She was wickedly capable with her sylvian, something the Klethos had not even seen yet. She'd do fine in the ring, and she had several years before the Brick caught up with her. But out there, out among the now 400 gladiators, a good portion of them would not be around a year from now. The ring and the Brick would take their toll.

Come one! Let's get into happier thoughts. It's the Marine Corps Birthday Ball, for goodness sakes! she admonished herself.

"Come on, girlfriend," she said, jumping up and taking her best friend by the hand. "Let's show these plodding heifers how Marines dance!"

Chapter 35

Beth lay in her bed, luxuriating in the lazy feel. The Marine Corps Ball had been a nice release, and she wasn't quite ready to let it go. She'd get a good workout in later in the morning, and she had an appointment with Master Abad in the afternoon, but for the moment, it was nice to simply lay where she was with nothing pressing on her attention.

When her PA buzzed, she was tempted to ignore it. Whoever was calling knew where to find her if it was important. It kept buzzing, though, refusing to stop. And as she'd picked the buzz to be particularly annoying, she finally gave in and reached to the side table to grab it.

A glance at the screen indicated it was an TAG, or "To All Gladiators." Probably another party in the making, she thought as she almost put it back down. When she heard a muffled "Shit!" from Jonna's room, though, she quickly sat up and keyed in the message.

"Oh my God!" she said aloud as she read it.

Fleetwood Case, the last male gladiator, had just died.

"Did you see the TAG?" Jonna asked, bursting into Tamara's room.

Tamara just held up her PA, at a loss for words.

"But he looked OK last night! We just danced with him a few hours ago."

But he hadn't looked OK. He hadn't looked OK ever since Tamara and Jonna had been nominated. He'd been a scarecrow of a man, haggard and gaunt as the Brick devoured him. He hadn't looked any worse at the ball, and he'd seemed in good spirits when Tamara and Jonna had stolen him from some of the other gladiators and danced with him, one on each arm as he spun his hoverchair.

Fleetwood had never fought in the ring, but he'd become a vital part of the sisterhood. Everyone's big brother, he was a symbol more than anything else. He's been their anchor. It had been very difficult for Tamara to get to know him, given her fear of the Brick, but he'd always been there for her, just as he'd been there for all of them. And now that he was gone, Tamara felt a hollowness inside of her.

Jonna started to cry, and Tamara held out her arms into which her friend gratefully melted. The two held each other for several minutes, saying nothing. Tamara could feel Jonna's hot tears roll down her shoulders and onto her breasts. She felt like crying, too, but she held back, afraid that if she started, the tears would only feed on each other.

"Let's get dressed. We should go over to the Man Shack," she finally said.

Jonna nodded, pushing herself up and away from Tamara. With a final squeeze of Tamara's hands, she left to return to her room. Tamara quickly threw on some running sweats, and a few minutes later, Jonna met her. Together, they left the house and started to walk to Gustavson Village, joining other small groups and individuals as they made their way. By the time they reached the Man Shack, where Fleetwood had lived alone, there were several hundred of them there, with more arriving every minute.

Auntie Ruth was at the front door of Fleetwood's home. Auntie Ruth was fond of old-fashioned physical make-up, the kind that was applied every day, and her mascara was streaked with tears. She was acting as the gatekeeper, letting in small groups of gladiators at a time into the house to pay their last respects. It took almost 45 minutes for Tamara and Jonna to make it into the house and into Fleetwood's bedroom.

Fleetwood was laying on his back in his heavy wood-framed bed. Most Brick-suffers looked bad in death with faces in rictuses of pain. Fleetwood, however, somehow looked better, as if death relaxed the muscles of his face, giving him a slightly softer look. Most people who died of the Brick had long, debilitating, and painful slide into death, and Fleetwood hadn't. He'd been as mobile and normal, whatever normal was, just the evening before. He looked like he'd simply slipped away in his sleep.

If the Brick is going to take you, that's the way to go, Tamara thought as she stood at the foot of Fleetwood's bed. *God be with you.*

Then it was time to move on so more gladiators could file in. Tamara and Jonna went out into the common room and out the back door into the garden, then looping back around into the front of the house.

"It was his time," Jonna said as they milled out in the street, unsure of where they should go.

"No it wasn't. He was 29 years old, for goodness sakes," Tamara snapped. "It's none of our time."

"I meant. . ." Jonna said before giving up and falling into silence.

The gladiators knew death. Five of Tamara's classmates had already died in the ring, along with eleven others from other classes since she'd been a gladiator. Over forty had died of the Brick. Death was a constant presence, hovering over the Chicsis campus. With the grim reapers scythe constantly hovering over them, the dead were not celebrated as on Orleans or with the Blackrobers, no parades filled with music and professional mourners. There was a simple ceremony before the cremation, attended by anyone who wished.

Except for a few cases where she'd had a real relationship with the deceased, Tamara didn't wish, especially when the death was from the Brick. She tried to avoid reminders of that grim possibility. She'd be attending tonight, though, just as would probably every other gladiator and staff.

Tamara and Jonna drifted back to the Sichko rec center. There were at least 50 other gladiators there, sitting around and talking. No one seemed to want to go on with their routine. Tamara knew that she should hit the gym, if for nothing else than clearing her mind. But she stayed, sipping tea and chatting about the most mundane things. The PA announced that the closed memorial service would begin at 1600, so they had another four hours to kill, and it seemed appropriate that they spend that time together.

Tamara was actually laughing out loud in the middle of a story Beth was telling about a paramour's advances to her the week before when Elei came into the rec center, pale as a ghost. She spotted Tamara's group and made a beeline to the couches the gladiators had arranged in a little tea klatch.

Beth didn't notice and kept going, pushing her description of the events into the more fantasy side of what probably had really happened, but those sitting on the couch with Tamara looked up, wondering what was up with Elei.

"It will be passed on the TAG in a few moments, but Grammarcy is dead."

"What? How can that be? She's not that sick yet!" Tamara protested.

"Suicide," Elei said as the entire rec center went quiet.

It wasn't common knowledge throughout the population, but more than a few gladiators committed suicide. Most recruits had been athletes of some sort, women in tune with their bodies, and to see those bodies break down into a painful regression was more than many women could take.

"She'd said more than once that she didn't want to become disabled," Elei went on.

"But she wasn't disabled yet," Tamara said, not wanting to accept it.

"Yet. And with Fleetwood today, I guess it pushed her over the edge," Elei said.

Tamara wanted to stand up and scream, to shout out her pent up emotions to the gods. But that would do nothing. They all volunteered for this, knowing the ramifications of their choices. They were saving humanity, but at a price.

But throughout human history, it was always that way. Soldiers protected their family, tribe, or nation, sacrificing their life and limbs in doing so.

Queen looked back at Beth, then pointedly asked, "So what did he say then?"

Beth looked surprised, then shook her head a few times before continuing, "Well, then he says to me, he says he wants to buy me a Hyundai Comet if I just have dinner with him. A Comet, like I can fit in one of those pocket rockets! Can you imagine that?"

Slowly, first with chuckles, then building to laughter, the group of sisters leaned back and let loose. The story wasn't really that funny, but their release was total.

Tamara started laughing a few heartbeats after the rest, but when she did, she let cut her emotions free. She would mourn Grammarcy later, but life went on, and with their life expectancy so short, she had to grab for all the laughter she could.

Chapter 36

"I've got my assignment!" Jonna shouted, entering the gym.

Tamara was on the bench, 600 kilos on the bar. She looked up as a happy gladiator came rushing over.

"It's on IGA 23," Jonna told her.

"IGA 23? What's that, where they mine the iridium?"

"Yes, siree! Almost 38% of all the iridium mined in human space. And I get to defend it."

"Not bad, Reindeer Girl, not bad."

Frankly, Tamara was surprised. She was very confident of her roomie, but the powers-that-be usually assigned braided gladiators to very important challenges, and with 38% of humanity's iridium, IGA 23 certainly would seem to be important.

"I guess they've been saving me," Jonna said, her happiness barely contained.

Jonna had been brooding for a good six months on why she hadn't gotten the call. With her extra training, she was a good year behind the rest of her class in getting a fight, and having a roomie with two braids reminded her of that every day.

Tamara got off the bench and gave her roomie a hug.

"I guess they have. I'm happy for you."

"And, of course, I want you to be my second."

"I would have had to fight you myself if you'd told me anything different," Tamara said.

"Look, I'm due for my first brief, but I wanted to stop by here first and tell you. And tomorrow night? Illy's?"

"I wouldn't miss it for the world, Jonna."

"OK, we'll talk later. I'm running late."

Jonna gave Tamara a peck on the cheek and ran out of the gym. Tamara watched her friend leave, happy for her, but with a tinge of worry. She was confident, very confident in Jonna's abilities. But even the slightest possibility of Jonna getting hurt gave her pause. She wasn't sure how she'd cope without Jonna's sunshine lifting her up. But she knew Jonna wanted this so bad. To go through genmodding without ever fighting for the cause was a horrible thought. It had been too much for Grammarcy.

Tamara lay back down on the bench. She wasn't done yet with her reps. Six hundred kilos were one of her middle days, and she had another set to go before moving to her legs. She almost considered that with the interruption, she'd just quit the bench, but she'd felt a tiny twinge in her shoulder earlier, and she wanted to get that worked out. As if in punishment for even considering such blasphemy, she gave herself two more sets on the bench, not just the one.

She's going to be fine, she thought before pushing Jonna out of her thoughts and concentrated on her workout.

IGA 23

Chapter 37

"You look great, Reindeer Girl," Tamara said, looking at her friend.

"White Ghost, there, lowly second," Jonna said, a huge smile on her face.

The press had taken one look at Jonna's official release holos, and the name White Ghost was immediately attached to her. She looked the part, Tamara decided. At Illy's Frank had kept most of Jonna's pale, pale hair untouched, with only a black and silver streak on each side of her head. Jonna had matched those colors with her shark suit: white with black and silver trim. With the chrome-like silver of her sylvian, she was the very picture of a superhero, one hot enough to invade the dreams of billions of teenage boys around the galaxy.

"I bow to the White Ghost," Tamara said, rendering a passable medieval court bow.

"You may proceed me, m'lady," Jonna said, affecting a high, snooty voice.

Tamara had to smile as she opened the hotel room door for Jonna. Her friend was not the bundle of nerves Tamara would have thought. Outwardly, at least, she was cool and collected. Too cool. She might as well have going out to see the latest Hollybolly flick.

The press, both the "regular" free press and the IGA public affairs press, had eaten Jonna up like a vanilla angel food cake. From the moment they stepped off the ship until they'd locked the door on their suite 15 hours before, they'd been hounded. The press instinctively knew Jonna was a star in the making, and they were circling like sharks in the water. A drone had even tried to holocord them through their 24th-floor window before the Four Season's security shot the thing out of the sky.

IGA security met them at the elevator, actually checking inside to make sure it was safe. Tamara tried to withhold a laugh, but when Jonna did laugh, Tamara lost it as well. Two gladiators, the best warriors humanity could create, and these security guards half their size thought they were protecting them?

Luckily, their size made the elevator too crowded, so none of the guards followed the two inside, and they had time to regain their composure before the doors opened and no less than 12 more company security escorted them out of the lobby to the applause of about 50 or 60 hotel staff and guests.

They were alone in the van, but when the doors opened at the combat site, the press seemed to outnumber the VIPs. IGA 23 had over three million employees on the planet, but close to 200 million non-employees had immigrated over the years. About half supported company operations, but the rest simply carved out a life as they deemed fit. But the planet was a company planet, and the VIPs were all IGA bigwigs or friends of the company.

The fight was to take place inside the company sports complex, Patterson Arena. Jonna gave a regal wave to the gathered observers in the stands as she slowly glided to the ring.

She's really eating this up.

Jonna had been a star basketball player back on Pohnjanmaa, so she'd been used to the spotlight, but Tamara knew Jonna was just having fun with it.

Several smiles cracked the faces of the witnesses, who were down on the arena floor as Jonna did her thing. Beth, Elei, Queen, and a few others who knew Jonna well knew that Jonna was playing with the spectators, treating them almost as a joke, and they appreciated being in on the joke as well.

Jonna reached the ring, and the playful Jonna vanished while the gladiator Jonna made her appearance. She carefully tested the footing of the sand, seemed to accept it as satisfactory, and then settled in to wait.

They didn't have to wait long. Within ten minutes, two Klethos strode into the arena from one of the tunnels. Tamara broke her frozen position to steal a glance at Jonna's opponent, and her heart dropped.

The d'relle entering the arena was armed with a mace.

There were only five fights in which a d'relle used a mace. Four of them had been defeated while only one won, and the Klethos seemed to give them up. The weapon, while extremely powerful, was unwieldy and slow. The four human winners had been able to counter the blows while dancing around it, scoring almost at will against their opponents. The one win, however, had come against a gladiator with a merrick, which was a type of foil. The much heavier mace had smashed through the merrick's parry and crush the chest of the gladiator.

Jonna's sylvian was a type of foil, and it just wasn't heavy enough to do much against the d'relle's mace.

"Just stay clear, Jonna," Tamara whispered. "Dance around it."

The d'relle marched right into the ring and launched into her initial challenge. She paused, then started her haka. It wasn't much as far as hakas went, consisting mostly of foot stomps and heavy spins. She lifted the mace high a few times, but didn't swing it with much force. Two minutes later, which seemed to be the minimum that a d'relle would dance, she was done, lunging forward and screeching.

Jonna stood still, then slowly reached back. Tamara place the hilt of the sylvian in her hand before retreating a couple of steps. Jonna almost languidly leaned forward into the initial lunge without the normal stomp. She rose back up and flowed, more than anything else, into a graceful ballet, all beauty and movement. Tamara had seen it before while Jonna practiced, but to see it here, in the ring of the Patterson Arena, Tamara thought Jonna was transformed into a deadly, but beautiful wraith. She spun, jumped, and moved through the ballet, all arms, legs, and mastery of her body.

Tamara had suggested that Jonna cut her haka shorter to save energy, but Jonna had resisted. This was her dance, and she wanted it done right. Billions upon billions of people were watching her, and she wanted to reach each of them.

Tamara thought she'd succeeded when she went into the last grande jeté and seemingly fell into the final challenge lunge.

Instead of screaming out, she simply said, "I accept your challenge."

If the d'relle had been surprised by any of this, she didn't show it. She lifted up her mace, holding with both left arms. That was unusual, and Tamara couldn't recall off hand if any other d'relle had used her upper arm in a fight.

The d'relle moved forward. The weight of the mace head looked to be almost 100 kg, and no matter how strong a d'relle was, that was a lot of weight to carry and manipulate. She couldn't expect to fight long and maintain her skill level. Jonna had to stay clear, looking for opportunities to strike and wear down her opponent.

Instead of backing up, though, Jonna moved forward to meet the d'relle.

No, Jonna! Circle and stay clear! Tamar silently implored her friend.

There would be no lightening quick strikes from the d'rella, but when the d'relle started her swing, instead of sidestepping her, Jonna raised her sylvian to meet the swing. Tamara almost took a step forward as the front quarter of Jonna's sylvian caught the handle of the mace.

The mace wasn't a sword, though. It did coulé down the length of Jonna's sword, but instead of being caught in the quillon, it simply smashed through it, snapping the super-strong ceramometal right off. The head of the mace passed within a few centimeters of Jonna's chest.

Jonna staggered but somehow managed to retain her weapon. She was out of position for a riposte that would take advantage of the d'relle's exposed position, and she danced back. Tamara watched Jonna unclench and clench her sword hand. The blow must have hurt her arm, she knew.

The d'relle raised her mace again, and any advantage Jonna might have had was lost. Jonna finally started circling, to Tamara's relief. She couldn't stand and be a target.

Use your movement, girl! Use your quickness!

The d'relle suddenly struck, quicker than Tamara would have thought possible, but Jonna danced out of the way. She danced in and slashed at the d'relle's exposed shoulder, scoring a long cut. Unfortunately, Jonna was not able to put enough power behind it to make it a killing blow. She passed the sylvian to her left hand, shook out her right hand, then passed the sword back.

She might have broken it, Tamara thought. *Just ignore the pain and finish this.*

Gladiators were genmodded to be able to handle pain. If the hand could physically work, Tamara knew Jonna would be able to still function. Pain alone was not going to be a deciding factor.

Tamara thought she could see just the tiniest slowing of the d'relle. She'd launched two attacks, which didn't seem like much, but that was a heavy piece of metal she was throwing about. Tamara felt a slight bit of satisfaction knowing Jonna was gaining the upper hand.

Instead of another lunge, the d'relle suddenly charged, mace held high. And instead of dancing back, the Jonna moved forward to meet her opponent, sylvian at the low guard, ready to skewer the charging Klethos queen. The tip of her sword hit the d'relle's belly, but it skittered across the armor until it caught and pierced through on the side, just as the d'relle hit Jonna like a linebacker, knocking her back on her ass. Jonna now weaponless, hit the sand hard, but she started to scramble to the side as the d'relle finally started to swing her mace down.

"Jonna!" Tamara shouted out, breaking all protocol.

Jonna rolled out from under the swing, but somehow, unbelievably, the d'relle was able to adjust the swing while it was already in motion, something Tamara would have thought impossible. The adjustment wasn't much, but it was enough for the mace head to catch Jonna on the upper back just below her right shoulder. Tamara could hear the shoulder blade break with a sickening snapping sound.

Jonna screamed out as the blow spun her around, face up. The d'relle, sword still embedded in her belly, stepped forward, putting one big clawed foot on Jonna's right leg, trapping her as she raided the mace high. Jonna kicked out with her left legs, trying to hit the exposed hilt of her sword to drive it deeper into her opponent and cause more damage.

Tamara took an involuntary step forward as the d'relle brought down the mace. Jonna tried to jerk herself free, but the mace head hit her in the chest just below the throat and crushed Jonna's rib cage. Just that quickly, Johanna Sirén, Tamara's roomie, best friend, and sister, was dead.

The d'relle reared back her head and screeched, then almost casually pulled Jonna's sylvian out of her side, dropping it dismissively on the sand before wheeling about and stalking out of the ring.

Tamara rushed forward, sliding in the sand to lift Jonna's head and place it in her lap. The shark suit was valiantly trying to put pressure on Jonna's open chest to stem the bleeding, but there was nothing on which to apply pressure. Tamara, tears in her eyes, kept trying to pull the edges of the suit together so as to hide the mess that had been Jonna's chest. Her sister-gladiator's beautiful face, pale and striking, stared lifelessly to the roof of the arena as if unsure what had just happened.

MALIBU

Chapter 38

Tamara's blow sent Master Abad to the ground where he grunted in pain.

He looked back up to his student, then said, "I think we're done here today," before he slowly got up, wincing, and left her in the practice ring.

Tamara knew it hadn't been fair. As good as the swordmaster was, he was still less than half her size, and without him being able to use his skill for a kill as if in a real fight, she had used that against him, beating him up pretty badly. It wasn't fair, but she didn't give a damn. In the week since Jonna had been killed, she'd turned into herself and presented a thoroughly nasty person, snapping at her friends and spending all her free time in her empty home, in her room with the lights off. Dr, Smith, the head psych, had tried to come talk with her, but she'd physically thrown him out, taking him by the shoulder and pushing him back out the door. She knew the staff was worried about her, she knew her friends were worried about her, but she didn't care.

At least three times before, gladiators had completely snapped, and everyone knew that the campus was protected by energy weapons—not for use against invaders, but against gladiators who posed a threat to others. Tamara knew she wasn't about to hurt anyone—well, not too badly, she thought as she watched Master Abad limp out of the practice facility. But she knew no one else knew what she would do, and she knew they would be taking precautions for any eventuality.

Crap, she thought, wincing at the pain in her right pec. *I think I hit him harder than I intended.*

She dropped the boctou, the practice sword, on the table and left, skipping lunch to go back to her home. For the hundredth time, she half expected Jonna to be there, either with a happy greeting or a practical joke. But the home was dark and silent. She didn't look at the door to Jonna's bedroom as she entered hers and flopped down on the bed without showering.

Life just isn't fair, she thought, her new mantra.

She'd known what she was getting into when she accepted the nomination; only she didn't know. How could anyone know until she was in the position? The last few weeks had taken their toll on her. Fleetwood, Grammarcy, Jonna, and now Bibi Manaus, another casual friend, killed the day before, also taken down by a mace-wielding d'relle.

We need to get heavier weapons to face them, her tactical mind noted.

That was always working no matter her mood, it seemed.

She knew she had to snap out of it. She was doing no one any good like this, neither her nor anyone else. But on one level, she wanted to be deep down in the pits. She wanted to feel miserable. It wouldn't be right to go on as normal with Jonna gone.

"Play *Alabaster Morning*, all songs," she commanded the house AI.

The hauntingly beautiful songs started to play. When *Dew Trap* started, a small smile creased her face. Jonna had thought the song was sappy and immature.

Tamara lay in bed all afternoon, and it wasn't until her growling stomach drove her out and into the dining facility. Her friends cautiously greeted her, but otherwise left her alone. She took a huge helping of yakisoba—the gladiator-friendly version, not one that any good Japanese chef would recognize—and wolfed it down. She needed the calories to support her big body, especially if she was going to fight again. And she knew she would fight. That was her only purpose in life anymore. And as she realized that, she knew she had to move on. Jonna was gone, but so were so many others. Things were no different for her than for any of the rest of them.

She dropped her empty tray in the bin and walked over to where Beth, Queen, Elei, and a few others were sitting. Several of them looked up cautiously, probably afraid of her lashing out at them again.

Tamara wasn't going to apologize, though. It was what is was.

Instead, she looked at Beth and asked, "Can you take me out tonight?"

The shock on Beth's face was evident as she asked, "Out? As in dinner?"

"No. Out. As in the Gryphon or wherever you go."

"Woah!" Queen said before purposely looking down at her food.

"The Gryphon? Are you sure?"

"Yep. I'm sure. I'm going one way or the other, and I'd like you to take me."

"Well, OK. But you are sure?"

"I'll see you at 2000, OK?" she said more than asked, then turned and left the dining facility.

She understood Beth's confusion. The Gryphon was a well-known paramour corral. More than a few gladiators frequented the place where anxious men adored and pampered them. Tamara had pictured in her mind something like a termite colony with a huge queen being served by a host of tiny workers whose only job was to make the queen comfortable. The thought had disgusted her, but now, for reasons about which she was unsure, she wanted to see what it was like.

Beth was the only one of her friends who went there often, and she was not too shy to show off the jewelry and gifts the men gave her. Beth had invited Tamara before, telling her it was innocent fun, but Tamara always refused. Now it was time to see what all of it was about.

Her thoughts went to her closet. She'd picked up a cute sundress in the commissary almost six months ago, but she'd never worn it. It might do for the evening. Surprised that she was feeling a little more normal, even a little excited, she picked up her pace.

She needed a shower, and she hadn't brushed her hair for three days. If she was going out on the town, she might as well do it right!

Chapter 39

Tamara sat in her seat at the auditorium and sneaked a looked at the small broach she wore on her chest. It wasn't much, and even her untrained eye knew the quality was poor. But Mark had been so sweet at the Gryphon, getting her drinks (gladiator-friendly of course—Beth had told her that the paramours were more cognizant of a gladiator's dietary restrictions than the gladiators were themselves), chatting about whatever topic interested her, and simply being there for her. To her surprise, she'd stayed at the Gryphon for almost five hours, and while the paramours made the rounds to meet Beth, Elei (who'd decided to come, too), and her, she'd spent most of the night talking to Mark. Over 60, slightly pudgy, and no Hollybolly hunk, he'd never-the-less been pleasant company.

She didn't know if she'd ever go back. There was no romance, and certainly there been no sexual attraction. She'd had the heat cut out of her, after all. But it had been nice simply to chat with an intelligent man who appreciated her for what she'd become. When he'd shyly offered her the broach, she didn't even consider refusing him. And now, it was a reminder of why she had become a gladiator. He was a paramour, so he was a different case. He'd like her no matter what. But he represented the teeming masses of humanity, and they were why she was fighting d'relles while waiting for the Brick to come visit.

She still missed Jonna terribly, but she thought she'd turned the corner. She was ready to get back into the saddle.

Her thoughts were interrupted when Warden Mantou walked up on the stage and behind the podium. The gathered gladiators, staff, and even the candidates quieted as the director cleared her throat.

"Good morning. As some of you know, I've been to the UAM headquarters for the last few days. I've met with the Secretary-

General as well as the heads of quite a few governments, to include the Brotherhood, the Confederation of Free States, and the Federation. We, that is our leaders, have come to a conclusion that will affect all of us.

"As you may know, since we have clashed with the Klethos, we have fought 398 times. We have lost 139 of those fights, losing 139 worlds. In this galaxy, we have over 2,000 worlds of interest, so if we continue along this path, we could lose the galaxy to the Klethos in about two centuries."

So what else is new? Tamara wondered. *The talking heads discuss this all the time.*

"However, as you are well aware, there has been an increase in the tempo in challenges. If this increase continues, we could run out of human worlds in about half a century."

That got Tamara's attention. Most of the people alive today could live to see that happen.

"So, with that in mind, we, humanity, are going to go on the offensive. We are going to challenge the Klethos to take back our lost worlds, and who knows, maybe after that, go after more prime real estate."

The was a complete silence for a moment before cheer sounded, reverberating through the auditorium. Tamara yelled out as loud an ooh-rah as anyone else shouting.

The director used her hands to quiet everyone down so she could continue.

"So how does that affect us? Well, some of that is to be determined. But we are going to start with Class 84-6. You'll be moving to Module 2 next week."

Even louder cheers sounded coming from the candidates.

Don't cheer too loudly until you know what you're getting into, Tamara thought, not seriously, but remembering the torture of the module.

"We will be expanding the school, and recruitment will increase to fill larger requirements. And all of you gladiators, those who haven't fought yet, your time is coming."

Beth was sitting beside Tamara, and she jumped out of her seat and cheered.

Tamara was no different than most of the people in the auditorium. She welcomed the news. It didn't seem logical on one level, to cheer a greater chance of an early, or earlier, in their case, death. But all of them were first selected for their warrior mentality. That had mentality had been artificially enhanced during the genmod. They were fighters, pure and simple, and that is what they had to do.

As a Marine, Tamara had been trained to attack, to be an offensive force. It felt good to her to take it to the Klethos instead of reacting as they controlled things.

This was going to be an interesting ride, and Tamara welcomed the change. If she was going to pay the price of her position with the Brick, she wanted to send as many of the bastards before her as possible before that time came.

BYB-10

Chapter 40

The first "Take Back" world attempt was the non-inhabited BYB-10 in the Brotherhood's Third Synod. BYB-10 had a workable atmosphere, but the rest of the terraforming had been halted at 62% after the Klethos had taken the world. Tamara had been rather surprised at the choice. She would have thought they would try and take back one of the more valuable worlds, ones with intact infrastructure and from which there were still large numbers of refugees.

From the little that made it way down the chain to Chicsis, there were others who felt the same as Tamara, but without knowing how the Klethos would react, it had eventually been decided that a relatively "valueless" world would be the first target. If there was an unexpected reaction by the Klethos, choosing BYB-10 made some sense. For all humanity knew, the Klethos might practice a scorched earth policy if they lost a planet. With BYB-10, if they did, there was just not that much to lose.

There was also the concern that there might be a minimum time between losing a world and when reissuing a challenge would be accepted, so BYB-10, which had been one of the earlier worlds lost, fit that concern better.

How the secretive contact team issued the challenge, or what were the Klethos reactions, Tamara didn't know. She didn't even know exactly how the Klethos issued a challenge. But evidently the Klethos accepted, and the fight was on.

The selection of a gladiator echoed the policy of "not much to lose." Warrant Officer Beth Hralto, UFMC, finally had her turn in the breach. Beth was overjoyed, and Tamara was glad for her, but she was angry at the implied lack of respect for Beth's value.

Beth decided on an amazingly jarring chartreuse, turquoise, and pink hair pattern, which Tamara was sure was her giving the proverbial finger to the staff. She had a chip on her shoulder, but she was not going to turn down the opportunity to fight. It just gave her more motivation to prove the doubters wrong.

Her choice for a second, Elei, had raised some objections, but she was the gladiator, and she had the final say. Well, not the complete final say. After discussions with the staff xenobiologists, it was decided that Elei had to take off her prosthetic arm. The fear was that even as a second, the Klethos might feel it was too close to an armored combat suit.

Tamara waited for the other witnesses at the ring. Five Klethos waited opposite of them, and the d'relle waited patiently in the ring. Other than the twenty witnesses, only five other humans were present, four UAM staff and a holocorder. Two Brotherhood ships were in high orbit over the ring, every sensor on recording the events through an entire host of spectrums, but there was only the lone holocorder at ground level.

All the procedures were being felt out as they went. Everyone knew how the Klethos managed their challenges, and the humans were attempting to follow most of the same pattern. One big difference, though, was that the human contingent had landed the day before at the designated spot, then erected portable habitats to wait for the appointed time. Beth and Elei were given their own habitat while the rest shared another.

When the witnesses and the UAM observers marched the 900 meters to the ring, the Klethos were already waiting. So the witnesses waited as well. Tamara thought it all rather surreal, the fate of a world in the balance, yet here they all were, human and Klethos alike, just sitting and staring at each other.

Finally, exactly on time, Beth and Elei marched up the hill to the ring. Beth was carrying her ichi-katana, and as soon as she entered the ring, she lunged into the challenge, complete with an ear-piercing shriek. Her kata was, well, unique. She'd evidently patterned it after the puckalicious dance movement, where "dance," which suggested some sort of style, was decidedly lacking. She looked like she was going into an epileptic fit as she shivered and shook around the ring, her sword an afterthought.

Oh, you go girl, Tamara thought, knowing full well that the UAM public affairs division were probably having a fit as they observed.

This wasn't the image of the noble, stallworth gladiator that they liked to project.

Tamara could give a flying fig. It was the sacrifice and the fight that mattered, not the hair color and haka.

Coming back in front of her opponent, it looked like Beth lost her balance. Tamara could hear the intake of breath from the UAM staff behind her, but at the last second, Beth stuck out her foot, landing in the correct challenge lunge.

If Beth's disjointed haka bothered the d'relle, she showed no signs of it. She broke out into a pretty standard d'relle haka, full of jumps and spins, full of whistling swords cutting through the air. Almost four minutes later, she stopped in her own lunge.

Challenge issued, challenge accepted. Nothing unexpected—so far.

Tamara tensed up as the two circled each other. Beth was a decent fighter, but she hadn't been the best. Jonna had been far better in the ring, and Jonna was now dead. Tamara didn't want to lose another friend.

Beth suddenly rushed the d'relle, her sword singing as it whipped through the planet's thin air. The d'relle parried, and the two broke apart, neither being touched. Beth immediately launched another attack, sword moving almost too fast to follow. Just as quickly, the d'relle parried and riposted. As the two broke apart, a thin line of red appeared on Beth's side. Beth ignored it as the suit pressed together to its memory position, the pressure dampening any blood loss. Still, that was not good. A cut, any cut, weakened and slowed down a swordsman. The advantage swung to the d'relle.

Someone must not have told Beth that, though. She moved in again, a flurry of blows aimed at the d'relle's legs. The Klethos countered, and with a sudden shift, Beth's sword went high, aiming at the head. The d'relle saw it coming and ducked back, the katana skimming just past its cheek, but cutting deep into the feathered crest, slicing off a third of the feathers in two. The d'relle screamed, then backed up a step.

Score one for Beth!

Tamara never understood why the d'relle fought with their crest displayed. It was a vulnerable part of their body, yet it had had no protection. Regular Klethos warriors often fought with flattened crests, as recordings of the first two full-scale battles revealed, but not the d'relle. They did try to maneuver to keep their crests out of reach of the gladiators, but sometimes, that just didn't work.

A little more blood leaked out from the cut on Beth's side, but she didn't let up. Pressing hard, she unleashed a flurry of slashes that the d'relle had to counter, and with its balance compromised, she was having a harder and harder time, and she was getting a tiny bit later on each parry. She wasn't going to give up easily, though. She tried to punch Beth with her right lower arm, but she was just out of reach, and the effort, along with her damaged crest, threw her off balance. Beth's next slash struck her across the left upper arm, and the one after that cut ten centimeters off of her beak.

The d'relle drove herself backwards to get out of range, but Beth was on her like tan on sand. She cut the d'relle's right thigh to the bone, then came back and cut through her opponent's neck, nearly severing the head. Blue blood spurted out while the d'relle tried to catch herself before toppling over.

Beth stood over the d'relle, katana high over her head, but she held the blow. It was over. With her sword hand, she reached over to the slash on her side and touched her blood. She bent over and rubbed her blood on the undamaged part of the d'relle's crest, then using the same hand, daubed up some the d'relle's blood. She rubbed that on her forehead, then bent back, face to the sky, and shouted out her victory call.

"Holy Mother of God," Zuneba, one of the other witnesses, said under her breath. "What will they make of that?'

Whether she meant the UAM, the public, or the Klethos, Tamara didn't ask. All of them fit the question, though.

Beth marched over to the witnesses.

Pointing her bloody sword through the gladiators to the head UAM observer, she said, "OK, I've done my job. Now it's up to you what happens next."

With that, she spun around, and with a beaming Elei in tow, marched back in the direction of the temporary, or maybe now permanent, camp. With one last look at the dead d'relle, Tamara turned to follow.

Beth was right. The world had been re-taken. Anything else was up to the civilians.

MALIBU

Chapter 41

Tamara stood looking in the mirror. She was naked, and she carefully watched her reflection as she slowly moved her left arm from outstretched to across her chest until her left hand touched her right shoulder. She switched to her right arm and made the same movement, then back to the left. Visually, she couldn't see a difference between the two. That didn't relieve her.

The pain that she had first noticed while lifting weights not only hadn't gone away, it had spread from her left pec up to the left side of her neck.

You're being paranoid, she told herself.

People who've been genmodded, especially those with an extensive genmod, often had little quirks with the results. The recipes were the same, but Mother Nature did not follow computer programming, and the genmod affected each individual differently. This was probably just one of those glitches in the programming. The pain was minor, and it didn't affect her fighting.

It was nothing, she kept telling herself. She simply refused to consider the possibility that it was anything else.

Chapter 42

Over the next two months, the UAM issued 19 challenges, and 14 worlds were won back. The Klethos only issued one challenge, winning San Cecilia. Instead of a slow but steady loss of worlds, humanity had reversed the tide and was regaining human homes.

The Klethos seemed unperturbed by the trend. No one except for a very select few knew what went on during the challenge process at the highest levels. Where or how the initial notifications of a challenge were issued was not something privy to the population at large; but on a very regular basis, Chicsis got the warning order, and a gladiator was given her notice.

With so many fights in such a short time, the witness party was reduced to ten fellow gladiators. Still, Tamara had been on three such parties, watching two victories as well as one loss. None of the three had been particularly close to her, but she still mourned the loss of Jillian Win, the new gladiator she'd watched die.

The new class had 300 candidates, but even on fast track, it would take them almost 18 months to become functioning gladiators. Simple math indicated that until then, if the tempo remained the same, pretty much all of the active gladiators would get at least one fight, probably more as their numbers were winnowed.

So it wasn't a surprise to Tamara when only a month later, she received her next fight: New Budapest.

New Budapest, where Tamara had been a witness when it was lost, was one of the most important worlds taken over by the Klethos to date. Given the fact that it hadn't been lost too long ago, the infrastructure should be mostly intact, and the hope was that the old inhabitants could rush back in and fall upon their old lives as if nothing had happened. Tamara wasn't sure that would be the case, but she was excited to be given the opportunity.

Tamara sat through the briefs, trying to will them to finish. She didn't care about the GNP of the two nations on the planet. She didn't care about the five major mountain ranges or the proliferation of Andean condors in two of those ranges. All she cared about was the fighting ring and when she had to be there. After a morning of briefs, she hurried to her medical checkup. Once that was over, she could get in a half day of training before embarking the next morning.

Her mind was more on who to pick as her second than anything else as she stripped and stood behind the over-sized bioscan projector. The scan was made, and the tech watched the readout screen intensely as Tamara started to get dressed.

"Um, Miss Veal? If you could, I'd like to run this again," she said.

Tamara shrugged and took off her shirt and shorts again and took her position behind the projector once more. The machine hummed for a few seconds, then went silent. Tamara stepped down, then went back to her clothes.

"Am I done?" she asked, tying here dungarees and stepping towards the door.

"Uh, Miss Veal, have you been feeling anything, well, different?" the tech asked.

A cold hand descended on Tamara's heart and slowly started to squeeze.

"Not. . .not really. Why?" she asked, trying to sound nonchalant and failing miserably.

"I. . .I don't think it's up to me to say. I'm a technician, not an MD. I think I'd better go get Dr. Vanderhorst."

As the young tech started for the door, Tamar moved to block her, 400 kilos of gladiator. The tech stopped and looked up at her with a frightened expression.

"Look, Tyra, is it?" Tamara asked, trying to put the girl at ease.

"Yes, ma'am."

"Tyra, you've seen lots of body scans while working here, right?"

"Yes."

"But does that machine over there make diagnoses?"

"Well, no. It gives us all the data and tells is what it thinks is wrong, but it takes a doctor to make the actual diagnosis."

"And that's because the machine can make a mistake."

"Well, not a mistake, ma'am," the tech said as she began to relax a little. "The B2050 determines probabilities based millions and millions of previous studies."

"But sometimes the option with the smallest probability is actually the case, right?"

"Well, yes. Sometimes, I guess."

"So I'm asking you know, what does the machine say about me. What is the probability?"

Tamara still refused to use the term. It was as if by not naming it, she could keep it at bay.

"Ninety-four percent, ma'am," Tyra said solemnly. "We can't know for sure without a different test."

Hell, that high?

Tamara felt defeated. Her will started to vanish before she bolstered herself.

"So that's six percent that I'm OK?"

"Well, yes, you could say that."

"And let me ask you this: did you see anything from your machine here, the 'B2050,' that would indicate I'm not capable of doing my job?"

"Well, no, ma'am. Not yet. But it will. You know that."

"But not now. Not today, not tomorrow."

"No, not today."

"So, let's just forget this for now. I'll come back in a week or so, and you can run it again."

"But Miss Veal! That's against the regs! And this is for your own good!" Tyra protested.

Tamara leaned her head back, closed her eyes, and took in a deep, calming breath. She looked back at Tyra and put her hands on the young woman's shoulders.

"How old are you, Tyra?" she asked.

"I'm 23, ma'am. Why do you ask?"

"That's how old I am. Only you have a long life ahead of you. I don't."

"And that's why we have to care for you. We need to give you as much of a life as possible."

"As an invalid? You've seen those of us who've wasted away, in pain as their bodies rebel against all that's been done to them. Tyra, I can't face that. I need to know that the sacrifice was worth it."

"But you've got two braids. You've done your time."

"And now I'm needed again. We need to recover New Budapest, and they think I'm the best-qualified gladiator to do it. Do you think we need to jeopardize that?"

'No, but if the Bri—"

Tamara put her hand over the girl's mouth, stopping her from vocalizing the word.

"We don't know for sure I have that."

"OK. If you have a condition that weakens you," she said after Tamara removed her hand, "then that could put New Budapest at risk."

She's right, Tamara admitted before firmly pushing that thought away.

"But you said nothing would affect me yet."

"I *think.* I don't know. I'm not a doctor," Tyra said, looking miserable.

"Look, I don't want to put you where you're uncomfortable with yourself. I'm just asking you, begging you, to put yourself in my position. Give me my one last chance to do my job. Let me go and fight. I'm sure you can 'accidently' misfile the results, and after I fight, you can find them, or I can come back, and you can take them again."

Tyra looked unsure.

"As one sister to another, I need this from you. A week won't hurt me one way or the other. So just give me this."

"And you'll come back? After you're done?"

"After I get back to Malibu, I'll see you. On my honor."

Tyra looked to the inner door, the one leading into the doctor's offices. Tamara could see the emotions play across her face.

Finally, she said, "OK, Miss Veal. I'll probably lose my job over this, but I won't forward this. I can pull your last one from the files and forward that one. But you have to promise, as soon as you get back, you'll come in for a new one."

"As soon as I get back, Tyra; as soon as I get back."

NEW BUDAPEST

Chapter 43

Tamara stood in the doorway of the temporary shelter. Soft snores reached out from inside as Elei slept in deep slumber.

We never got her back. Jonna, yes, but not Elei, Tamara thought with a smile. *I could always do it now.*

Instead of a practical joke, however, she stepped out of the shelter. The night was warm, and the greenery-filled air with pleasant, if elusive, smells. Tamara idly wondered if the Klethos had established any of their own vegetation to compete with the human-established Earth trees and plants (or if they even did that on planets they took). The planet's twin moons gave far more light than Tamara would have expected, something more evident out here in the forest than when she was in the brightly illuminated city a year-and-a-half before.

This was a far cry from the when Marta had fought. There were fewer than 30 humans on the planet now instead of billions. There were over a million Klethos, however. On most worlds, the Klethos often abandoned them soon after taking them. Not so on new Budapest—the Klethos seemed to be making it into a home.

Tamara had seen the cities as they came into land. They looked intact from her vantage point. Out here, in the wilderness though, there was an entirely different feel of the planet, one more attuned to nature than to the hustle and bustle from before.

Tamara knew she should get some sleep, but it eluded her. Too many thoughts filled her mind.

The pain in her shoulder had started radiating down her left arm. It was probably psychosomatic; it was just too coincidental that it could spread so quickly right after the scan. But in her mind or not, it was a constant reminder that this would be her last fight, one way or the other. In this case, winning the fight scared her more. She couldn't imagine the coming year or two, watching her body fall apart.

Neither Jonna nor Grammarcy had to experience that, and the more she thought about it, the more attractive that seemed. A quick death under the blade would be a far better outcome than sitting in a home in Sunset Acres, waiting for the reaper to claim her wasted body.

If she died in the ring, however, as sweet as a release it might be for her, humanity wouldn't regain the planet, and that could be forever. No, she'd fight, but there was that certain siren's call that promised a sweet relief.

The slope in front of the human camp led down to a creek, she knew. It was on the banks of the creek that the ring had been built. On the other side, about 500 meters away, a couple of hundred Klethos waited, which was a very large number for them. With over a million of them on the planet, though, that number really wasn't that impressive. Tamara didn't understand how they could seemingly show such a decided lack of interest in the future of the—their—planet.

It wasn't just Tamara who didn't know what made the Klethos tick. Excepting for a handful of xenobiologists, and probably not even them, humans just didn't understand their foe. It had taken a warrior, Ryck Lysander, to realize their martial intent, but since then, not much else had been added to the depth of human knowledge. And a lack of understanding could lead to drastic consequences. Humanity was quietly increasing their military capabilities, but an all-out war with the Klethos now would almost certainly end in a complete defeat.

Without a conscious decision, Tamara's feet led her down to the ring. It wasn't the huge arena in which Marta had fought, but it seemed more fitting to her. There was something basic about single combat, something humans had been doing throughout their history. Romans notwithstanding, it usually wasn't in an arena with cheering crowds. More fights had been fought in the plains, in the forests, in the mountains, with little more at stake than rights to a hunting territory, access to a spring, or to start a family. Tamara and her unknown opponent would fight tomorrow for stakes a little bigger than that, but the basic concept was the same.

Tamara hesitated, then stepped into the ring itself. She settled her feet in, shifting her weight back and forth.

"I believe you will find the footing satisfactory," a voice said from behind her.

Tamara jumped forward, away from the voice, and out of the ring, whirling to face whoever had spoken.

To her utter amazement, a Klethos stepped out of the shadows of a copse of fir trees along the creek.

"Does it meet your approval?" she (he) asked, as calmly as if a waiter was asking if the coffee was OK.

"You can speak," was all Tamara could say, stating the obvious.

"Of course, we can speak. What a curious statement. How else do you think we communicate?"

"But, you've never spoken before. Does anyone else know you can speak?"

"I'm afraid you are misinformed. We are an intelligent race, and to our knowledge, no race can attain intelligence unless it can communicate."

Tamara was shocked, to say the least. And she wasn't sure what to say next. Here she was, speaking Standard to a Klethos as if nothing was out of the ordinary.

"And to answer your other question, yes, humans know we can speak. That is how we issue and accept challenges. I must repeat, that is a most curious question."

"I've never heard your kind speak. I haven't seen you speak even on holos, either."

"Well, I guess that isn't too surprising. When under *ceelos,* that is, when we are conducting a challenge, we follow the precepts and traditions from long ago. It is not the time to speak in other than the mother tongue."

"But you screech."

"To your ears, perhaps. To us, there is meaning to the words."

Tamara stared at the Klethos' beak. She knew it was hard and bony, and she wondered how it could form human words. Then again, parrots could make human sounds.

"So I ask you again, is the footing to your statisfaction?"

"Oh. Uh. . .yes, I guess it is."

"I am pleased, then."

A thought hit Tamara. "You must be either the ring-maker, or you are a d'relle."

"True. I am this challenge's d'relle," she said, although her pronunciation of "d'relle" was decidedly different from how Tamara had always heard the word. "And you are Iron Shot?"

"I am Chief Warrant Officer Tamara Veal," she answered, standing tall. "Iron Shot is only a nickname."

"Are you going to fight tomorrow?" she asked after a quick moment.

"Yes, I am. We only have one d'relle at a formal ceelos. You and I will meet right here," the d'relle said, sweeping both left arms around to indicate the ring.

Tamara should feel wary, she knew. But somehow, she didn't feel the slightest bit threatened. As a species, the Klethos seemed to be protocol-bound, and she suddenly knew she could march right now into the Klethos camp without fear for her safety.

"Can I ask you your name?" Tamara asked for lack of anything else to say.

"I am d'relle, and d'relle is me. Once we become d'relle, we lose who we were before."

That made no sense to Tamara at all. The d'relle might be able to speak Standard, but that didn't mean she could convey meaning as well.

"So Klethos have no names at all?" she asked, trying to understand.

"Klethos-kee, yes, they have what you have in names. Not the same and the same. But d'relle become d'relle."

"So what do I call you?"

"If you must, you can call me d'relle. Only I will answer here and now.

"The night is lovely to me. I was born under twin moons, and this brings back memories of the crèche. Is the night also lovely also you?"

Geez almighty! Now we are waxing poetic?

"Uh, yeah, it's lovely."

"We are not so different, humans and Klethos. It is an honor to meet another race who understand us."

"But we don't understand you," Tamara protested. "We don't understand why you take worlds, why you insist on single combat."

"Yes, you do. You are a gladiator. You understand the ring, the pull of combat. You have won twice, and you know the thrill of victory. How can you live without it after once tasting the sweetness?"

"I don't—" she started, before stopping.

The thing was, she did understand that part of it. She'd already been competitive, and winning was paramount. After genmodding, the ring called out for her. She needed to prove herself.

"I do, I'll admit. But our race doesn't."

"Like with the others, it takes time to understand what is needed. But while others failed, Ryck Lysander did not. He understood what was needed. And was he not human?"

They know his name? Well, they can speak, so why not?

"He was a Marine. He was trained to fight."

"Yes, your Marines. A tribe, but still human, no different, if more capable. And we have now studied your history. Your kind, like ours, lives to war each other."

"But we don't kill off whole people. You've wiped out two entire races!" Tamara said, trying to distance humanity from the Klethos.

"Seventeen races, not two."

"Seventeen?" Tamara asked shocked.

"We are an ancient race," the d'relle simply said.

"Why? Why do you do that?"

"If we did not, we would die. We are also a warlike people, constantly fighting. We developed the ceelos to try and stem our self-genocide, but if the Utapurkra had not appeared, we would have killed ourselves off."

"The who?"

"We called them the Utapurkra. They invaded our home system, so we killed them. It took us centuries of your time to develop the spacefaring abilities, but once we did, we hunted them down and exterminated them."

As simple as that?

"And after? The other races?"

"We needed other enemies to stem our own fighting between ourselves. As long as there were others, we could survive."

An owl hooted in from the depths of the forest, almost in counterpoint to the d'relle's statement. But what the d'relle said had more than a degree of logic—brutal logic, but logic still-the-same.

"And humans? Do you want to exterminate us?"

"We don't want to exterminate anyone. We need a worthy foe, and you are the first to prove to be so. We were more than pleased when we realized that you understood honor in conflict."

"You wiped out an entire human world. Why single combat when you have the power over us," Tamara asked, wanting an answer.

"What honor is that? That is merely the slaughter of food animals. There is honor in ceelos, honor in the ring."

"But we beat you more than you beat us. We've gen—" she said before stopping, unsure of what she might be revealing.

"Your genmodding is a false evolution, in our opinion. We prefer our natural evolution, not that done with artificial influences."

"So why do you allow it?" Tamara asked, curious.

"We may be wrong. But more than that, we need strong opponents as triggers."

"I don't understand."

"We were once small, the size of one of your dogs. During the long wars, we, I don't know the word in your language, but maybe 'encouraged' evolution, growing larger and stronger. When the Utapurkra appeared, we needed to become stronger still, so we encouraged more evolution. But for the last thousands of your years, we have found no worthy foe, so we have stopped evolving. As a d'relle, I am no different physically than my many times predecessors."

"And with us, I mean gladiators, to face, you have to get stronger, in case you ever meet a race much stronger than you."

"I told you we are the same. You understand. We know only two galaxies. Who knows who else it out there?"

"But why not genmod? You can see how quickly we've been able to develop into your worthy foe, as you say it."

"As I said, we find it unnatural. Our method is more *estosias*, which is another word for which I don't know in your language. More honest, more genuine, one that breeds true. Your genmodding is an assault on nature, as your BRC shows."

So they even know about the Brick? Who let that out?

"And that is why we agreed to the process, but only if you could not reproduce."

What? What was that?

"Can't reproduce?"

"Yes. Surely you know you cannot reproduce."

"Yes, of course I know that."

I just didn't know that was part of the deal! she thought, feeling the anger build up inside. *Why didn't they just tell us?*

"So you gladiators pose no real threat to us. To me, perhaps. To the d'relle. But not to the Klethos-lee. But our improvements, they will breed true, to every Klethos-lee, and then to those who ascend to d'relle.

Tamara's mind was churning. She had no reason to doubt the d'relle, who seemed amazingly open, especially given that they were enemies, but she didn't want to believe the UAM was pulling their strings like that. She did believe, it, though, she realized. She believed she'd had the heat cut out of her not for medical reasons, but for politics. It was all part of some secret agreement between the human governments and the Klethos.

The d'relle might have been correct in that humans and Klethos had similarities in warfare, but she doubted the Klethos could be anywhere as devious and as underhanded as human politicians.

"D'relle," she started, unsure of what else to call her, "you have told me a lot tonight. Do other humans know all of this?"

"I am certain your kind knows all of this and more. I am only a d'relle. I have limited knowledge beyond my scope. But I do know that the contact between your kind and mine is extensive, and we hide nothing about us. Your people know much. Without that, how could we arrange ceelos as we do? How can we have protocol as we do?

"D'relle and gladiators, we are merely the instruments of our people's will."

"Instruments is right," Tamara said bitterly.

"But the most exalted of instruments," the d'relle said. "Who else is allowed to express herself in single combat? Who else is allowed to reach for the glory?"

That statement was so wrong on so many levels, but it was also so right. Whether from her genmodding or her own natural warrior personality, she understood the d'relle's point. There was no greater glory in her mind, even if 95% of humanity would vehemently disagree.

"Can I ask you, have you personally fought one of us before?"

"Yes, I have. I fought the Gladiator Tall Cliff."

That hit Tamara hard. "Tall Cliff" was Jillian Win. She'd been at that challenge, and she'd watched Jillian die. She should be angry, but the anger somehow didn't surface.

"You have defeated two d'relle. It is my great pride to have you as my opponent. Tomorrow, we will meet as honored foes, but if I may presume, as respected *sisters-of-the-soul*, as we say in the d'relle fashion?"

The d'relle held out her lower right hand, as a human would. Whether Klethos did that as well or if the d'relle simply knew human customs, Tamara didn't know. But she took the proffered hand and shook it.

"Yes, honored foes and respected sisters-of-the-soul."

Chapter 44

"Are you ready?" Elei asked as they stood just outside the doorway of their shelter.

"Yes, I am."

And she was, she knew. For whatever happened. When she woke up in the morning, she'd almost thought she'd dreamt the night before, it had been so surreal. But while her meeting the d'relle had been revealing in many ways, it changed nothing. The powers-that-be were pulling her strings, pulling everyone's strings, evidently, but she was still a gladiator with a job to do. And the thing was, she wanted to do it.

At that very moment, if she'd be given the option to go back to her nomination and refuse it, to never become a gladiator, to never fight in the ring, to never contract the Brick, she'd refuse it. Her time was coming to an end, whether in a few minutes in the ring, or in a year from the Brick—if she didn't follow Grammarcy and take the quicker way out. But how many people were given the chance to fight for something so important? As an infantryman Marine, she could have been part of something bigger, true. And she could have been killed in combat. But there was no way that her individual effort would have such an impact on humanity.

"Well, let's get going," she said, leading the way down the slope to the waiting humans and Klethos.

The sun was warm on her face, the breeze cool. What had been a beautiful night had turned to an even more beautiful morning. This was far more appropriate than fighting in a stadium with the teeming masses cheering.

Elei walked behind and one step to her left. Tamara had told her about the meeting, but she'd withheld most of what she'd learned. Elei was teeming with questions, and Tamara hadn't decided how much she'd pass on. Would it do any good for her sister-gladiators to find out why they couldn't have children? She wasn't sure. Just the fact that the Klethos could speak Standard was revelation enough, and with humans now issuing the challenges, Tamara was pretty sure other gladiators, either by happenstance or by seeking them out, will meet their opponents as well. If done before the actual challenge, the d'relle would not be constrained to the Klethos language. Once more and more conversations took place, well, secrets were pretty hard to keep, especially when one side didn't even consider them secrets.

As they neared the creek and came into view, the witnesses turned as one to watch her approach. At least a couple of hundred Klethos crowded around their half of the ring, some of them on the other side of the creek and partway up the far bank. Tamara's eyes, though, sought out the lone d'relle, kneeling at the edge of the ring. Her eyes were not trained to pick out individual differences in Klethos, but she knew this was her d'relle.

Tamara gave a slight nod to the witnesses, then marched to the edge of the ring. She reached back, and Elei handed her her mameluke, but still sheathed in the silver and gold scabbard. There was a slight murmur from the witnesses. Tamara knew they'd be wondering about her haka, and this had to surprise them.

Tamara, with exaggerated, long-legged steps, moved to the center of the ring, drew her sword, the placed the scabbard on the sand, one end facing her opponent, the other back to her gladiator witnesses. She then placed her mameluke on the ground, making an X with the scabbard. She slowly backed up, and raising her arms gracefully over her head, started her Scottish War dance. Stepping slowly, she touched each of the four quadrants made by the X, feet barely touching. Gradually, she built up the speed, her legs blurring into motion while her upper body remained still. She kept her face calm, but she was concentrating on the intricate movements. She was a gladiator, not a dancer, after all. Still, she was an athlete, and her feet flew through the steps, landing in each quadrant in turn, barely missing the sharp blade that lay there, waiting to damage an errant foot. Then she added bending to the side, one upraised arm reaching almost to the sand before coming upright to repeat the move on the other side, all the time her feet beating tattoos.

When she added spinning, she could feel her blood pounding, she could feel her face flushing. She hadn't been too sure about the Scottish dance when she selected it. It was not as martial-looking as her Maori haka or Turkish sword dance. It was far more of a ballet or Irish step dance. But with the added danger of a wickedly sharp blade, it just felt right. And she was living the dance, not performing it.

With a final flurry of spinning and steps, she hooked the hilt of her sword with her foot and lifted it spinning in the air. As it came back down, she snatched it out of the air and converted the move into the challenge lunge with a loud shout.

She'd nudged the scabbard twice with her feet during the dance, so it hadn't been perfect, but she could live with that. She felt exhilarated.

I'm a lean, green, fighting machine! I'm a lean, green, fighting machine!

The d'relle waited almost ten seconds before she got up. She almost slid into her initial lunge, then started spinning around the ring, a planet in orbit around Tamara's sun. She did twelve huge spinning jumps in a row, her sword singing through the heavy air. Tamara made no pretension of not watching. She followed the d'relle though each move, watching and somehow enjoying the dance.

It made no sense. The two warriors would be battling to the death in a few moments, but not only had Tamara had an absurdly friendly chat with her opponent the night before, she was watching and appreciating the d'relle's haka.

And the dance was beautiful. It was power, it was grace, all rolled into one. When she finally stopped and fell into the challenge acceptance, Tamara was sorry it was over.

Then, the d'relle did something unusual, very unusual. Instead of retreating to the edge of the ring, instead of launching an immediate attack, she bowed low at the waist, pulling all four arms up at the elbows, exposing the back of her crest and neck. With one easy slash, Tamara could have put an end to the fight before it even started.

The d'relle slowly straightened up from her honor bow and stared at Tamara. Tamara stood still, then repeated the bow to her opponent—to the gasps of the humans behind her. She stayed low for several heartbeats, her neck exposed, before straightening back up herself. The d'relle nodded once at Tamara before raising her sword.

Tamara kicked her scabbard out of the ring and raised her mameluke to her guard.

With her heart singing, she joined the battle.

Epilogue

As Crystal Kovács stepped off the tram, a laughing little girl of about four accidently ran into her leg and bounced off.

"Easy there," Crystal said, helping the little one to her feet.

"Oh, I'm so sorry," a harried-looking woman said, a baby on her hip. "Ali, say you're sorry to the lady."

"Sorry," the girl said, looking up at Crystal's 2.2-meter frame in awe.

"It's OK," Crystal said, watching the woman gather her daughter and lead her into the visitor's center.

Crystal watched the small family for a moment before shaking her head. She wasn't sure she could handle two kids like that. She liked kids as a general concept, but she wasn't sure she was the mothering type.

She wasn't here for the visitor's center, though. She'd been on the required class trips to the monument before, so she'd already been inside the center more than once. She knew the history of the place. That wasn't why Crystal had made the two-hour maglev trip, then taken the tram from the station. She wasn't entirely sure why she had come, but something deep inside told her that it was necessary.

Crystal bypassed the visitor's center and the people crowding inside and started on the winding walkway that led down the slope. The place was beautiful, she thought, and she was glad that the government allowed no commercial development of the area. It was unsullied and pure, as it should be.

Her long legs quickly ate up the distance, and as the brick path led around the last bend, the monument itself came into view. Her heart quickened as she saw the statue, then the ring. A number of people were gathered around, some at the edge of the ring itself, some in the benches set back. More than a few older people in hoverchairs sat together chatting. A ranger was talking to a small group of primary students, pointing across the creek to the far bank.

Crystal took in the scene for a moment, then ignoring the rest of the people, marched straight up to the statue in front of the ring. She had to wait a few moments as a young man posed in front of it while a young woman snapped a few holos, but when the two finally were satisfied and left, she stepped right in front and looked up at the oversized figure.

Tamara Veal, the *Megmentő*,[16] stared off into the distance, her mameluke held across her chest. Crystal had seen the real weapon displayed at the New Budapest Museum of History, but to her, the almost three-meter-long sword in the statue's hand seemed more real somehow. A sword was nothing, after all, without the person wielding it.

Crystal shifted her gaze to the statue's face. The fabrisculptor had done an outstanding job of programming, she thought. Crystal could almost feel the intensity of the gladiator's thoughts. She wished she could have known the real person, to know what she felt, to know just who she was. Instead, she was left with the statue, the Hollybolly flick, and the urban myths that tended to spring up around heroes.

She'd watched the recordings of the fight, of course. It was required viewing for all secondary students. Where some other students had broken down and cried at the bloody battle, Crystal had been mesmerized by the violent beauty of their dance, gladiator and d'relle moving almost like dance partners in synch with each other, scoring minor hits, but carrying on their ballet. Sure, Crystal jumped back when the d'relle's sword almost severed the gladiator's left arm at the wrist. She anguished when the d'relle pierced the wounded gladiator's side, but then there was that gorgeous overhand swing where the gladiator, the d'relle's sword still deep inside of her, connected at the base of her opponent's neck.

She'd almost cheered, but stopped when she realized that the other students were more in shock than anything else. Everyone knew the history, but seeing it in its bloody glory was different.

---

[16] Megmentő: Savior in Hungarian

The two opponents, their weapons trapped in each other's bodies, slowly started to fall. Then came the arm clasp. The two reached out to each other, clasping hand to forearm, and together, supporting each other, they sank to the sand.

Despite the urgings of a couple of the UAM observers, Tamara did not carry on the fight. Neither did the d'relle. They both sat together, facing each other as blue and red blood flowed down to mix together in the sand.

Crystal vividly remembered watching the holo, feeling the tension even if she already knew the outcome. She remembered feeling the outpouring of relief as after eight long minutes, the d'relle started to lean forward until she could no longer withstand the pull of gravity, and she fell face first into the gladiator's lap. She was dead.

The humans in the holo erupted into cheers, and across the creek, the Klethos farthest away from the ring turned and started to leave. Tamara Veal, though, held up her one good hand to stop her witnesses from entering the ring, and then slowly smoothed out the crest of her opponent. With her hand still on the d'relle's crest, she started leaning forward as if to look into the d'relle's eyes, but she didn't stop the lean. She fell on top of the d'relle, covering her, and Tamara Veal, the *Megmentő,* was gone.

Crystal stepped over the low rope that circled the statue and walked up to the base.

"Miss? Miss? Please get back behind the rope!" the ranger, who was still with his tour group, shouted at her.

Crystal ignored him.

"Was it worth it?" she asked as she reached up and put her hand on the statue's shin as if she could use the physical contact to pull out an answer.

Of course, from humanity's viewpoint, it was worth it. New Budapest was regained, and at almost no cost. Tamara Veal had died, but as it turned out, they discovered after the fight, she'd already contracted BRC. What was another year of one person's life when compared to an entire world? Lives had been wasted freely for much less in return.

But Crystal was not asking about the fight itself. She wanted to know if becoming a gladiator, of going through genmod, if the process was worth it. Nature didn't like such a drastic perversion to her plan and inflicted BRC as punishment on the puny humans who were arrogant enough to try and challenge her will.

"Ma'am, you have to leave," the ranger said, starting to walk over to her.

"Was it worth it?" she asked again. "Is the glory ever worth the suffering and sacrifice?"

But she knew the answer to that. She'd always known it. She just needed to come out to this hallowed ground to confirm that.

She dropped her hand from the leg and stepped back so she could see the entire statue.

She looked Tamara Veal in the face and shouted out, "I'll accept the nomination. I will become a gladiator, and I hope I do you proud!"

Thank you for reading *Gladiator*. If you liked it, please feel free to leave a review of the book in Amazon or Goodreads.

This is the first book of a planned three-book series. The other two books will be about two other minor characters introduced in this book and will feature more Marine Corps-type action.

If you would like updates on new books releases, news, or special offers, please consider signing up for my mailing list. Your email will not be sold, rented, or in any other way disseminated. If you are interested, please sign up at the link below:

http://eepurl.com/bnFSHH

Other Books by Jonathan Brazee

The Return of the Marines Trilogy
The Few
The Proud
The Marines

The Al Anbar Chronicles: First Marine Expeditionary Force--Iraq
Prisoner of Fallujah
Combat Corpsman
Sniper

The United Federation Marine Corps
Recruit
Sergeant
Lieutenant
Captain
Major
Lieutenant Colonel
Colonel
Commandant

Rebel
(Set in the UFMC universe.)

Women of the United Federation Marines
Gladiator
Sniper (Coming soon)
Corpsman (Working Title)

Werewolf of Marines
Werewolf of Marines: Semper Lycanus
Werewolf of Marines: Patria Lycanus
Werewolf of Marines: Pax Lycanus

To The Shores of Tripoli

Wererat

Darwin's Quest: The Search for the Ultimate Survivor

Venus: A Paleolithic Short Story

Non-Fiction

Exercise for a Longer Life

Author Websites
http://www.returnofthemarines.com
http://www.jonathanbrazee.com